I0545281

VINTAGE SOUL

The DeChance Chronicles Volume Two

By David Niall Wilson

"You have a better reason to remain locked away than most," the little man chuckled. "She is magnificent, as well, but you know this. Even my Ligaya watches Vanessa with hunger."

Johndrow laughed. The little man, whose name was Joel, had traveled the world with his lover Ligaya for centuries, and nothing born of darkness or light could part them. They were insatiable, incorrigible, and Johndrow found that he had missed their company more than he'd realized.

"It is good to see you both," he said, taking a sip.

A scream rose from the hallway where Vanessa had disappeared, and everyone in the room froze. The sound cut through the rhythmic heartbeat flowing from the stereo and slapped conversation to silence. It echoed, rose a second time, and then fell away. Johndrow dropped his glass and was at the door the hall before it touched the polished wooden floor.

He reached the kitchen in seconds, but it was empty. There was a crashing sound in further down the hall, and Johndrow launched himself toward it. It came from the direction of the elevator. As he hit the hall, he saw the doors closing, but before he could reach them, they had sealed tightly. The small man who'd served the wine and sealed the door lay on the floor. He was broken. That was the only way to describe it. His arms and legs jutted at impossible angles. Blood soaked the floor and leaked from his pale lips. His eyes were open wide, staring up at the ceiling in abject terror.

Johndrow turned to the panel on the wall to alert the drivers. Where the panel had been there was nothing but a molten mass of circuits and wire fused into a single, shapeless lump. Nothing remained. He knew this would alert the drivers as well as he might have, but he screamed in frustrated anger. The corpse beside him told him the intruder was no ordinary threat, and he knew there was nothing the drivers could do.

"What is it?" Joel cried, joining his friend in the hall.

"Vanessa," Johndrow growled. "Someone got in here and they've taken Vanessa."

Copyright © 2014 by David Niall Wilson
Cover art by Cortney Skinner
ISBN 978-1-949914-26-9
All rights reserved. No part of this book may be used or reproduced in any manner
whatsoever without written permission except in the case of
brief quotations embodied in criticalarticles and reviews
For information address Crossroad Press at 141 Brayden Dr., Hertford, NC 27944
A Mystique Press Production - Mystique Press is an imprint of Crossroad Press.
www.crossroadpress.com

First edition

Dedication

This one is dedicated to all the children of the night I have known, and to all who still share a fascination with vampires, magic, and mystery. In particular, I would like to dedicate this one to Kay Reynolds, whose novel *American Vampire* is one of the least read and best written vampire tales of all time - Robert Eighteen-Bisang for sharing Dracula with me for so many years, the old guard of White Wolf Publishing who did not want this book as a cross-over for their worlds of Mage and Vampire the Masquerade, and yet did not discourage me from writing it anyway - and to wine...whatever the vintage.

Author's Introduction

This is a book with a history, and it's always a shame to me when history is kept in private. It is probably one of the most significant works I've completed, not because of the content, or even because it was originally the first Donovan DeChance novel...but because it was one of the supports I grabbed hold of when I pulled myself out of the longest period of writers bleah (I don't believe in writer's block, but I was going through a lot and not writing) that I've ever encountered.

There was a time when I wrote mostly licensed novels for franchises like Star Trek and White Wolf Publishing. I pitched some really cool ideas to those folks at White Wolf, but it never seemed to be the right story at the right time. One story I pitched was...well...this one. A crossover between the worlds of magic and vampires.

In 2004 I wrote during Nanowrimo for the first time. My family had just survived Hurricane Isabel, and I had a story to tell. That story became the novel *The Mote in Andrea's Eye*, a science-fiction thriller about a woman whose efforts to stop a hurricane sent it spinning out of control, and into The Bermuda Triangle. Then it came back. That book sold almost immediately to Gale, Five Star publishing, and did very well. It went through hardcover, trade paperback, and large print editions, and it was a redemption of sorts. It was another story I'd been told not to write – my previous agent wasn't interested.

Then November swung around again, and I started digging through the folders on my hard drive. I found the pitch I'd sent to White Wolf so long ago, and started thinking. How much fun could I have...how much better a story could I create...

without the rules and annoyances of a licensed, rules-bound world hanging over my head? I didn't know, but I knew the time had come to tell the story, and so, Donovan DeChance was born.

You'll think this sounds like a success story. Stick around. I wrote the novel, and again –it was bought by Gale, Five Star. They had it slated for their horror, fantasy line. Then – they killed their horror fantasy line. They still wanted to do my book, they said, but they were going to release it – since it was at its heart – a mystery – as a mystery. Great, I thought. It took another six months to get it through the hoops and into print, but they made it happen.

No one ordered it. They didn't know what to do with it. It was a mystery list, it was clearly NOT a mystery, it was either not marketed at all or just fell through the cracks. If I recall – 60 copies of the books shipped. Then it was picked up by Roy Robbins at Bad Moon Books as a signed limited edition. That did well enough, but it was limited. Again, very few people read the book, and there I was, four years into the creation of a "series" that no one knew existed.

Another Nanowrimo came around, and I dug out a story of mine that I'd always loved, but felt was not fully told. The original story was "In His Heart Live Dragons," and it was published in *Deathrealm* Magazine. I took that story, and I turned it into another Donovan DeChance story- *Heart of a Dragon*.

I did not, at the time, have the rights back to *Vintage Soul*, and I'd only just started Crossroad Press, so I decided that, in anticipation of getting the other book back, eventually, I would write *Heart of a Dragon* as a prequel. That is what I did, and so, this new, revised, improved edition of *Vintage Soul* is Book II of The DeChance Chronicles. *Heart of a Dragon* is Book I. If you read and like them, you'll want to check out Book III – *My Soul to Keep & Others* – available soon. If you can't wait, *My Soul to Keep* is available now, but the other two novellas that will be added to the book are important background for Book IV – *Kali's Tale*, which *also* draws on my fictional North Carolina town of Old Mill, and leads the brand new novel – Nevermore –a tie-in of sorts.

I've learned that, much like my tattoos, which I jokingly tell people are only one tattoo that has blank spots in it, my stories, if I write long and well enough, blend and come together in one giant world. I like that idea...because it's my world – a place where you are welcome.

Now, on to the story...to cats and crows and magic, vampires and fine wine. I hope you enjoy the journey...

"Age is just a number. It's totally irrelevant unless, of course, you happen to be a bottle of wine."

–Joan Collins

ONE

The private elevator had been busy since sunset, shuttling guests from the sub-basement parking area to the top floor penthouse suite. Long, sleek limousines and dark roadsters were lined up like soldiers, and their drivers had gathered in the comfortable lounge provided for them just to the left of the elevator entrance.

By nine, the outer doors had been closed and secured, and the last well-dressed couple had been ushered into the plush elevator and deposited on the upper floor. As the elevator door closed for the final time, a short, wizened man stepped up to the doors, laid his palm across an intricately designed panel imbedded in the metal and dropped his head forward. A greenish glow seeped out around the edges of his fingers. His lips moved slowly in an almost silent incantation.

None of the guests paid him the slightest attention. In the garage below, the drivers watched in silence as the wall where the elevator doors had closed only moments before grew dark, shimmered, and solidified. No trace of the elevator's existence remained. The outer wall of the parking garage made a similar transformation, leaving the drivers alone in the comfortable lounge.

"That's that, then," a sallow, pale faced man said, turning to the driver next to him with a grin. "It's a long time until dawn...cards?"

The other man nodded, and they broke into groups. Some took seats around the single round table in the center of the lounge, others gathering near a small but high-end television in one corner. There was a panel on the wall with a light corresponding to each parking space. When the owner of one of the vehicles was ready to leave, the light beside their number would flash, and the driver would know to prepare the vehicle and prepare for departure. None of them expected to leave for a very long time.

Many stories above, the guests gathered in the center of the penthouse's large living room. The furnishings were Victorian; plush velvet and dark mahogany glittered in the dim light of candelabras spread across every available horizontal surface. The air throbbed with a hypnotic beat that emanated from rows of speakers and originated from a stereo rack tucked into a dark recess half-shrouded in the fountain-like fronds of dozens of potted spider plants. The stereo's controls and multi-colored LEDS peeked out past the deep green leaves and dangling vines creating a pleasant, jungle-like separation of technology and luxury. The music had no lyrics. It pulsed rhythmically and turned the room into a gigantic, beating heart. The guests swayed gently, transfixed by the sound.

The outer wall was a slick, ebony curtain. It glimmered like obsidian, casting the dancing flames of the candles back at the room. Preston Johndrow, the host, stood with his back to that wall and faced his guests. He held a glittering bottle in one hand, and in his other, a crystal goblet. Johndrow was tall. He was a slender man with a trim waist and deceptively broad shoulders that filled out his tailored suit immaculately. His hair was as black as the smooth wall behind him, flecked with just the hint of gray. His smile was wide and expansive.

A slender blonde woman stood to his right. She was dressed in a shimmering black evening gown that clung to her like scales and. Her heels were so tall it seemed impossible she could balance on them and walk, but she showed not the slightest discomfort at the tortuous pressure on her ankles. Her hand rested on the wall beside another control panel. The room was riddled with such devices, each cleverly hidden by plants, curtains, or various pieces of sculpture. Everything blended perfectly, and though they were out of period, the control panels and glowing indicators were swallowed by the overwhelming opulence of the room's ambiance.

Johndrow tapped his goblet lightly on the bottle in his hand, and the room grew silent. He turned to the blonde woman with a loving smile, and nodded.

"Vanessa," he said, "will you do the honors?"

Vanessa Di Caprio did not answer. Instead she pressed her palm flat on the switch. The wall behind Johndrow split down the center. It parted and rotated to either side, disappearing into recesses shaded by crushed velvet curtains that might once have hung in a great theater. In fact, that was the effect. The curtain of wall opened, and the night sky beyond was revealed. Stars glittered brightly, winking at those gathered. The moon hung low on the horizon, yellow and full. In the brilliant contrast of pitch black night and winking stars, with the glow of the city seeping up from below, the moon appeared heavy and sluggish; it's off-white color out of place.

Johndrow's guests gasped in appreciation of the tremendous view. He turned, stared out over the city for a moment, and then turned to face the group once more.

"Amazing as it is," he said, "I know you all haven't come here just to admire my view. Shall we begin?"

The others murmured assent, and Vanessa stepped to Johndrow's side. She had the smooth, flawless skin of a seventeen year old, and if it hadn't been for the practiced grace of her movements, and the direct, almost arrogant power projected by her gaze, it would have been easy to imagine that she was Johndrow's daughter. This illusion was quickly dispelled as she wrapped herself around him, insinuated her head beneath his arm and wrapped her leg around him seductively, the spiked heel of her shoe caressing the inner edge of his calf.

Johndrow's smile broadened perceptibly, but he concentrated on his balance, and on the bottle in his hand. He held the stem of the goblet between two extended fingers, and gripped the neck of the bottle firmly with the same hand, being careful not to crack the two together. It should have been difficult to hold the full bottle in this manner, but Johndrow showed no strain or sign of concern. He reached down to a decorative table beside him and picked up a gleaming, golden corkscrew.

His performance was almost theatrical, and his guests

followed his actions appreciatively. He twirled the sharp metal corkscrew in and popped the cork. The sound of its release was wet and rich. He handed the corkscrew to Vanessa, who unwound herself, lifted the instrument to eye level and licked the cork, very carefully, teasing every dark drop of liquid from its surface and then holding it in front of her like a lollipop as Johndrow, trying not to show the effect her actions had on him, poured a splash of glittering ruby wine into the goblet.

"Meredith?" he said, holding the glass out with a slight bow.

A red haired woman stepped from the crowd. She gripped her escort's arm for just a second, released him, and approached Johndrow.

"Such an honor," she said. Her voice was breathy and deep. She wore an emerald green silk dress that reached nearly to the floor, but was slit up the sides nearly to the tops of her thighs, revealing flashes of dark, tanned skin as she walked. To his credit, Johndrow watched only her eyes as she approached.

"We took the liberty of holding a drawing before any of you arrived," Johndrow explained. Vanessa thought it would be more fun to announce both contest – and winner – in the same instant.

Meredith reached for the goblet, but Johndrow pulled it back out of reach. "Do you know what this is?" he asked.

"Wine?"

The room erupted in a short burst of laughter, and then quieted again.

Johndrow's eyes sparkled. "Wine, indeed," he replied. "Very astute of you, but – of course – this isn't just any wine. If it were, well, I would not be standing here, and most of you," he swept his arm in an arc that encompassed all present, "would likely not be either."

Johndrow sniffed the wine experimentally, closed his eyes and rolled his tongue slowly over his bottom lip. His eyes flashed open once more, and he held the glass up for all to see clearly.

"The last time this wine touched the open air, Lord Byron himself was present. It was a party, much like this one, though with considerably more...mortality."

Every gaze was locked on the glittering goblet as Johndrow spoke. There was no sound. No breath. No whisper of air, or shift of feet.

"The wine was already in the bottle at this point, ready to be sealed, but before they could do so, I begged this single bottle from the vintner, who was happy to part with it. I would say the small bag of gold I presented him had something to do with his good humor, but that is another story entirely. The grapes that year were particularly sweet, and bottles of this wine have sold on the collector's market for in excess of ten thousand dollars.

"This bottle," he softened his voice slightly, though he could be heard clearly throughout the penthouse, "would bring a hundred times that amount, were it available for sale. Before it was sealed, on a dare, I convinced Byron himself to contribute seven drops of his own blood."

"How in the world did you do that?" a man called out from a back corner of the room. He was tall with spiked platinum blonde hair and a long, egg-shaped platinum earring dangling from his left ear. More rings glittered up and down the sides of his cheek, and across his eyebrows. Some were gold, others copper, and still others glittered with jewels. "What would you say to a man of such power that he would willingly gift you with what must so often be taken?"

"That is a tale for another day," Johndrow declared solemnly, "but let me state for the record: the difficulty was not in securing the blood, but in controlling my nerves once the vein had been opened. I do not know if such blood exists in these later days… if so, I have not found it. I would have had more than the seven drops, but if I had not sealed the bottle and taken it from the room, I would have a different bottle for you tonight and a far different story of my time with Byron. Even now…"

Johndrow took another whiff of the wine, and trembled visibly. He extended his hand to Meredith, who took the goblet eagerly. Johndrow snapped his fingers sharply, and the short man who had sealed the elevator stepped forward. He held a tray upon which one more goblet, and several ranks of slender, fluted cordial glasses were clustered. Johndrow poured half a glass into the goblet, and then a small splash into each cordial.

The little man stood still as stone, and within moments the single bottle of wine had been divided into more than two dozen small portions. Vanessa twined elbows with Johndrow and they waited, gazing into one another's eyes over the top of the larger goblet Johndrow still held.

The short man turned smoothly on his heel, not even jostling the precious glasses, and wound his way slowly around the room, dispensing the cordials carefully and quickly, until everyone was served. There were no extras. If there had been, Johndrow would have been outraged at the waste.

He stared at Vanessa a moment longer, and then he spoke.

"She walks in beauty, like the night,
Of cloudless climes and starry skies,
And all that's best of dark, and bright,
Meet in her aspect and her eyes..."

He nodded at Meredith, who took a quick sip, and then downed the heady tincture in a single gulp. Johndrow smiled and nodded at the lucky guest. There were murmurs of jealous appreciation throughout the room.

Johndrow tipped his goblet to Vanessa's lips and watched as her head fell back, blonde hair shimmering over her shoulders. Her eyes closed, and she stretched up on her toes, the heels of her too-tall shoes actually lifting from the ground. Her back arched and he watched as she drank. She took exactly half. He drew her to him then and lifted the goblet from her lips, which she pulled back reluctantly. When their bodies met, he drew the glass up and drank. In that moment, Vanessa's eyes flashed open and her gaze locked with his. They melted together and Johndrow drained the glass, flipping it distractedly over his shoulder. The short man appeared very suddenly, plucked the glittering projectile from the air, and placed it on the tray without a sound.

"Enjoy," Johndrow called to the others in the room. "Enjoy, and there is more to come. I have brandy, I have the blood of kings...I have the exsanguinated voices of an entire choir in three cases, from bass and contralto to the shiver of soprano.

Tonight, we will celebrate the blood. Tonight I will feed my passion, and sate your hunger. To life, and those who grant it. To the blood."

As he fell silent, two dozen glasses were raised and drained. Moans of pleasure and cries of delight rang out through the room. The conversations that had fallen silent when Johndrow stepped before them returned to full volume. Couples moved about the room, as bottles were brought forth and their cordial glasses were replaced by tumblers and goblets. The music rose slightly in volume.

Johndrow noticed none of it. He held Vanessa close. Their tongues danced, teasing the last droplets of the wondrously spiked blood from one another and blending it with the kiss. Vanessa had an inexplicable talent for caressing his body with hers, every inch of her a part of the motion and every raw nerve he possessed burned with the need of her. She knew it, and pressed closer, matching his heat but besting his control. She could keep this up all night, and he feared – and dreamed – that she would do so.

"Enjoying yourself, love?" she asked, pulling back slightly.

"Standing here like this, you ask me such a question?"

Vanessa laughed and stepped back, whirling away from him. The dress rippled with every shift of her well-muscled form and caught the candlelight perfectly, sending tiny reflected flames across her back.

"There is plenty of time, darling," she admonished. "You have guests. You have cognac and whiskey. She turned back and pointed at him with one long nail. "You'd better steer clear of the soprano tonight. I believe I prefer you closer to bass."

Then she was gone, and Johndrow shook his head to clear it. He had trouble imagining a world that did not center on Vanessa. Even his collection would be an empty pleasure if she weren't there to share it. This concern troubled him, because he knew it was a weakness. Any addiction, no matter how pleasant, was a handicap.

Johndrow turned to the wall beside the stereo alcove. There was another control panel tucked in behind a potted fern. He reached back, flipped a switch, and a portion of that wall slid back to reveal a mirrored bar. Lit with dim, blue bulbs that were there more for effect than for any need of illumination, the bar was magnificent. Bottles of odd shapes and sizes lined four tiers of shelves. Johndrow reached to the bottom shelf, pulled out a round-based bottle of cognac, and tipped two fingers of the contents into a flat-bottomed tumbler. He thought briefly of the priest he'd first shared that bottle with. He closed his eyes – just for a moment – and the scent of the liquor brought back the man's grey eyes.

"Take, drink," Johndrow whispered, "for this is my blood." He took a slow sip of the cognac, though he was reluctant to wash away the magnificent savor of Byron's wine blended with Vanessa's kiss.

The music shifted through a syncopated variance on the original heartbeat. Blood scented candles in various corners of the room fed the illusion that they all stood within the walls of a giant, beating heart; the speed and regularity of the music orchestrated subtle changes in the mood of those gathered. It was going well. The wine had been a major coup, a one time chance to present them all with something they had never had, and could never hope to have again. It was a moment's distraction in an eternity gone bland, and he knew they would talk of it and relive it for days, years, possibly centuries to come.

Johndrow watched Vanessa move among their guests. She had a knack for coming just close enough to make the men uncomfortable, and to bring the women to the brink of anger, and then slip away, or pull back, or say something – more than likely about Johndrow himself – that set whoever she was talking to back on his heels, or at her ease. Every eye followed her when she was near.

Johndrow saw her turn into the hall that led to the kitchen, and he smiled. He wished, suddenly, that there was no party. He wished he had her to himself, that he could track her down that hall, corner her, and taste her again -- thoroughly. He felt the ghost brush of her teeth on the skin of his throat and took a long gulp of the cognac, cringing at the waste. It should have been sipped – savored one small swallow at a time. A hand brushed his elbow lightly, and he turned, startled.

A short, very thin man with long moustaches, a beak-like nose, and dark eyes smiled up at him. The man held a small tumbler cupped between his palms, and Johndrow caught the scent of the bayou, Cajun blood. The drink was whiskey, warm and raw, served at room temperature. Johndrow smiled.

"It is marvelous," the little man said. His voice was soft, but it carried easily. He surveyed the room and took a sip of his drink. "Truly marvelous."

"Thank you, old friend," Johndrow replied, turning and refilling his own glass. "I wanted it to be special. Vanessa and I don't get out as much as we once did. There are some here tonight we haven't seen in years. It isn't good to remain cooped up too long. There is too much to forget, and once it's gone – you never really get it back, do you?"

He glanced thoughtfully at the cognac in his glass. It held a fleeting glimpse of the past. It held the essence of a lifelong fallen to ash, but it was a pale image of the reality that had spawned it.

"You have a better reason to remain locked away than most," the little man chuckled. "She is magnificent, as well, but you know this. Even my Ligaya watches Vanessa with hunger."

Johndrow laughed. The little man, whose name was Joel, had traveled the world with his lover Ligaya for centuries, and nothing born of darkness or light could part them. They were insatiable, incorrigible, and Johndrow found that he had missed their company more than he'd realized.

"It is good to see you both," he said, taking a sip.

A scream rose from the hallway where Vanessa had disappeared, and everyone in the room froze. The sound cut through the rhythmic heartbeat flowing from the stereo and slapped conversation to silence. It echoed, rose a second time, and then fell away. Johndrow dropped his glass and was at the door the hall before it touched the polished wooden floor.

He reached the kitchen in seconds, but it was empty. There was a crashing sound in further down the hall, and Johndrow launched himself toward it. It came from the direction of the elevator. As he hit the hall, he saw the doors closing, but before he could reach them, they had sealed tightly. The small man who'd served the wine and sealed the door lay on the floor. He was broken. That was the only way to describe it. His arms and legs jutted at impossible angles. Blood soaked the floor and leaked from his pale lips. His eyes were open wide, staring up at the ceiling in abject terror.

Johndrow turned to the panel on the wall to alert the drivers. Where the panel had been there was nothing but a molten mass of circuits and wire fused into a single, shapeless lump. Nothing remained. He knew this would alert the drivers as well as he might have, but he screamed in frustrated anger. The corpse beside him told him the intruder was no ordinary threat, and he knew there was nothing the drivers could do.

"What is it?" Joel cried, joining his friend in the hall.

"Vanessa," Johndrow growled. "Someone got in here and they've taken Vanessa."

"How do we get down?" Joel asked, turning and looking for a door, or a panel that might open on a stair.

"There is no other way," Johndrow said flatly. The elevator is the only entrance. It can be operated manually, assuming anyone is left alive below. If not, I'll have to send someone down the shaft. It could take hours, and by then?"

Joel didn't answer. Others poured into the hall, some clutching drinks, some half-amused, wondering if this was a new and unexpected amusement. With a snarl, Johndrow pounded his fist into the wood paneled wall. The wood cracked and buckled inward.

Several floors below, the huge garage door slid open silently, and a single dark Mercedes coupe rolled out into the darkness. The door did not close behind it, and no one followed.

TWO

It took Johndrow the entire night, and his staff working throughout the day, to arrange a meeting of the council. It had been several years since they'd last convened, and many members were reluctant – particularly those in attendance at his party the previous night. Threats had grown fewer and less likely in recent times. Electronic security, for those who could afford it, had progressed to incredible levels, and, as Joel had bemusedly put it, people just weren't as frightened. The human race had reached a point in its evolution where they were as likely to seek and embrace the way of the blood as they were to reject or fear it. They were as likely to attract groupies and talk show hosts as any form of modern slayer.

None of this changed the fact of Vanessa's disappearance. When Johndrow's staff managed to free up the elevator, the guests had dispersed quickly into the fading night. Johndrow had rushed from the main door of the garage, but there was no sign of forced exit, and none of the drivers remembered seeing anything out of the usual. In fact, their memories were sufficiently clouded that Johndrow was certain they'd been wiped, hurriedly and without much thought to what consequences such an act might have on their minds. Most of them vaguely remembered arriving at the party. A couple were able to tell him what hand they last remembered holding in their poker game.

None of them remembered anything out of the ordinary, nor had they seen Vanessa or anyone unexpected. In the chaos that followed the elevator repair, no one thought to check for an empty space in the lot, and by the time they did, half the guests had disappeared into the night, and there was no way to sort it all out. No one remembered opening the outer door or hearing any alarm from the penthouse above.

On top of this, there was the matter of Stine, Johndrow's head of security. The man had been ancient and quite skilled at his duties. Whoever had taken Vanessa had brushed past the gnomish wizard with no more thought than one gave a mosquito, and the result of that encounter had been astonishingly violent – and final. Stine's people had worked over the body for twelve hours straight, but the effort was wasted. There was no chance of resuscitation, and despite intricate charms and incantations, they'd been unable to extract any information from the corpse.

Since Johndrow's penthouse would not be fully secured for several days, the elders had opted to meet in Joel's office. His quarters were not as ostentatious as Johndrow's, but the security was tight. Joel occupied the seventeenth floor of a twenty story office building in downtown San Valencez, California. Below were the vaults and offices of the bank Joel had built and held full controlling interest in. The eighteenth floor was vacant, not accessible by public elevator or stair, and housed offices for security and other dealings that required separation from the financial institution below. The upper stories were apartments Joel leased to relations and associates. Each had its own private security and access. There was a helo pad on the roof.

The last time the council had met, there were sixteen in attendance. Tonight, there would be only ten. The Resendez brothers were in Argentina on business, and though their people had, of course, been alerted, and warnings passed, they were unable to return in time to be present. Claudia Forsythe and her current paramour, who Johndrow knew only as Benjamin, were in Europe and could not be reached. Copper and Alicia Contreaux were still in Louisiana, and there were reports that the two had troubles of their own in the bayou.

Johndrow glanced up and down the hallway as he entered the large conference room Joel had cleared for the meeting. Two of the small, gnomish men and one gnarled woman, a good foot shorter with piercing blue eyes and a hooked nose reminiscent of a buzzard, were stationed at intervals up and down the hall, and there were others at every entrance. At Johndrow's apartment, Stine had been alone, and had fallen to the element of surprise. It was obvious that his people considered the threat a serious one. Johndrow had never seen such a concentration of the security force. He knew it must have cost a fortune, and he knew as well that a bill would arrive at his penthouse shortly for his part in it. Joel was a good friend, but business was business.

Joel stepped up to greet Johndrow at the door, laying a hand on the taller man's shoulder. "They will be sufficient," the old man assured him. "They take what happened last night as a personal affront. I would not like to try and breach their defenses tonight."

"I would have had them there last night, if I'd had any idea..." Johndrow's features darkened. He was angrier than he'd been in over a century, but there was nothing on which to vent his rage. He wanted to roar up and down the hallway, smashing anyone and anything that got in his way, but it would have served no purpose, and he knew that Joel was right. If he tried something crazy like that tonight, it would be *his* bones scattered haphazardly over the carpeted floor.

"Come in," Joel said, stepping aside. "Corwyn, Ballard, and Jensen are here already. I just received word that Grimshaw and Nystrom are in the garage. Lydia and her Adriana will be fashionably late, of course, and that only leaves Ligaya, who will finalize security. We've commissioned extra wards. It's an inconvenience, I know. No one will be able to leave before the charms are raised, but it will afford us the extra level of security we need to be certain we are not disturbed."

Johndrow nodded distractedly. He'd expected as much, and knew the others would as well. Only extraordinary circumstances could have dislodged them all from their comfortable holdings at such short notice, and anything less than perfect security would not do at all. They would see it as their due.

They were ten of the most powerful creatures on earth. They were men, or had been men, and women, but now they were more. Sixteen floors beneath them were corridors and offices where the finances of the world were bartered, traded, negotiated and sealed. Huge vaults held the vast fortunes of those who ruled the daylight hours. The wealth of minor foreign countries was stored safely beneath the polished marble floors, and centuries of treasures, secrets, and lives were tucked into row after row of secure safe deposit boxes, some so old and intricately guarded that the building could withstand anything short of nuclear attack and not breach their integrity. That was what the world saw.

Beneath those secure vaults, beside them, sometimes even within them, were other vaults. Joel had gathered wealth, treasure, and power of his own. Centuries of it. There were secrets held safe within his walls that kings would ransom their holdings to acquire, that wars could be and had been fought over; artifacts that required such deep concentration and dedication to control and secure that the task boggled Johndrow's mind. And Joel was only one of the ten.

Before long the first nine were seated. Ligaya entered last, drawing the doors closed behind her. Just for a moment the gnomish security woman's fierce eyes filled one pane of the glass paneled door behind her, glared into the room, and then were gone. Ligaya seemed not to notice. She took her seat beside Joel, and Johndrow rose slowly, getting right to the point.

"There's no sense in my going over the events of last night in detail," he said. "Most of you were there, and those of you who were not have no doubt gathered the details through your own people. Vanessa was taken, right out of my penthouse, right out of my party. Most of you know – knew – Stine. He was one of the oldest and most trusted of his kind. There was only just enough left of him for identification. My elevator system was thoroughly fried, and at least a dozen drivers had their memories wiped. All of this took place in the span of only a few moments time, and the intruder left no trace."

"It's bad about Vanessa," Nystrom called out. He was a trim man in a gray suit, and as he spoke, he slowly filed a long, sharp fingernail. He didn't meet Johndrow's gaze. In fact, he looked somewhat bored by the entire proceeding, though it would have been a mistake to believe he wasn't paying scrupulous attention. "The two of you have been together a long time now," he went on. "I remember a time when you were not, though. In fact, most of us remember that time. Vanessa has disappeared in the past, what makes you so sure someone took her this time?"

Johndrow's hands shook and he dug his nails into the hard, smooth surface of the conference table. Had it been wood alone, he'd have splintered it, but it was reinforced against just such extreme treatment. He kept his voice even and calm. Nystrom and Vanessa had been involved with one another for a short period, perhaps fifty years, before Johndrow had met her. He knew Nystrom was testing his nerves, but they were dangerously frayed, and he had to fight to keep from launching himself across the table and gripping the smug bastard by the throat.

"I am as aware of Vanessa's history as any of you," he said. "Probably more than any other, I understand her nature, and it is true that in the past she has been – somewhat less than reliable."

There was a soft snicker from one corner of the room, but it fell to silence before Johndrow could pinpoint the source.

"This is a serious threat," he said. "You can sit there and make light of it if you want, but I don't think there's anyone here who believes that Vanessa, even in a fury, could have done what was done to Stine, let alone what happened to the elevator and the drivers below. She's old, and she's powerful, but none of us is that powerful."

Nystrom glanced up, as if he took offense at this statement, but he held his tongue. He stared pointedly at where Johndrow still clutched the conference table in a death grip, chipping his nails from the pressure. Nystrom went back to his manicure, shaking his head.

"What would you have us do?" The speaker was Andrew Corwyn, a peevish, bookish little man with large glasses perched on his nose that he no longer needed, but wore in memory of a mortal life he claimed to miss. No one believed him, of course, but neither did they suggest he cast aside the spectacles. "I mean," the man said, glancing around at the others for support, "It's your problem, not ours. It was your party, your security, and, to be blunt, Vanessa was your lover. How does this affect me?"

"You were at the party," Joel cut in evenly. "It could as easily have been you, or your Meredith, that was taken. Would you feel differently then? How is security at your place, Andrew? A few gnomes short of a quorum, I'm betting, since they won't work unless you pay them fairly."

Ligaya reached out and laid her hand gently on Joel's. "They don't like to be called gnomes, dear, you know that. Considering how much is riding on our contract...?"

"What are they then?" Nystrom cut in, "Height challenged? Charisma challenged? They certainly aren't human."

Corwyn slowly pulled his spectacles off and began cleaning them, doing his best to take on the indifferent air that Nystrom pulled off so effortlessly – and failing. He fumbled the glasses back onto his nose and glared at Joel.

"I don't care what we call them, or for that matter, what they want to be called. My point is, it wasn't my place that was attacked, was it?"

"Not this time," Johndrow said softly. "How do we know it's an isolated attack? We have no idea who, or what, pulled this off. We have no idea where Vanessa has been taken, or why. We have no way to know, in other words, that this threat was to her in particular, or to any one of us, rather than a sign of things to come. It may have just been a warning shot."

"Warning of what, exactly?" Grimshaw cut in. "Not to be quarrelsome, but we seem to be particularly short on facts to have called a meeting over this. Wouldn't our time have been better spent tightening security and trying to find out who this mysterious intruder might have been? As powerful as he – or she," he nodded to Ligaya with a smile, "might be, they are not beyond detection. The list of those with the power and intelligence to pull such a thing off is a short one."

"There is no time," Johndrow replied wearily. "Vanessa may already have passed to final death. I believe we've been together long enough for the blood bond to form, but I can't be certain. I have not felt her pass. If she is out there in trouble, we owe it to her as one of our own to find her and bring her back."

"A tall order," Nystrom observed.

"That is why I suggest we put it in capable hands and tend to our own defense," Joel interjected. "There is one we can call at such times, and though we have not needed his services for a very long time, I believe that extraordinary circumstances call for extraordinary measures."

"You mean DeChance, Preston?" Lydia Hollinshead asked. She pursed her lips and steepled her hands, delicate elbows perched on the surface of the table. Lydia never spoke without striking a pose, and it was such long habit that none paid her odd habit the slightest mind.

"Yes," Johndrow replied. "DeChance, of course. I took the liberty of checking to be certain he's in town."

"And he is," Joel cut in. "I agree with Preston. This is serious business, and not something we can afford to ignore. We are all far too busy to complicate our lives by constantly watching over our shoulders, and I for one have no time or resources to devote to this full time. DeChance has served us well in the past, and as long as we meet his price, I see no reason not to trust him. Besides," Joel scanned their faces, "which of you believes they know more about the sort of power we are talking about here than Mr. DeChance?"

"What about the gnomes?" Nystrom asked. "We've already paid them quite a lot – couldn't they be persuaded to look into this?"

"Possibly," Ligaya replied, taking over for her husband. They all knew she was the bank's liaison with the security firm, so none objected when she interrupted. "But it isn't their specialty. They protect things. They covet things, and when they cannot have them for themselves, they help others to covet more safely. They aren't detectives, and they aren't good on the offensive. Whoever we are up against already bested them once, and without much difficulty, it seems. I, for one, don't feel safe in letting them handle this without help. Particularly," she glared at Nystrom, "if you continue to insult them."

"And they aren't cheap," Grimshaw cut in. "DeChance has his price, but it's always been fair, and it's certainly less than the – um – security wizards? -- would ask to go so far beyond their normal tasking. I say we bring DeChance in and be done with it. Security will be over-taxed answering our additional concerns for the immediate future, no sense straining them to the breaking point."

There were murmurs of assent, and Johndrow took advantage of the moment.

"Then, unless there are further concerns, I recommend that we draft a letter immediately and send it by messenger. The more quickly DeChance can get on this, the less likely it is that whoever we're after will have time to simply vanish into thin air."

"Again," Grimshaw added.

"Well," Joel, said, "We have time. The wards will not lift from this room for another twenty minutes. He stood, pulled a bottle out from some alcove beneath his seat at the head of the table and placed it in front of him. "There are glasses on the small shelves beneath the table. Please help yourself. The letter itself should not take long, because we don't know enough to drag it out. Short and simple."

There were no more questions, or concerns. The moment Johndrow pressed pen to paper, the others in the room withdrew into their own little worlds, already planning upgrades to their personal security, or trips out of the country. All things considered, it had been one of the shortest and least difficult meetings the group had ever conducted, and Johndrow was pleased. He knew he didn't have the resources to hunt Vanessa down in time, and he was fairly certain that he didn't have the power to do anything about it if he did. He'd met DeChance only once, but it had been enough to impress him.

He signed the letter, passed the paper and pen to Joel, who then slid it in front of Ligaya, who signed and sent it around the table. By the time the ward lifted and the short, fierce-eyed gnomish security woman opened the door, the letter was sealed, and Ligaya laid it in her hands without a word. The woman glanced at the name, nodded curtly, and was simply...gone.

Johndrow watched in silence as the others filed out of the room and off down the corridor to the elevators. He lingered, and Joel walked him to the door.

"Don't worry old friend," Joel said. "We'll find her. If it can be done, he can do it."

"I know," Johndrow replied. "I know. He turned to Joel. "Will you hunt with me tonight? If I don't tear the throat out of something, I'm going to be quite insane, and it has been a very long time since I spent a night on the street."

Joel glanced sidelong at Ligaya, who nodded with a worried smile.

"Certainly," Joel said. "It has been too long."

Johndrow nodded and started down the corridor. Joel handed his jacket to Ligaya and followed. Moments later, as she stood watching them, the jacket clutched in her arms, the elevator door closed, and they dropped slowly to the ground floor.

Ligaya stared at the elevator doors a moment longer, then turned abruptly and headed deeper into the bank complex. "Be safe," she whispered. "And be back soon."

In a small office on the 18th floor, the small, gnomish woman held the letter and its envelope to the lit end of a black candle. Smoke curled up from the dancing flame and filled the room, making breathing difficult. She paid no attention to this, concentrating her will on the point where paper met fire. As the envelope caught, she whispered two words.

"Donovan DeChance."

The paper caught, burned in an instant to black, dusty ash, and before it fell, she blew on it. The ash formed itself into a cloud, took substance and form and spread. A dark wraith-like form stood staring back at her, then turned, and with a soft "pop" was gone.

THREE

Donovan DeChance sat in a comfortable chair, beside a very warm fire and stared out over the city skyline, thinking. On his lap a sleek, silver-white cat with dark leopard-like spots purred contentedly, her feet asprawl and her tail dangling over the arm of the chair. The cat was a large creature, an Egyptian Mau named Cleopatra, and while Donovan watched the glitter of the stars, she watched the firelight dance through the ice cubes in the whiskey tumbler he held, contemplating her chances in an attack.

The room was an organized jumble. Heavy wooden bookshelves lined the walls from the floor to just below the ten foot ceiling. A rolling ladder clung to the face of the shelves, about halfway down one wall, but its progress was impeded on either side by cartons and stacks of more books waiting to be shelved. They would wait a long time, as not an inch of empty space could be found on any of the shelves. It was a problem, and Donovan knew he'd have to address it soon, or be pushed out the front door of his own home by the sheer volume of clutter.

A short altar stood in an alcove in one corner of the room. This, too, was cluttered. It held an ornate, silver goblet in the form of a robed woman with demons clutching her feet, a crystal ball on a wooden stand carved of a single branch of olive wood, a book open somewhere near the middle and marked with a heavy gold-colored ribbon, a small brazier black with ashes, and a dagger. The dagger was long and curved. Its handle glittered with jewels and was trimmed in four metals, gold, silver, copper and platinum. These were woven equally into a pattern that circled the hilt in concentric rings.

Charts and maps dangled and jutted from the shelves. A few of these were rolled, or folded, but still others were attached to the wood by tacks or small nails. One shelf held an assortment of divination equipment, Tarot cards, joss sticks for reading the I Ching, a small geomancy box and a leather bag of stone runes. In a jeweled case a set of animal bones rested at odd angles.

Still another shelf had a small rack attached beneath it where talismans, crystals, pendants and charms dangled. There did not seem to be any particular order to them, and there was no index or label to differentiate one from the other. Their chains and thongs were tangled together, snarled hopelessly and all-but-forgotten.

Two doorways opened out of this main room, which served as office, library, and sitting room. One was the hallway that led to the two bedrooms and the bath in the rear of the apartment, the other led to his small kitchen. Both were separated from the main room by heavy wooden doors, and both were closed. A third door, larger and more ornate, led to the hallway beyond and, in turn, to the world below and beyond.

There was little light. A few feet to the side of where he sat in his arm chair stood a battered old desk. It was the one uncluttered horizontal surface in the room. On it sat a computer, a telephone, a pendulum dangling from a small metal stand, and a single lamp. The lamp was old. Its base was carved metal in the form of a tree. The tree had ten branches, and from each of these a small and very ancient coin dangled. A rod ran up the center to a spiked finial, which screwed down to hold the fragile slag-glass shade in place. The glass itself was thick and lustrous. It was violet, giving off an odd, soothing radiance similar to that of a weak black light. Around the rim of the shade, formed of inlaid bits of colored glass, ran the twenty-two letters of the Hebrew alphabet.

The lamp, as most of the other objects in the room, had been a gift received in return for services rendered. Also, as was true of most of the other objects, it served more than its obvious purpose.

Donovan raised his whiskey tumbler and took a sip. As he

did so, the violet light from the lamp pulsed. It flared more brightly for a moment, and then returned to its normal glow. Donovan turned and stared at it with a slight frown. He placed his glass on the table beside his seat, shooed Cleo from his lap, and stood.

He was six-foot three inches tall with broad shoulders and an athletic build. His long dark hair swept back over his shoulders in waves, and when the light caught his eyes, they flashed a violet shade of their own. His clothing, dark pants, a rather ornate jacket over a shirt open at the neck to reveal several chains that disappeared beneath, and dark, polished boots might have seemed eccentric or affectatious on most men, archaic on others, but not on Donovan. He wore them like a second skin. He didn't move quickly, but his motions were deceptively graceful. The lamp pulsed a final time, and then settled back to its normal violet hue. Donovan, who had crossed the room in that space of time, reached for the ornate knob of his outer door.

Behind him, Cleo leaped back to the seat of his chair and bounded up to the back cushion. She seated herself and began to wash her face casually. Donovan heard the thump as she came to rest, and knew she was watching. It was good to know she had his back.

A soft chime rang, and Donovan opened the door before the sound could die. He liked to have the advantage over visitors, and knowing they were at the door before they rang the bell was one method of achieving this. This particular time, his effort was wasted.

A very thin apparition stood in the hall outside the door, and he – it – held a thick, ornate envelope in one hand. At least Donovan assumed it was a hand. The robes concealed the messenger's features, so that it was impossible to tell if it was a man, or a woman, or if there was anything below the billowing cloak at all. Donovan thought he caught a flash where the eyes should be, but it was impossible to be certain. The same was true of the point where the envelope dangled from the creature's arm. If there was a hand clutching it, that hand was concealed beneath the dark material, and Donovan was fairly certain that, either way, he just didn't want to know.

"Good evening," he said. He held the door open slightly, filling the gap with his own form. The messenger said nothing. It wavered slightly and extended the envelope.

Donovan frowned. No verbal message. He reached out and accepted the envelope. The second he touched the paper, whatever force had held it evaporated. Donovan stepped back with a start as the cowled form disintegrated into a cloud of black dust. It maintained the vague form of a man, just for an instant, and then whirled into a funnel that resembled a small tornado before roaring down the hall in a rush of wind. Donovan's hair lifted from his shoulder, and a sensation like being pricked with ice cubes danced down his spine. He glanced at the envelope, frowned again, and stepped back into his apartment, closing the door behind him. As many times as he'd received such deliveries, the sensation of unease they caused never diminished.

Cleopatra regarded him cautiously from her perch atop his arm chair, but he ignored her, stepped around his desk, and sat down. He dropped the envelope into the soft pool of light from the lamp and stared at it. His name was carefully penned across the center of the envelope. There was no name attached to the return address, but he knew it well enough. The envelope was standard stationary from the Bloodstone Financial Group, and he only knew one member of the administration of that fine institution. He kept most of his valuables in the institutions vault, but somehow he didn't believe this missive related to his personal account.

Donovan pushed his keyboard and mouse aside to reveal an intricately carved design on the wooden desktop that covered most of the wooden surface. It was a circle within a circle, the outer of which brushed the bottom and top edges of the desk and curved just inside the lamp. Between the two concentric lines, symbols had been carved. Within the center circle, an eight pointed star stretched so that each of its longer points, north, south, east and west, touched the ring. Smaller points bisected the joint of each of the longer tines.

He placed the envelope in the center of the circle, and then reached into a drawer to his right and pulled out four small metal braziers. He placed them at the four large points of the star. Next he filled each with a small measure of powder. He laid a tiny, ornately decorated dagger in the circle beside the envelope, and cleared everything else from the desk. He muttered a name under his breath and touched the tip of his right index finger to the powder in the first brazier. It caught, blazed brightly for just a second, and then faded to a deep orange glow. Tendrils of smoke rose, scenting the air with sandalwood.

Donovan repeated the process with the other three braziers, chanting a different name each time. When all four were lit the smoke whirled, trapped between the two carved circles. The symbols, and the desk, were obscured from view, and as Donovan sat back and concentrated, the envelope floated into the air as if plucked by invisible hands. Donovan's hands mimicked the motion. He then reached down and lifted an invisible dagger from the air. The dagger in the circle rose at the same time, and he wasted no time pressing the thin blade beneath the flap of the envelope and slicing it open.

The dagger floated back to the desktop, and the paper within the envelope slid out, then unfolded to float about an inch above the circling smoke. Donovan shifted slightly so that the violet light from the lamp caught the paper just right. The first thing he noted was at the top of a list of signatures at the bottom of the letter. It was signed, Preston Johndrow. Beneath Johndrow's bold script were nine other signatures, including that of Joel Bloodstone himself.

Donovan knew Johndrow, though the two were not close. He'd performed a few tasks for the council in the past, and though he was never fully comfortable in their presence, he respected their power and authority. In any case, they were not wizards, and though they employed a small army in the name of security, it was not likely they would resort to a cursed letter if they intended Donovan harm.

He snuffed the braziers with a quick gesture of one hand. He slid them aside with the tip of the dagger too cool and placed the blade itself back in the drawer. Then he leaned over the desk to read. It was not a long letter; the facts were laid out quickly and with a slightly shakier hand than the signature beneath them. Donovan scanned the note quickly, and then read it over a second time more slowly. When he reached the part about Stine's death he stopped and frowned.

Donovan knew the small wizard by reputation. Whoever, or whatever, had brought off this kidnapping was no slouch. Stine was not only old and powerful, but he was a stickler for detail. If his defenses were breached, there were only two ways it could have happened. Either someone, or something extremely well versed in stealth and combat had crashed that party, or it was an inside job. No ordinary wizard – and certainly none of the death-challenged guests at the party could have breached a gnomish defense shield, even if security had been light with only Stine himself present. There had been no reason to expect trouble for many years, and things had grown slack in some quarters, but not with Stine. Every job was as important as the last, and the next. The security firm's motto was "Nothing lost, ever." Donovan wondered if they'd be changing that now.

Cleo leaped down from the chair and padded across the floor. With a quick, graceful leap she landed on the desktop beside the lamp, narrowly avoiding sending the small braziers tumbling in all directions. Donovan looked up at her.

"What is it, Cleo? More company?"

Donovan glanced at the lamp, and it flared so suddenly and so brilliantly that he was blinded. He dropped the letter and drove back from the desk, cursing. As the flash of light faded from the room, Donovan recovered and scanned it quickly. Nothing seemed out of place, but he had only a fraction of a second to take it in. The room went dark. The lamp hummed. There was still a faint glimmer of radiance from the bulb, and for an instant it tried to rekindle and blaze, but its effort failed.

The fire, which had snapped and popped merrily only moments before was silent. Warmth fled with the light, and Donovan felt as if he'd been doused in ice water.

As the room went dark, he crab-walked to the side as quickly and silently as he could manage. He drew up with his back tight to one of the book cases. He remained there, immobile and silent, waiting. Sweat rolled down his collar and he repressed a shiver as cold sweat slicked his arms and chest. Salty drops rolled into the corners of his eyes, burning, but he kept them open, and he remained still.

Cleo meowed mournfully across the room, but he made no move to find, or comfort her. Donovan held his breath and concentrated. With no light, his eyes were useless, so he closed them and concentrated his other senses. His heart pounded loudly, and he worked on calming it. He needed silence. Cleo meowed again, and he let out a slow breath. Whoever it was hadn't found or harmed the cat.

At first he heard nothing; then it came. A whistling, whining sound echoed down the chimney, low at first, but rising in pitch and volume until, within moments, it was so loud he had to cover his ears against the pain. With hearing cut off, he instinctively opened his eyes.

The fireplace flashed with flaming light, and Donovan dove around his desk, rolled once and spun. As he rolled, he drew one of the talismans that hung about his neck free and held it in front of his face. Still blind from the flash, he couldn't see it, but he knew he had the right one by touch. Cleo brushed his back and curled around him, hissing at the fireplace, and Donovan blinked, trying desperately to regain his sight.

Then the whining died to a hiss, and, as his vision cleared, Donovan saw it. A white, flaming face hovered just above the logs in the fireplace. The face was featureless with the exception of two black pits that served as eyes. The flames burning around them made them look like lumps of fiery coal. As Cleo flattened herself against Donovan's back and dug her claws into the carpet, the face began to shimmer.

FOUR

The burning coal eyes of the hovering face glared out of the fireplace, but there was no sign of further intrusion. Calming himself, Donovan mentally ran over his defenses. The fireplace should have been safe against such an invasion as this. Donovan had placed the wards himself, and he checked them regularly. He had plenty of enemies, and they possessed a variety of powers. There were further magical barriers still in place between the fire and the rest of the room, but this was no time to check their efficiency, if he could avoid it.

The talisman he'd drawn from the front of his shirt and gripped tightly in his hand was a powerful one. Instead of attempting to foil one or another type of magic, it was designed to reflect whatever was cast upon it, magnified. It had saved his skin more than once in such an encounter, and was always the first thing he reached for.

Donovan had purchased the charm from a young man and his wife, who was considerably older; by centuries. The talisman had been purchased from a gnomish wizard named Tobias Langston in a small shop down town. The woman had been trapped in a crystal until she agreed to wed Langston, which she never would have done. Only the accidental sale of this talisman to the young man had helped to free her. Ironically, Langston sold the talisman because he was unable to determine its abilities. Every time he cast a discovery spell on it, his mind was filled with nothing more than the desire to know what the talisman was.

Cleo curled around Donovan's ankle as he stood slowly to face the flaming apparition in his fireplace.

"You could have knocked," he said, forcing his voice to sound casual.

There was no immediate answer. The fire had resumed its crackling and popping. The lamp on Donovan's desk hummed very quietly and had resumed a very dim violet glow. Donovan clutched his talisman more tightly. Either his visitor had relaxed, for the moment, or the effort to overcome the entire home's defenses had proved too much, and the lamp was a sign of that weakness.

A voice crackled out of the flames, distorted and amplified. There was something hauntingly familiar about it, but Donovan could not quite place it.

"I have come for a book," the voice said.

"Well," Donovan replied, waving his free hand about the room, "you've come to the right place to see many books, but I'm not a lending library, or a bookseller."

"It is a particular book," the voice continued, "that I know you, and you alone possess. I have been able to find no other copy."

Donovan held his silence. He had several books that fit this description, but saw no reason to offer information freely.

"I need the journal of Jean Claude Le Duc," the voice demanded. "You will give it to me now, if you wish to be left in peace."

The glow of the lamp had strengthened somewhat, and Donovan stood a bit straighter. He knew that the longer he kept this intruder speaking, the more energy would be dissipated, and the longer the spell remained active, the better his own chances of overcoming it. On top of that, the melodramatic presentation, rather than filling him with dread, as was no doubt it's intended purpose, was beginning to amuse him. Who was he talking to, the lost son of Shakespeare?

"Le Duc," Donovan said, rubbing his chin with the talisman thoughtfully. "Le Duc. I seem to remember such a book; He was a Frenchman, wasn't he? I believe he was last seen around the time of the Crusades…"

"Do not toy with me," the voice boomed. Sparks shot out at odd angles from the fireplace grate. One large ember landed on the seat of Donovan's armchair. It glowed and hissed, but did not burn the seat. With an impatient wave of his hand, Donovan cooled it. The remaining ash exploded in a soft puff of air and vanished.

"I don't know who you are," he said, "but you really do need to work on your dialogue. I mean, really, what do you think this is, a Victorian Romance? Next you'll be warning how I'll 'feel your wrath,' if I don't cooperate, right?"

There was no immediate answer, and Donovan took a step forward.

"My god," he said, "you really *were* going to say that. Who the hell are you?"

"Give me the book," the voice said. This time there was no false bravado behind the words.

"I don't think so," Donovan replied. "As I said, this isn't a library, and I'm not a bookseller. If, in fact, I have the book you are looking for, I guess you are out of luck. If you'd come to my door, knocked, and asked politely I might have let you look at one of my books – or I might not – but unless you've got considerably more up your sleeve than an illusion of a flaming face in my fireplace, you're wasting your time, and mine."

Cleo suddenly dug a claw into Donovan's ankle. He flinched, but did not look down. Something had moved deep inside the flames, something dark and not associated with the face. Donovan glared directly into the fire face, hoping that his eyes hadn't given away what he'd seen.

"I did not come here to look at your book, or to ask a favor," the voice said. The tone was sibilant now, and the hissing intonation sent sparks skittering and dancing through the air. The motion of the flame gave substance to lips that had – until that moment – been totally obscured by flames. Whatever glamour it was that kept the intruder's features hidden was failing slowly. The shadowy hint of a nose poked out from between the glowing eyes. It was impossible to make out any features, but the face the fire hinted at wavered just beyond recognition.

"Who are you," Donovan asked, taking a step forward.

Whatever it was in the fire moved again; it flitted behind the flames and darted to the side.

"Step back," the voice commanded.

Donovan ignored it and took another step forward. He didn't speak, but he silently mouthed a shield charm. He didn't know how much of the fire was illusion, and how much was the real fire with an illusion impressed upon it. If he leaped forward and the face vanished, he faced the very real danger of setting himself on fire. If, on the other hand, the fire had been put out to protect whoever stood within the illusion, then Donovan might be able to leap onto the grate and drag them out into the open.

He hesitated, and all decisions became moot. The flames crackled and flared. The heat from the fire might have been an illusion, but if so that illusion was very real. Donovan stumbled back with a curse. Fire engulfed the eyes in the flame and soared up the inside of the chimney with a roar. The defense held. Donovan knew that his unwanted visitor was battering against the spell containing it within the fireplace. So far he had not proven strong enough, but if he continued as he was, he might cause the entire structure to explode from the contained energy.

There was a snap, like a rubber band drawn too tight and parting. A hideous scent of sulfur permeated the air in the room, and the fire, no longer bottled up, spurted from a fissure in the center of the fireplace grate, shooting from mid-air. Donovan cursed and drew a symbol with his free hand. Where his finger passed the air glowed silver, and when he finished with a flurry, the glow formed a fine mesh of luminescence and shot across the room, directly into the path of the escaping jet of flame.

When the mesh he'd created settled over the fiery leak, Donovan cried out. Light, feathery threads of illumination shot back to his fingers from the net he'd formed, and they glowed brighter where the two forces collided. Donovan closed his eyes and concentrated. He knew he needed to close off the breach in his defense, and that he had to do it quickly. The flames had already leaked out and dripped along the fine lines of power toward his hand. If they reached him before he was able to patch the spell, he would lose control of it entirely.

Distracted, he missed the first flash of shadow against the light of the fire. Two glittering eyes launched from the fireplace and soared over his head. Donovan staggered, straightened, and concentrated. Out of the corner of his eye he saw that the shadow had wings, and was soaring about the room, narrowly avoiding walls and curtains. Each swoop took the creature lower, until finally, with a great cry, it alighted on the third shelf from the top along the wall behind Donovan and began picking frantically at the spines of the books there with its beak.

Donovan curse and spun, grabbing for the bird, but he could not reach it, and in the second his concentration shifted, the flames roared. He whirled to face them, saw with shock that in that second of dropped attention the fire had dripped down the threads toward his outstretched fingers like molten wax. He muttered a single word and stepped forward. The droplets cascading toward him quivered, hovered in place, and then slowly retreated toward the glowing mesh.

Donovan pressed his advantage, and within seconds he had moved a step closer to the fire, and then another, pressing the fire relentlessly back. There was no hint of the glowing eyes, or the ethereal face in that fire. All of the intruder's strength had been diverted into that single breach in Donovan's defenses.

Cleo leaped to the first shelf and launched herself upward. A long swipe sent the bird fluttering upward, but as the cat passed, already spinning for a second lunge, the bird cawed in triumph and reached out with both taloned feet. Gripping the spine of a thin, leather tome, the raven wheeled back and up, narrowly missing a collision with the back of Donovan's head.

Cleo bounded off the shelves, planted her rear feet on Donovan's shoulder and launched herself after the fleeing bird. Donovan saw what was about to happen and let out a hoarse, choked cry. He sprang forward and concentrated every bit of will power and strength he had to the tips of the fingers of his left hand. The threads swelled, became strings and then sticky, ropes of energy. He dove at the fire, ignored the danger, and pressed his seal over the escaping flames.

Before he reached the hearth, a black flash shot past. The bird, seeming not to struggle at all with the heavy book, dove into the fire like a black arrow. Cleo flashed past Donovan in pursuit, and he drove his legs into the floor, launching after her in a headlong dive of his own. As if aware of its pursuers, the bird gave another great cry and slashed the air with its wings, narrowing itself and diving straight at the heart of the fire. It disappeared into the rift just as Donovan's hand pressed the ropy tendrils of his charm to the invisible wall of the ward spell. There was a bright shimmer, another crackle of energy, and as Cleo bounced off the now solid ward, Donovan leaned into it, seeming to rest against solid air, and sagged weakly, sliding down to sit on the floor.

He growled in frustration and pounded his hand on the hearth. There was no sign of the bird, the book, or the flaming face behind it all. Donovan sat for a moment, regaining his strength. Cleo shook her head, meowed plaintively, and then crawled into his lap. Donovan cradled her there, turned, and glanced up at the bookshelves behind him, already certain what he would find – or not find – when he did.

Two books had slid out and hung precariously over the edge of the shelf. The space between them, where the journal of Jean-Claude Le Duc had been tucked safely away, was empty. Donovan rose and deposited Cleo on his armchair, then walked to the bookshelf. There were scratches in the wood where the bird had scrabbled for purchase, and there were peck marks on the spines of the two volumes on either side. Donovan frowned.

Under normal circumstances, even an extremely talented bird would not have been able to slide a book off the shelf and carry it away. It was too heavy, for one thing. It had to have been enchanted, or more than a bird to begin with. He glanced around.

On the floor at his feet two black feathers rested. One had been trampled when he launched himself forward at the fireplace, but the other was clean. Cleo must have come closer to the mark than he'd realized with her first leap. He gave her an appreciative grin, but the cat was busy washing her left foot and paid no attention to him at all. She looked up when he lifted the feather from the floor and let out a soft yowl of disapproval.

"I know, Cleo," Donovan said, carrying the feather back to

his desk and returning to his seat. "I don't like it either, but what can we do?"

Donovan stared at the feather for a moment, and then sat up straighter. He placed it in the center of his desk, where the letter from Johndrow had rested only a few moments before, and set to work. Within moments he'd set the wards and placed his spell. It was a long shot, but some essence of the bird, and its master, should still be lingering either in the room, or the fireplace.

The feather rose, spun lazily in the air, and then pointed at the fireplace. Donovan rose, stepped around the desk, and gazed in the direction the feather pointed. He saw nothing, but stepped forward to the grate and glanced back over his shoulder. The feather jerked once, and then twisted a few degrees to Donovan's right. It pointed at the upper right corner of the fireplace grate. Donovan saw nothing on the metal grate itself, nor had anything dropped to the floor as the bird passed. He frowned.

He placed his hand on the brick wall beside the fireplace and whispered the incantation that released the security spell. The warmth from the dancing fire increased, and Donovan stepped closer. He didn't see Cleo, who had leaped up onto the desk chair and sat, paws on the surface of the desk, watching the feather twitch in lazily in the air. Cleo's tail whipped back and forth in time, and her muscles quivered.

Donovan leaned down. There was something tucked in behind the grate that held the logs in the fireplace. It was dark and flat, like a piece of cloth, or paper. There was just enough room on the side of the fire for him to reach one arm around behind, but he had to be very careful not to get too close to the flames. He knew his hair could catch in an instant, and he wasn't used to dealing with the open flame.

Just as his groping fingers neared the object behind the fire, Cleo leaped. There was a surprised yowl as the protections Donovan had set on the circle repelled her, sending her crashing to the side, knocking Johndrow's letter, the pendulum on its stand, and two of the small braziers askew as she scrabbled for purchase on the desktop.

Donovan spun, narrowly missed whipping his hair into the fire, and gasped. When the braziers tipped, the circle fragmented. Released from the circle, but not from the enchantment, the feather shot across the room at dizzying speed. Donovan rolled aside as it passed, narrowly missing his cheek. The feather passed through the fire, burst into flame, and drove into the object behind the grate with such force that it shattered in a flash. Donovan made a grab for the object, but he was too late. It was nothing but a small heap of ash by the time his fingers reached it. He brushed this out without much hope and collected it on a scrap of paper, but it was difficult to tell if the ashes came from burned paper, leather, cloth, or flesh, and he knew at least part of what he'd gathered was the remnant of the feather itself.

"Damn it, Cleo," he complained, clambering back to his feet. "That might have been important."

Cleo glared at him from the corner of his desk. She was seated in the exact spot where the small pendulum usually dangled on its stand. She looked indignant, and Donovan, despite his irritation, laughed. He bent down, picked up the pendulum, and examined it carefully. Nothing seemed broken, and once he'd straightened the metal stand a bit, it was as good as new. He shooed Cleo off the desk and returned the instrument to its proper place.

He leaned down to retrieve Johndrow's letter, remembering what he'd been doing when things had gone south, and before he could stand straight again, he stopped, still as stone. He thought of the missing vampire, Vanessa, and then of the contents of the stolen book. He'd read it only once, and it had been many years in the past, but the minute the pieces fell into place in his mind, he knew he was correct.

"Oh my god," he said softly. "The Perpetuum Vitae Serum; he's after Le Duc's formula."

He scooped up the letter, scanned its contents again, and then dropped it on his desk. Next he strode back over to the bookshelves and slid a large, leather bound tome from a shelf at shoulder height. He carried it back to his desk, opened it, and began to skim the index quickly.

It didn't take long to find what he was looking for. It was a reference to Jean-Claude Le Duc's life. In fact, it was the very reference that had sent Donovan off in search of the journal that had just been stolen. It was short, but there was enough detail to confirm his fears.

"Jean-Claude Le Duc," it read, "spent his entire life in search of a single spell. Rumor has it that he succeeded in developing a potion that would grant the recipient eternal life, but that he died trying to acquire all the proper ingredients. Among the things he gathered were certain crystal formations, ashes from the grave of a particular type of priest, and several more standard items. The final ingredient proved his undoing, as it apparently involves draining the blood of a vampire of a certain age. Le Duc was killed by vampires in 1832, and was not brought back as one of the undead, as far as any record can be found. His journal contains his studies, but to date no one has attempted this particular magic to our knowledge."

There was more, but Donovan had read enough. Cleo leaped up to the desk again, more delicately this time, and sat, regarding him.

"This is a bad one, girl," he said. "It may be the worst yet. I'd better get started, eh?"

As Cleo batted at the cord, Donovan took up the phone and dialed Johndrow's number. It was shaping up to be a very long night.

FIVE

Donovan reached Johndrow's assistant on the third ring, and was patched straight through. His call was obviously expected, and though Johndrow kept his voice calm, tension crackled at the edges of his words. It was the first such breach in the other's icy persona that Donovan had ever detected, and he knew from this that things had not improved since the note had been penned. He almost wished he didn't have to deliver worse news of his own.

"You'll look into it then?" Johndrow said immediately. "I knew you would, but I was worried you'd be tied up with something else, or ..."

"I would look into it even if you hadn't asked me," Donovan replied, measuring his words carefully. "I've had a visitor of my own. I think there's more to this than a simple kidnapping."

"What do you mean?" Johndrow asked. "I had a hard enough time convincing certain of the elders that Vanessa didn't take off on her own. How could you already know something?"

"Because," Donovan said, "whoever took her was here, as well."

There was a momentary silence, and then Johndrow asked. "You were robbed while you were away?"

"No," Donovan replied. "I was here, right in the room, when it happened. All that was taken was a single book. I didn't get a good shot at the intruder, though Cleo tore a few tail feathers out of his familiar. It was a crow, a very large one, maybe a raven. I've never seen it before."

There was silence on the line again, and Donovan knew that Johndrow was considering the wisdom of putting his faith into someone who'd already come face to face with the one he sought – and had not come out on top. It was a natural reaction, but still irritating.

"It took all he had to get a breach large enough for his bird to enter," Donovan said. "If I'd been ready for him, we'd have caught the thing and put an end to it. As it is, he made it in through the fireplace, and he escaped with an old journal."

"A journal?" Johndrow said. "What does a journal have to do with Vanessa? How do you know it's the same person at all?"

"It wasn't just any journal," Donovan answered. "It belonged to a French alchemist named Jean Claude Le Duc. He was a very single minded man – the volume is not a thick one. It is concentrated on the formula for a single spell, and Le Duc never lived to see that spell put into use."

"What spell?" Johndrow asked. "That name is familiar, but I can't quite place it."

"It should be familiar," Donovan said. "The formula is for the Perpetuum Vitae potion, and the ingredient that caused Le Duc's death?"

There was a hiss on Johndrow's end of the line. "The blood drained from a vampire," he whispered. "From a very old vampire."

"Vanessa fits that description," Donovan said, softening his tone. "She's in more danger than you realized."

"But surely," Johndrow said, "There are other difficult items on that list. Could he have gathered them all without drawing attention to himself?"

"It might have been a problem to find that out," Donovan replied, "if technology hadn't become so advanced. I scan all of the books I acquire into my computer before putting them on the shelves. It allows me to preserve very old and fragile texts, and to protect against an emergency. I have a copy of the formula, and I don't believe he's quite got everything he needs. We have some time, though not a great deal of it. The blood must be extracted immediately preceding the mixing process, so we can expect he is keeping Vanessa – alive -- until he's ready."

"What does he need?" Johndrow asked. "If I knew…"

"Let me handle that," Donovan cut in. There was silence on Johndrow's end.

"This is what you are hiring me to do," Donovan continued. "I will have a better chance of tracing this without others blundering around muddying the waters, and despite what just happened here, I have the better chance of saving her once I've found her. Even if you managed to track him, what would you do? I have your letter – I know what happened with Kline."

"What happened with Kline is the reason I don't feel comfortable trusting this to only one man," Johndrow replied. "Kline's people have resources, and I can call in my own people..."

"Kline's people are not trained to work in the field," Donovan replied calmly, "and your own people aren't trained for this type of work at all. Let's be honest, Preston, it's been a long time since any of your kind has needed to march into real battle. Even the elders, yourself included, are decades from the last serious conflict. This is what I do, let me handle it."

"I will give you two days," Johndrow replied. "I won't lose her through foolish trust."

"I understand," Donovan replied. "I don't want this guy succeeding any more than you do, though admittedly for selfish reasons."

"Keep me informed, Mr. DeChance," Johndrow said softly. "Don't leave me sitting at home and wondering. Idle hands, you know..."

"I'll be in touch," Donovan replied. He hung up the phone and stared at the wall.

He slid the computer's keyboard and mouse back into place and tapped the keyboard. When prompted, he logged in and watched as the machine loaded. He smiled as mechanical drives whirred, lights flashed, and complex patterns of logical numbers whirled through machine. Men could say what they wanted about magic not existing, but they understood the concepts of ritual and reaction quite well. Their methods were slow and relatively crude, but the outcome was solid and workable. The Personal Computer was one of the finest magical achievements of the age.

Once the logon sequence ended he opened the encryption

software he used to scramble the more esoteric texts he'd scanned. The computer had more than standard firewall protections, and a number of enhancements that had nothing to do with microchips or wires. A series of symbols rotated into place on the screen, and in the center a large gold colored disk spun lazily. At each point corresponding with the correct pattern, Donovan tapped the button on his mouse, and the disk slowed, stopped, and then spun the opposite direction. After seven flip-flops, there was a sound like a key sliding into a lock, and the disk spun inward, disappearing from the screen. What appeared was a single folder, and Donovan opened this quickly.

He flipped through the directories until he found one titled "Journals" and opened this, then chose Le Duc's manuscript. The pages had been scanned in at very high resolution, and the program he viewed them in had singularly amazing magnification properties, as well as a translation algorithm Donovan had designed himself. Alchemy in the twenty-first century, he liked to call it. An electronic philosopher's stone.

The manuscript was not difficult to read. The French was archaic, but the script was clear and clean, and Le Duc had taken great pains to separate the lines evenly and to make no mistakes. Mistakes in such a text could be disastrous, at the one end causing a spell to fail with no result, and at the other sending forces crashing out of control. Le Duc had been meticulous to the end.

The formula itself had been developed over a long period of trial and error, gathered piece by piece from a wide variety of sources. Donovan recognized several of the sources cited, and had to admit that for a fanatic, Le Duc had been very clever. It was unfortunate when such genius coupled itself with a sociopathic disregard for life or the fragile lines of balance that held the world together.

There were six ingredients in all. Two of them were simple powders that anyone could have located. Donovan knew he could assume that these had already been collected. That left three ingredients to go. One of those, Vanessa, had already been scratched off the list. The remaining three might pose more of a problem.

A certain crystal was required for the wand that had to be

manufactured for this spell. It was one of the rarest of stones, and Donovan knew the location of the only store of it that was known. It was, coincidentally or not, held in San Valencez – very likely this unknown magician knew this well enough, and had planned his assaults to confine them to the smallest area possible. Either that or it was pure luck. In any case, Donovan did not worry immediately about the theft of the crystal. He turned his concentration on the final ingredients.

Next was an extremely rare item. The spell required a pair of perfectly matched Timeline Crystals. These were used in the creation of certain higher level portals, and were cherished for their rarity, and for the complexity of preserving their potential. There was a pair in San Valencez, but it was not accessible. Not without an army, anyway, and certainly not after Donovan warned their owner of trouble to come.

That left the final ingredient. He frowned. "The dust formed of the marrow of the spinal cord of a priest who has performed both last rites and exorcism."

This was a truly problematic ingredient. It would only be stockpiled by a necromancer, and there were less than a handful of these unsavory wizards in existence. It was possible to retrieve the powder without the aid of necromancy, but grave digging posed problems of its own, and the circumstances of the priest's life and death needed to be rather singular. Of the existing necromancers, Donovan could think of neither an easy mark for extortion, nor one likely to give this sort of assistance to any other. Necromancers were more comfortable with their once-dead companions.

That left the more direct approach. If he could locate a priest that fit the description in the formula, the thief could extract the powder himself. It wouldn't' be easy. The Last Rites were not rare, but there had been few sanctioned exorcists over the past century, and a crackpot wouldn't do. There was also the fact that relics recovered from such graves were rare, powerful and valuable. That meant that every collector in existence would cherish them and the older graves from days when exorcism was more common, would have been sought out and violated long ago.

In modern times, the ritual was still practiced, though rarely. If he moved quickly enough, Donovan knew he'd be able to localize possible gravesites for a source of the powder. Maybe, with his connections and the additional electronic resources he commanded, he could find such a grave more quickly than their unknown thief could manage it. It was hard to believe that others would band together with anyone proposing to cast such a spell as the *Perpetuum Vitae*, because it benefited only he or she who cast it. It wasn't the kind of magic one shared, and if he was forced to work on his own, or with secretive mercenary assistance, then Donovan's new enemy was at a disadvantage. No one who heard what was going on would want the spell to succeed.

There was no time to lose. Donovan rose, gathered a few objects from the shelves that he tucked into his pocket, and double-checked the security wards. Before he left, he picked Cleo up unceremoniously and plopped her into the center of the symbol on his desk. The cat meowed at him, possibly in complaint, possibly just in irritation, but he paid no attention.

"I need your help, Cleo," he said softly. "You need to find Amethyst. Tell her I miss her, and then warn her about what happened here. Tell her I'll be in contact soon."

Cleo returned his gaze unblinkingly. Donovan closed his eyes and raised one hand. In an intricate and graceful scrawl, he drew symbols in the air. These gathered substance, like silver mist, or smoke, and when he drew his finger down with a final slash and spoke aloud, reciting in ancient Egyptian, the mist whirled in a circular motion around Cleo, who sat very still, never breaking eye contact. The mist spun faster, thickened into a milky white wall, and then, with a sudden release of energy that sounded like the popping of a huge bubble, it was gone.

No trace of Cleo remained on the desktop. Donovan turned, opened the door, and stepped out into the night. The sun was just dipping beneath the horizon, and he knew Club Chaos would soon be opening their doors.

SIX

Vanessa swam lazily up through darkness toward consciousness. Her thoughts were a cloudy fog of half-memories and unlikely images. She remembered the party. She remembered the beat of the music, flowing through the walls and the floor and shimmering through the air. She remembered Preston's speech before he shared the bottle he'd been so proud of, the wine with Byron's blood. Had it been too strong? Had she taken her share, admittedly larger than the others had received, walked blithely away, and passed out?

No. There was more, she knew there was more, but she couldn't bring it to the surface of her mind. She opened her eyes and the room before her spun. She blinked, tried again, and managed to focus weakly. The walls were dark and gray; cold polished stone where there should have been deep, rich paneling. The air was dank, and she was hungry – hungry like she hadn't been in years. She was also alone.

Vanessa drew on the strength of centuries and focused her mind. When she moved, there was a clink of metal. She glanced down and found that her wrists, and her ankles, were manacled. The chains that were attached to these bonds disappeared into small recesses in the stone wall to the left of the cot she lay upon. She sat up, sending the chains rippling over the side of the hard, thin mattress to pool on the floor.

The room was empty. Other than the cot a long, empty table, and a massive wooden door on the far wall, nothing broke the stark emptiness of the cell. That was what it was. For all its size – the walls stretched what must have been twenty feet to an arched ceiling. Was she in a tower? It seemed so, but she hadn't seen such a tower since castles had been in vogue.

As she sat, taking in her surroundings, the last of the cobwebs cleared from her mind. Whatever had happened, it wasn't because of the effect of a mixture of blood and wine. She vaguely remembered having stepped into the kitchen. There had been a younger guest, perhaps a century, though for some reason it had been difficult to be certain. He had asked to see more of the house, and though she knew he was only flirting, and that she would have to extricate herself fairly quickly, the urge to tease him had been impossible to ignore. She'd stepped through the kitchen and into the hall. Kline was there, standing beside the elevator, and she'd been about to speak to him when something hit her from behind.

The blow wasn't a physical one. Her mind had simply blanked. She had no idea what had happened to Kline. She vaguely recalled the face of the young one she'd been with, but she couldn't remember who he was, or why he'd been invited. She knew that she'd never seen this tower before.

The chains clinked again, and Vanessa stared down at them contemptuously. Whoever had put her in this room was a fool. She rose, gripped the chain where it snapped onto a ring on one manacle, and yanked at it with incredible strength. The metal, rather than snapping, gave slightly under the pressure. Vanessa frowned. She tried again, twisting this time to break the link closest to her wrist, but again the chain proved flexible. It spun with her twist, and when it snapped back into place the jolt threw her across the cot and into the stone wall.

Real fear stole through her for the first time. She tore frantically at the chains, pressed her feet into the wall and dragged at them, but they did nothing more than flex slightly. They were enchanted, and whatever effort she made to remove or snap them reversed painfully, until she was crying out with rage and pain.

The door opened and a man stepped into the room. He stayed carefully out of reach near the door, and smiled at her. Vanessa stopped struggling, slid off the cot in a single fluid motion and stood. She returned his gaze evenly. She was frightened, but she wasn't going to give her captor the satisfaction of seeing it in her expression.

She still wore the evening gown she'd turned heads with at
Preston's party, and the seemingly impossibly high heels were
still strapped around her slender ankles. She stood very still
and gauged the distance between them against the length of
her chains.

He was not undead. She knew this the second he entered
the room. His blood pumped hot and inviting through veins
very much alive. It was rich blood, and old. She scented power
and tasted strength.

Vanessa took advantage of the silence to study him. He was
at least six feet tall, had long, silver blonde hair and gray eyes.
He was slender and moved with casual grace. She thought he
was used to giving orders and being obeyed. She'd seen the
same haughty arrogance in others. Most of them were dead.
She saw just the hint of the guise he'd worn when he tricked
her into the hallway. Whoever he was, he'd slipped past Kline's
defenses and spirited her right out of Johndrow's supposedly
secure penthouse.

"So," he said at last, stepping a bit closer, "you are awake
at last. It's a pity we have to meet under such circumstances.
I've heard stories for years of your beauty, but never had the
opportunity to verify it for myself. The rumors did you little
justice."

"You brought me here to admire me?" she asked, turning
toward him, but making no move to approach. "Surely it would
have been easier to contact my husband and arrange to meet.
He is a very social creature."

"And not," the man countered, "overly bright. He should
check his guest lists more carefully."

"You weren't on that list," she replied with certainty.

"No," he admitted with a slow smile, "I was not. However,
appearances can be deceiving. Your lover's security was quite
good – the best in the business, I'm told, but they were not
looking for your guests, were they? They were looking for
something, or someone, unexpected."

Vanessa remained silent.

"No guesses? Well, I'll tell you then. That old friend of
yours, Margot, is that her name? She took a new lover recently.

But of course, you knew that – the two of them were invited to the party. He wasn't long 'in the blood,' but he was certainly good for her ego. I believe that's how she put it, anyway. It was a shame to end his existence so soon – so early in his second life. Less than a hundred years since his death, and now he's gone. Margot never knew the difference.

"It's not an easy charm, but for a certain amount of time, while a spirit lingers between worlds, their shape, identity, even personality can be stolen. Did you know that? Kline must have known it, but for some reason, he didn't check. I admit that he disappointed me. It was arrogant of him to attempt the security for your party by himself, and even more foolish to assume that your guests were beyond reproach. I wonder if Margot has found the remains, or if she's had the courage to tell Johndrow about it. Do you think he'll kill her?"

The man raised a long, slender eyebrow and glanced at Vanessa with what appeared to be real interest. The conversational tone of his voice chilled her more than his words. He was supremely confident, and if remorse was part of his makeup, he had hidden it well.

"He will kill you," she said softly. "The elders will not stand for this. You may have gotten past Kline, and you may have sent one of the young ones to his final death, but you will not find Preston so simple to brush aside."

The man actually laughed at this. His voice tinkled like broken glass; it was empty of mirth and dripped contempt.

"Do you really think so?" he asked. The sarcasm in his tone sounded brittle, like his laughter. Vanessa didn't want to know what would show through if it shattered.

The man glanced over his shoulder, and then scanned the room, feigning nervous fright. "Do you think they're onto me yet? I'd better go and check my security. Maybe…" He hesitated, dropped his charade, and fixed her with an icy stare, "I should call Kline's people."

Vanessa held herself in check. Anger nearly drove thought from her mind, but he was still out of reach. Then, as if reading her mind, or answering her silent request, he stepped forward.

"Who are you?" she asked. Her voice was low, and she

fought to keep the anger out of her tone.

"That's not really important," he said. "You won't be around to learn what it means, I'm afraid. I have plans for you, my dear, and I'm afraid they don't include further longevity, at least not for yourself."

He had taken three slow steps toward her as he spoke. His movements were slow and languid. Vanessa didn't know if he was stupid, or if his arrogance was justified, but she knew that she would have to find out. He might not give her a second chance. Cocking her head seductively, she put one hand on her hip and leaned on it just enough that her gown slit to show the full length of one slender leg.

"Are you sure there isn't some other arrangement we could come to?" she asked. She tried to give her voice a coy lilt, but was afraid it came out too high pitched and a little shrill.

The man smiled and took another step toward her. "Interesting," he said. "I suppose you have something in mind?"

Vanessa coiled and sprang with all the preternatural speed and strength the centuries had granted her. The chain trailed behind her like the tail of a kite, and though heavy, it did not appear to slow her attack. The man backpedaled and nearly lost his balance. Vanessa flew headlong, hands extended like talons. She gripped the edge of his robe, just as she hit the end of the chain and it drew her up short with a horrible snap of bone. Her right wrist shattered, but she clung to him with her left. Crying out in rage she dragged that robe toward her, but he was seconds too quick. With a gasp, he spoke, and the word hovered between them.

A clattering sound filled the room, and Vanessa was jerked backward. Her captor's robe tore, and she held that bit of cloth in her hand, but the chains retracted into the wall, slowly and relentlessly. Vanessa gritted her teeth against the pain and drove forward, fighting her bonds. It was no use. She slid back, step after inexorable step and the man, back on his feet and with his composure regained, followed her. He kept just out of reach and smirked as she snarled and scratched the air, trying to reach him.

Within moments the chains had drawn tight. Vanessa was pinned flat against the wall, her wrists out to her sides and her ankles immobile, slightly spread. She fought, but she could barely twist her wrists in the charmed manacles, and the one was only partially healed. It would be hours before it mended properly. The force drawing the chains back into the wall was impossibly strong. The man had continued his slow, deliberate pursuit, and now that she was held helplessly to the stone, he stepped closer still. He was careful to keep his throat out of the possible range of her fangs, but he pressed his leg between hers and rested his chest against the material of her gown so her nipples brushed the rough fabric of his jacket.

"Very good," he said. "You are faster than I expected, much faster – and stronger. I have done even better than I'd hoped."

Vanessa didn't reply. She continued to struggle. She tried desperately to pull away from him and at the same time ground the already tortured bones of her wrists and ankles against her bonds. She gritted her teeth against it the pain, unwilling to give him the satisfaction of knowing how great it was.

"You can smell it, can't you?" he asked, turning his head to the side so that the pulsing vein in his neck was in clear view. "I know you can – probably smelled me the moment I entered the room, didn't you?"

He pressed closer, and Vanessa began to panic. His voice droned on, but she only caught the words between the thunderous, crashing beats of his heart. She'd been this close to many throats, fed many times, though not to the death – not in three hundred years. This was like nothing she'd ever experienced. His pulse blanked thought, and the heady, powerful scent of his blood – the taste of it, even through his skin, maddened her.

Her gums retracted to show long, pearl-white fangs. Her jaws worked convulsively, trying to latch on and drive those fangs home and drain that sweet, hot blood. She felt him brush a hand through her hair and lunged, like a wild beast, toward his wrist, but he was far too quick now, and her mind had dropped into a slow-motion world of fuzzy vision and humming sound. He stroked the other side of her throat, and she lunged that way, lashing her hair back and forth across his face. Each time she tried to clamp onto him, he evaded her, and throughout it all, he caressed her cheeks, her throat, and her hair. His voice never ceased, and she realized vaguely that he was chanting.

Then something slipped between her lips. She tried to turn from it, but it was too late. Blood spurted in over her tongue, washed down her throat, and she latched onto the metal tube like a baby suckling its mother. She couldn't stop herself. It was his blood, she knew the scent, the taste, and it was as sweet as she'd imagined, though cold – so cold.

"That's right," she heard him say. "Take it all."

She did. He pulled back from her with a satisfied smirk on his face and surveyed his work. Vanessa hung limply from the chains. Her bones had knit themselves and healed, her complexion had grown rosier. Her strength returned, but along with it a strange, inexplicable lethargy.

Her captor waited a few moments longer, then stepped forward again. She watched him, but did not try to reach him. Her thoughts were shifting very slowly, and she couldn't quite remember why she'd wanted to escape, or who he was. He stepped close again, pulled something from his pocket, and slipped it around her neck.

Glancing down, she saw he had hung a circular gold pendant on a chain around her neck. He held the ends of the chain together behind her and whispered two words she didn't understand. When he stepped back, the chain was joined in back. The chains on the wall grew slack.

Vanessa allowed him to lead her to the cot by the wall and sat beside him. The chains trailed behind her and hung limply down over the edge of the cot. She knew she should be doing something, but could not bring it into focus. Her eyelids had begun to flutter, and she was very tired.

"I couldn't have you attacking me every few minutes, you know," he said conversationally. "You really are far too fast to be trusted. I think things will go more smoothly now, don't you?"

Vanessa nodded her head, though she had no idea what things he meant. She hoped he'd leave her so she could lie back on the cot and rest. She thought the sun must have risen outside and sapped her strength. If the building had proper shielding, this wouldn't happen. She tried to tell him, but he shook his head.

"It's fine. You get some rest, and I'll be back to see you with more blood. We have to keep you healthy, don't we?"

She nodded.

He reached out and traced her throat with a long fingernail, lifted her chin, studied her face, and then stroked her skin gently. "Before long," he told her, "I'll be taking my blood back, you see. All of it, and more. I'll be taking all of that wonderful, powerful blood of yours, and that exquisite immortality, and I'll be keeping it for my own. I'm afraid I can't share, and it's a pity, but you understand, don't you?" She nodded, though she really didn't understand at all. He couldn't have said what she thought he did, how was that possible? She was the one who took blood – she didn't give it back. What a funny thought.

The man stood and laid her back on the cot, and Vanessa closed her eyes at once. On her chest, the gold medallion glowed with a dim golden light. He watched for a moment, nodded, and tucked the small bottle with its metal tube spout back into a fold of his robe.

"How fitting," he said, brushing his fingers a final time through her hair. "They sell these for the feeding of pets, you see."

Without a backward glance, he left the tower room and the heavy stone door closed behind him. On the cot Vanessa lay very still. Her eyes were closed, and other than an occasional twitch at the corner of her mouth, nothing disturbed the crypt-still air, or the total, lifeless silence.

Miles away, seated in his living room staring at the smooth obsidian shield on his window, Johndrow jerked so hard he nearly dropped the wine glass in his hand. He lurched, caught himself, and managed to place the goblet on the table beside him.

"What is it?" The younger man across the table from him

shot to his feet. He was dark, swarthy and thin. He appeared to be no more than about seventeen years old, though he'd walked the streets of this same city for more than a hundred and fifty years.

He stood beside Johndrow, who recovered quickly, and watched as his elder sat up straight, eyes blazing. Then he felt it too, and his eyes widened.

"He has fed her something," Johndrow said. "I don't know what it was, but it was powerful. I can almost taste it. I…"

He fell silent, and the younger man cursed.

"This is too much," he said. "First he steals Vanessa from your home, now he invades our minds, using hers. We can't just sit around and wait, hoping this DeChance will find him. We have to act ourselves, and quickly."

"I told him he would have forty eight hours," Johndrow said, reaching for his glass. He steadied himself, then took a long gulp of the wine, and then put the goblet down again. "You must be patient, Vein, we all must be. Donovan is not just any man, and this job is beyond our knowledge. I'll ask you what he asked me; what would you do if you found this thief? If he can control Vanessa, drag her out of here like a toy, and controls her still – what chance would you have?"

There was no insult or contempt in Johndrow's question, but the younger man scowled. "You are too quick to let others make your decisions," he snapped. "I would not go alone. There are others – many others. We'll find the one who has done this, and we'll put an end to this once and for all."

"You will wait," Johndrow said. He rose to his feet and glared at his visitor. "You will not do anything to jeopardize her safety. Is that clear?"

The young man stood silent, glaring at him, and Johndrow repeated the question.

"Am I clear, Vein? No interference. None. When the time comes that we have no choice but to take this matter into our own hands, you will be the first I call."

Vein said nothing. He drained his own wine goblet, and placed it on the table beside Johndrow's.

"I've got to go," he said. "I'm expected downtown."

Johndrow watched him for a moment, as if judging the other's silence.

"Stay in touch," Johndrow said, turning back to the window. It was growing dark out. Soon he'd be able to open the shield and watch the stars. "Don't do anything foolish. Two days is not such a long time – particularly for us."

Vein turned on his heel and vanished from the room. Moments later a soft chime indicated that he'd found his way to the elevator and been granted access.

"Where are you, Vanessa?" Johndrow asked.

Silence was his only answer, and he punctuated it by pouring another glass of wine.

SEVEN

Most of the citizens of the world travel through cities by the main roads. Heads down and collars pulled up against the growing chill of night, they slide past the mouths of alleys and turn away from shadowed stairways, particularly those leading down. Deeper in, where the veins of civilization are narrow and more easily clogged, where side streets and garbage-strewn tributaries trail off into unknown darkness, another city thrives.

The two coexist in reasonable peace, the citizens of each rarely crossing into the other's world or brushing shoulders on purpose. Still, there are gray areas. Life has certain requirements, and some of those requirements exist on the other side of boundaries otherwise avoided. At such boundaries, you sometimes find a crossroads. That's what Club Chaos had become.

The only way to reach the club was through an alley. You walked down to where a neon sign said PHONE, and you stepped into the phone booth. Right off the bat it was strange, because there is no reason a phone booth would be located in a dark alley. Who would use it? Once inside, you dialed a number, and the booth spun like a revolving door and deposited you inside. There were several distinct numbers you might use to access Club Chaos.

The first, the number you'd find now and then on the streets, in phone booths or inked onto bathroom walls; the one in the fine print at the bottom of posters announcing live entertainment and cheap drinks; that number was obvious. You dialed sixty-nine and you spun into a world where morality was checked at the door. The music was loud, usually heavy gothic or industrial, pounding so loudly that the most important skill patrons developed was an ability to read lips and a willingness to communicate on a more primal level.

This was the area of the club where worlds mixed most freely. The undead haunted the shadows and held court with pale, thin children and aging junkies. Musicians searched for their own crossroads down chemical highways, always providing the backbeat and the melody required to sustain the groove. Donovan had spent plenty of time there, though not as much in recent years.

If you dialed the more complex 360, your entrance was different. When the booth spun, it didn't stop at the one hundred and eighty degree point, as you'd expect, but spun on around. Logic said you'd step back into the alley, but logic was on hold at Club Chaos. What you entered with the 360 code was a very dark bar. There were no mirrors, few lights, only ranks of dark tables where quite conversations were carried on in low tones. The air was always smoky, and the music was always soft. It ranged from blues to light jazz, from Robert Johnson to Charlie Johnson and back again.

They called this central bar The Crossroads, and there was no set clientele. It was a place for business transactions and private liaisons. It was neutral ground where the two halves of the club, and of the city, met in relative peace. There were no bouncers in sight, but Donovan knew from experience that they would miraculously appear if they were needed. Trouble was rare, and when it erupted, was handled quickly and with great force.

Donovan stepped into the phone booth and punched in the second code without hesitation. He knew three codes personally, and knew of the existence of at least two others. He imagined the club as a giant wheel with alcoves all around its circumference, but he'd never had opportunity or reason to look into it. He had access to the third, more private club, but his business lay elsewhere this day. He needed information, and he needed to find it quickly. He might have found the information by dialing sixty-nine, but he wasn't in the mood to scream over the music, and he didn't like using other means of communication in such an exposed place.

Scattered patrons lined the bar and leaned in close over the tables. As he entered The Crossroads, a few heads turned in his direction, but no one spoke. There was no bell over the door, and there were no greetings shouted from the bar, or the tables. He was simply absorbed by the smoke and Billie Holiday's crooning voice, and then deposited on a stool at the bar without ceremony.

The barman approached, polishing a glass tumbler carefully with a gleaming white towel. He had long hair, and the way he squinted with his right eye gave his face a sort of sideways, off-kilter aspect. He didn't speak, just stopped in front of Donovan, who ordered bourbon and water on the rocks, nodded, and spun.

There were three others at the bar. Donovan turned and inspected them quickly. He didn't let his gaze linger on any one person, or table, because it just wasn't done. This was a place you came to if you needed privacy, as well as a private hideaway for making deals and sealing pacts. A lot of what happened here was never intended to be spoken of or described once a patron walked back out through the door and into the alley, and it was better still if they managed to develop a case of amnesia.

Donovan had been coming to The Crossroads for many years, and he respected their policies. He'd made use of the place several times in his own business dealings, and had always appreciated that they were courteous and discrete.

At the far end of the bar, a very thin woman leaned over a cup of something hot. It might have been herbal tea, but Donovan didn't think so. When he'd entered the room, she'd turned to the door – maybe hoping to see someone else slip in – and he'd seen her eyes. They reflected what light was available in the room and flashed silver. They were a seer's eyes, and every time Donovan met such a gaze he had the urge to turn away. For a brief moment he considered approaching her – it was possible she could find his answers for him without the personal risk and trouble other methods entailed, but he decided against it. Consulting a seer had its perils, and was never cheap.

A couple of stools down from her two others sat together.

They leaned in close and brushed shoulders as they whispered. One rose abruptly, pushed back from the bar, and headed for the door. The other signaled the bartender to refill his beer glass. Donovan didn't hesitate. He rose, slid over a few stools to sit beside the man, and indicated to the barman that he was buying.

The man seated beside Donovan didn't look up at his approach. There was also no complaint when the bartender refilled the beer glass and stepped away down the bar, discreetly out of hearing.

"Hello Windham," Donovan said. He took a long, slow sip of the bourbon and water and watched the other man in silence.

Up close, the man's profile took on stark angles. He was razor thin. His long hair wasn't exactly greasy, but it also wasn't clean. He wore a dark trench coat, despite the fact that in San Valencez there were only a few days of the year cool enough to warrant it. There were gloves on the bar beside him, and Donovan noted that the man's hands were uncommonly long and slender. His skin, where it was visible, was very pale and tinged a light yellow. A quick assessment by one who didn't know him would have placed Windham in Johndrow's group, but it would be a mistake.

Jasper Windham was a collector. He made his living finding things; ingredients for potions, amulets, missing persons, things that others didn't want found. Windham wasn't the only collector in the city, but he was one of the best. Donovan was pleased to have found him so quickly and easily.

"You come here just to buy me beer?" Windham asked, turning to face Donovan at last, "or you need something?"

Windham's voice was very dry, hardly more than a whisper, as if the vocal chords that formed its sound were made of aged parchment. He wrapped his fingers around the fresh beer, and Donovan saw that they circled the glass completely and folded in under his palm. The nails were yellow and chipped.

Donovan met Windham's gaze and smiled thinly. "You know me too well, old friend," he said tipping his drink gently in Windham's direction. "I don't have much time for casual drinking these days."

Windham continued to stare pointedly, not speaking. He sipped his beer, and then placed it back on the bar.

"There are strange things happening," Donovan continued. "They are things that concern me and quite a few others as well. I'm looking for some information."

"I don't deal in information," Windham replied, dropping his gaze. "I find things, you know that."

Donovan nodded, despite the fact his suddenly reluctant companion was no longer looking at him.

"Yes, I know." he said. "I also know that if someone wants something, you are one of their first choices for finding it. That's why I'm here. There are a lot of things ending up – missing. Did you hear what happened at Johndrow's party?"

Windham's head swiveled snake-quick.

"I had nothing to do with that. I wouldn't even have tried with Kline there, and I don't do kidnapping."

"I didn't suggest that you did," Donovan replied, taking another sip of his bourbon. "I'm not sure who was behind it, but the same person visited me, and now it's personal."

Windham watched Donovan carefully, but no longer seemed inclined to interrupt.

"Something of mine was taken," Donovan continued, "and if my suspicions are correct, there will be more things taken before our thief has finished. I think I know what he's after... what I'm trying to find out is if he's tried to get you to find it for him."

Windham held his silence. He had grown very still, and Donovan knew he was poised to defend himself, or run.

"I know you don't share information on your clients," Donovan said. "I'd be pretty unhappy with you myself if you did, but I'm thinking the one I'm looking for might not be a client yet. Maybe he talked to you . . . or someone you know. Maybe you didn't like what you saw, or heard. Maybe you're still thinking about it. Maybe I have enough money backing me to make you think twice."

"I'm listening," Windham said. His whispery voice was almost lost in the soft jazz. It dropped into the conversation like a ghost lyric behind the saxophone.

"I think he's looking for bone marrow dust," Donovan said, getting straight to the point. "But not just any dust. This would be from a very particular bone, and a very difficult donor. I'm not going to give you any more details until I know where we stand, but I bet I've said enough."

Something flickered across Windham's expression, just for a moment, and then he sat still and silent as stone again. Donovan sipped his whiskey, and waited.

"I might have heard something," Windham said at last, turning back to his beer. He spoke quickly and kept his head down, muffling his words further with the proximity of the polished wood bar, and punctuating his words with quick sips of cold beer. "No one contacted me directly, you understand, but there is a general call out on the street, if you know where to find such requests– very handsome wages, I might add – for such an item. It's difficult, and the last I'd heard no one has attempted to fill the order. Whoever does won't have to work for some time to come, but the risks…"

"Assuming we're talking about the same item," Donovan said, "how many sources would there be – locally?"

Windham glanced at him, trying to read his intentions, then replied with a shrug.

"One." He said, dropping some of the secrecy. "There is only one such grave within a hundred miles. It's in the older section of the Shady Grove Cemetery, between here and Lavender. I'm sure you're familiar with the location."

Donovan nodded. There had been all sorts of strange occurrences at the particular graveyard Windham had named.

"That place is pretty well guarded," he said. "I can see how the job could be complicated."

"Are you looking, too?" Windham asked.

"I'm looking, but not for someone to do the work," Donovan replied. "I want to see to it that the one who is seeking it doesn't come into possession of this particular item."

"He won't get it from me," Windham said with a shrug. "I doubt he'll find a collector in the city who'd go for it. There's too much chance of getting caught, and the records for that section of the graveyard are sketchy. It might take hours just to find the right grave, and what if someone took him long ago? There's no way to tell without digging him up, unless you're a necromancer, and no one wants to attract attention."

"That's understandable," Donovan replied. "You're certain these bones ... meet the criteria?"

"Absolutely," Windham said without hesitation. "On that much the records are solid. The grave belongs to Father Antoine Vargas. He was one of the first priests to serve at the Cathedral of San Marcos, by the Sea. I'm sure you know the place?"

"I've seen it," Donovan said.

"Father Antoine was, apparently, very sensitive to demons. He was retired at an early age by the church for performing exorcisms. This would make him unsuitable, except that the first few of these ceremonies were sanctioned by The Church. The records I found show that he was unaccountably successful in these rituals, though the church never acknowledged it. He made quite a stir in other parts of the city at the time."

Donovan nodded thoughtfully. "Why is it so difficult to find his grave, then?"

"He was not in favor with the church for the last decade of his life. Apparently, despite the success rate his exorcisms claimed, The Church didn't like the idea that there could be such a concentrated, acknowledged burst of evil in one place. He was replaced with another and given a small cottage by the beach and enough money to live off of, which it seems he used little of before one of his rituals finally claimed him. The grave was paid for by parishioners – not by the church – and it is marked only with a flat stone. The inscription, according to my sources, reads simply 'Gone to God.'

"Of course, locating the grave is the least of the problems," Windham sighed. It was obvious he would have loved to accept this particular assignment, and Donovan had to fight back the frown that threatened to crease his brow.

"You said the price for this job was high," he said, controlling his voice. "How open is the call?"

Windham glanced up at him sharply.

"You aren't thinking about horning in on the business?" he asked. His voice had grown suddenly shrewd, and sharp.

Donovan laughed and took another sip of his whiskey. He turned fully in his seat to face the thin, cadaverous man beside him.

"Not a chance," he said flatly. "I like what I do just fine. I have only two reasons for being here. The first is to see that this thief doesn't acquire what he needs to complete a particular ritual, and the second, if possible, is to find out who he is. If I had what he needed, he'd have to come to me again, wouldn't he?"

"I suppose he would, at that," Windham said, nodding thoughtfully. "I'm not going after this one, in any case. Security is tight on that graveyard, and though there are always ways around it, most of them are too costly and difficult to make it worth my while. I'd have to cut someone else in…"

He glanced at Donovan shrewdly.

"It won't be for sale when I'm done," Donovan growled.

It was Windham's turn to laugh. "Can't blame me for thinking about it. I'll keep checking, but last I heard, most of the collector's felt the same as I do. It's too risky. We figure he'll have to go out of state, maybe out of the country to get what he needs, and that could take a long time."

"He doesn't strike me as very patient," Donovan said. "My guess is that if he can't get someone else to collect this for him, he'll go himself. He's certainly got the skill. I don't suppose you'd just tell me who it is and save me the trouble?"

Windham drained his beer and stood.

"I'd love to help you," he said, "but the call that went out is anonymous. The instructions are clear, and payment is secured through a third party – one I won't be naming – but I doubt even he knows the face of the buyer. I guess your new friend knows you're coming."

"I'd be disappointed if he thought otherwise," Donovan said. He reached into his pocket and pulled out a small, folded wad of bills. He peeled two off the end and held them between his thumb and forefinger.

"If you hear anything more about this, I want to know. If someone else takes the challenge, even if they fail, or if your contacts happen to notice a particular order going through channels out of state, I want to know about it. Don't wait, send a messenger. If the information is good, I'll double the usual fee."

"I told you," Windham said softly, slipping the bills from between Donovan's fingers and sliding them into the pocket of his trench coat. "I don't deal in information."

"Still," Donovan flashed a smile that wasn't quite a smile, and Windham nodded.

Donovan watched as the thin man turned away and scuttled to the door. It spun and he was gone. No one looked up at his passing.

Donovan turned back to the bar and paid for the two drinks. He had what he needed, now it was time to put it to use before his window of opportunity – and Vanessa's – closed.

He turned to the door, but before he could step away from the bar, it swung open. A pale figure in a dark sports coat, mirrored glasses that mocked the shadows, and dark hair stepped from the booth. He was followed in quick succession by four others, each so much like the last that they might have been pressed from the same mold.

Donovan spared them only a glance, and then headed for the door.

"DeChance?" the thin, dark man said. It was inflected like a question, but Donovan knew better.

Donovan glanced up and, as he drew nearer to the man who'd spoken, he saw it was a vampire. More correctly, it was five of them. They all appeared to be in their early to mid twenties, but Donovan knew better than to make age assumptions in such a situation. He stopped and smiled as politely as he could manage while sizing them.

"I'm Donovan DeChance, yes," he said at last. "You are?"

"Just call me Vein," the slender young vampire said. "That's what everyone calls me."

"Vain?"

"You heard me." The vampire stepped closer, but Donovan held his ground. None of these had the aura of age that Johndrow and the elders possessed, and he suspected most of them were not long in "the blood."

"How can I help you…Vein?" Donovan asked.

"We know you've been hired to find Vanessa," Vein replied coldly. "We don't think much of that decision. We've decided to take the matter into our own hands, and we've come to find out what you know."

"Does Johndrow know you're here?"

Vein hesitated, and Donovan had his answer. "I didn't think so," he said. "Well, since he hired me – and you didn't – and I don't know who the hell you are, vanity aside, I don't see how I can help you."

"Oh, you'll help me," Vein replied. "If you don't tell me what I want to know there are other ways I can get the information – and there are other uses for one of your...vitality."

Donovan chuckled. "You're kidding me, right? First off, son, even Johndrow knows better than to confront me like this. You are out of your league. In fact, what are you, a hundred? A little more? You aren't even old enough to address me without calling me sir."

Vein took a step forward, and the others spread out at his shoulders, glaring at Donovan from beneath their own dark shades.

"What are you guys, The Men in Black?" Donovan asked dryly. "Area 51 isn't too far...head down Highway 5 and cut across on Interstate 10 – you can't miss it."

"You're a funny man," Vein said. "I didn't know that about you."

"This is a lot of fun," Donovan said, steeling himself, "but I really do have to get going. I have a job to do, as you well know, and I doubt very seriously if the Council of Elders would appreciate you wasting their money by getting in my way. If you'll excuse me?"

The five who had spread out closed in around him and Donovan slid his hand into his pocket, wrapping his fingers around the crystal pendant coiled there. He hadn't expected such an encounter, and hadn't really prepared for it, but he always carried basic defenses.

A shadow flickered across the wall behind the five. Donovan followed the motion with his eyes, but didn't move his head. It happened again, and he breathed more easily. Vein and the others hadn't noticed, but behind them, to either side of the strange entrance to The Crossroads, hulking, shadowy figures had materialized. They might have stepped from the wall their entrance was so sudden, and so silent. Donovan wanted to know how they did it, but he knew better than to inquire into it too closely. It wasn't any of his business, and in situations like the one confronting him, it was a godsend. There would be no 'altercation' in the club today, or any day. It was part of the club's appeal.

"You'll think this is just a cliché attempt to get out of a bad situation," Donovan said conversationally, "but I really think you should look behind you."

Vein stared at him, unblinking, but one of the others glanced back and let out a startled sound. Vein turned, more slowly. He saw the bouncers gathered to either side, weighed their size against that of his followers, and glared.

"I wouldn't try it." Donovan said.

Vein turned back with a snap of his head, and his eyes blazed.

"I don't' need advice from you," he said.

Donovan shrugged and took a step back toward the bar to distance himself. Vein turned back toward the shadowy bouncers, who were closing in, and he scowled.

"Come on," he said to the others, as if it had been his purpose all along. "Let's get out of here."

The dark shapes stepped aside as the five vampires, one by one, stepped into the booth and spun out of sight. Donovan watched them go. Vein was the last.

"We'll see you later, DeChance. You can't stay here forever."

The booth spun, and Vein was gone. Donovan glanced around at the bar. The bartender was polishing another glass and staring up into the rafters as if nothing out of the ordinary had taken place. No one else in the club had paid the slightest attention to the commotion at the door, or if they had, they'd managed to get their eyes directed at their tables before Donovan turned.

Donovan turned back to the phone booth, and found that he was alone. There was no sign of the bouncers. He hesitated.

He thought about heading back to the bar for another drink. If he left them out there long enough, he figured they'd get bored and look for him later. He could always buy the seer a drink and spend a fun half hour avoiding her gaze.

There was only one way in or out of the club, unless you went to a lot of trouble and paid a lot of money, and even the more secretive exits could be watched. He didn't know if Vein knew any of them, but it didn't matter. He had no time to go looking for someone to let him out, and he wasn't inclined to run from such a ridiculous challenge.

With a sigh of resignation, he arranged his charms, gripped a dark, green crystal pendant in his right hand, and stepped into the booth. He lifted the receiver, and then placed it back in its cradle. The booth spun, and he stepped into the alley beyond the club and stopped. Vein and his followers stood waiting. The moon was rising, and there was no one else in sight.

"Hey fellas," he said, taking a step closer and smiling as he lifted the green crystal over his head, "did you miss me?"

EIGHT

The narrow alley afforded little room to move. Vein stood dead center between Donovan and the streets beyond. The others formed two small phalanxes, ranks of two, on either side of the phone booth, blocking both ends of the alley. One end was, or at least appeared to be, a dead end, but apparently Vein was in no mood to take chances. It was likely he knew more about Donovan than he was letting on, though he didn't seem concerned.

"Always the funny man," Vein said. "We'll see if you can keep that smile in place. You are going to tell me what you know, or we'll make you wish you'd seen the light. Am I clear?"

"Oh, I understood you the first time," Donovan replied. "You know, inside the club, when the bouncers showed up and you all ran like whipped puppies? I was hired to do a job by your elders, and I intend to finish that job as contracted. You can get out of my way and let me proceed, or I will proceed through, across, and despite of you, and your elders will be informed of your stupidity. It's your call...Vein."

Maybe it was the thought of a living, breathing man, regardless of how old or powerful, giving him orders. Maybe it was the calm delivery, which Donovan had perfected over many years and much worse situations. Probably, Donovan reflected, it was the sarcastic inflection of his voice when he pronounced the affectatious name. Whatever it was, the vampires lunged.

Donovan raised his hand, swung the green pendant in a slow arc, and chanted softly. Greenish light, matching the hue of the crystal, appeared in the air, trailing after the circling chain. The light crystallized, and the first two attackers met that barrier head on. Sparks flew, and they cried out, stumbling back. Donovan started toward the head of the alley. He lowered the crystal in front of him like a shield and the shimmering barrier of light preceded him as he ran straight at Vein.

Young and foolish as he was, Vein was fast. He didn't back away from Donovan's attack, but instead leaped straight up. It was a graceful motion, like you'd expect to see in a bad kung fu movie, the leap taking him so high, and the whirling motion of his body so precise, that it gave the impression of slow motion. As Vein hurtled back to the floor of the alley and landed with his booted feet spread, already running forward, that illusion was shattered.

There was still one black-suited vamp between Donovan and the mouth of the alley. The shield of light divided them, but Vein was coming up fast from behind. Donovan knew he had to think fast, and make no mistakes. He didn't have the strength or speed his adversaries could bring to bear, and he had to make a quick decision now and pray it was the right one. It would be hard to explain to Johndrow and the elders how he'd been ambushed and taken down by their own whelps in an alley.

Vein was moving much more quickly than he was, and Donovan knew he had no chance of reaching the other vamp blocking his way before he was caught from behind. With an odd gesture of his left hand, Donovan wove a character in the air. He spoke the name *Pachacamac,* and relaxed absolutely. He closed his eyes, blanked his mind and focused, and his body dropped like a stone to the floor of the alley.

Vein was moving so quickly that stopping wasn't even an option. He roared over the point where Donovan had stood and plowed into his follower full tilt. The other cried out and raised his hands, but it was far too late to provide any protection. The two crashed to the ground and fell, thrashing and fighting to untangle themselves.

Donovan floated within the stone and brick and soil beneath them. He felt the earth elemental's hold tighten, and with a quick mental push disassociated himself. While he lacked the innate agility and strength of the undead, Donovan was not weak. He arched his back, executed an admirable kip up and scanned the alley.

Vein was back on his feet, though his companion still sat on the ground, shaking his head. Their glasses had been knocked free, and Vein stared down the alley at Donovan in unfettered rage. His eyes glowed red and predatory in the dim light. Donovan glanced back toward the dead end and saw that any ill effects from his crystal charm had worn off. He had a decision to make. He could try getting past these three, who didn't seem overloaded in the brains department, and find his way up or through the walls at the far end of the alley, or he could give Vein a second chance, hope he got lucky, and sprint for the streets. Angry as they might be, Vein and his "posse" wouldn't dare to follow if Donovan made it onto the crowded streets. It would draw too much attention.

"That was a mistake, magic man," Vein said. His voice was low now, grating and dry like it had been filtered through charcoal. "I wanted to talk, now I 'm going to kill you."

This time there was no mad rush. Vein and his companion, who'd finally managed to get back on his feet, not bothering to brush off the dust of the alley floor, strode purposefully toward the phone booth. Donovan considered slipping back in and dialing, but he knew they were too fast. One or more of them would be in the booth with him, and in their mental state even the thought of the bouncers waiting inside wouldn't be enough to deter them from ripping out his throat. That meant he'd have to kill them, and he didn't want to explain that to Johndrow any more than he wanted to explain his own defeat.

From the other side, the three remaining undead mimicked Vein's slow approach. They spread out, like a dark curtain, so the only open space was the blank wall directly in front of the phone booth. Donovan considered this, and frowned. He hadn't brought as much protection as he should have, and hadn't even considered his present danger, considering it was Johndrow who'd hired him. The danger was very real, though, and he had to think quickly, or he might not live to get back to his office and the charms he should have brought with him in the first place.

He could try the wall. If he were quick enough, he might summon another elemental, slip into the brick, and take his chances in its arms until they reached the far side of the wall. He didn't like it. The Elementals were unpredictable in allegiance, and in strength. If he caught the wrong one at the wrong time, he would spend the rest of his days embedded in that wall, the essence of his spirit joining with the elemental, and that would be the end. It wasn't the death he had in mind for himself – not that he'd give his preference much thought.

He could try levitating, but with the speed and agility of his attackers, he wasn't certain he could get out of reach before they scaled the walls and dragged him back down.

"Not so funny now, are you magic man?" Vein asked. His smile widened, and Donovan saw the fangs fully extended and the dripping, drooling hunger fairly foaming from that yawning, arrogant mouth.

Cold sweat trickled down the back of his neck. His skin was clammy, and he knew his heartbeat thundered in the ears of his attackers. Even if they wanted to stop, it was beyond that point now. He knew enough about vampires to understand that, civilized as they appeared; they were a slave to the hungers that defined them. Once certain limits were reached, and exceeded, there was no turning back.

Then it hit him. Without waiting to gauge the wisdom of his actions, Donovan concentrated on his heart. He dropped his breathing into rhythm with that pulsing beat, and he incanted a short, monotonous chant, being very careful to match the inflection of his voice to that steady pumping of blood through his veins.

The vampires didn't hesitate, they surged forward. Vein's grin widened and his eyes filmed red. Donovan chopped one hand through the air, as if slicing his own words into equal pieces, and there were two of him standing in front of the phone booth. The vampires hesitated, mesmerized by the motion of his hand and the pounding of his heart, which he continued to magnify through the deep, sonorous accompaniment of the chant. He chopped his hand down again, and again. The six undead stood stock still, staring from one to the other of four flickering images. Donovan slipped forward, and before they realized what he was going to do, he joined the other three versions of himself in a slow, whirling dance.

"Kill them all," Vein whispered. His voice was hoarse, and his gaze flicked first one way, then the other. The pounding heartbeat confused his senses, and with it magnified to such intensity, it was impossible to attribute it to one, or the other of the dancing Donovan DeChance figures whirling before his eyes.

Donovan knew it was only a diversion, and he knew it wouldn't stop, or fool them for more than a moment. As he reached the outer edge of the ring of images, he broke out around the far side of the slower vamp to Vein's left. As he moved, the images wavered, and seconds later there was nothing but a scent of acrid smoke floating in the center of the alley.

Donovan skirted the wall as closely as he could and sprinted for the mouth of the alley. He knew he had a second, maybe two, before Vein would recover. Maybe a bit longer for the others, but their leader was sharper than he'd first appeared, certainly more formidable than Donovan had given him credit for.

There was no sound, but he knew they were coming. The alley extended another ten yards, and Donovan ground his boots into the alley floor and launched forward. He heard traffic on the road beyond the alley's mouth, and the honk of a horn. He needed to stagger into traffic, fade into a crowd, something – anything – to distance himself from the red glowing eyes and starved fangs of the young idiot on his heels.

Someone grabbed his jacket from behind, and he drew his arms in instinctively, sloughing off the outer garment in a graceful lunge. As he dove forward again, he expected to feel strong, cold hands on his shoulders, or his arms, or the colder bite of ivory through the flesh of his neck. He prepared himself for a final curse, something to leave his mark in defiance.

Someone screamed. Then there was another. Donovan ran another step, frowned, and whirled, pressing his back to the wall of the alley. He gasped as he caught sight of Vein, gripped at the throat by long, slender, gloved fingers that held him easily, lifting him from the ground. Vein and one of his followers were held aloft by a tall woman with flame red hair and eyes that flashed like ice chips in the dark alley, despite the lack of light.

"Amethyst?"

Donovan grinned. His breath came in deep, heaving gasps, and he wanted to collapse onto the ground and clutch his gut, but he stood his ground. For some reason, this particular woman's presence made him want to appear strong and brave. He knew this was an illusion even he wasn't going to pull off in this situation, but he did what he could.

"What are you doing here?" he asked her.

"What does it look like I'm doing?" she asked. One of her eyebrows rose, and she smiled lazily back at him. "Men are never good at this sort of thing." She informed him.

Vein, who had overcome his fright at being snatched from his feet unceremoniously, whirled and lunged at her neck. Amethyst flung him to the side, slamming him into the brick wall of the alley so hard that Donovan was afraid they must have heard the collision inside the club. Amethyst tossed the second vamp to the far wall and strolled indifferently down the alley to where Donovan leaned on the wall and watched in amazement. He'd seen her in action before, but never like this. She had never exhibited more than normal strength in his presence, and he was wondering what other secrets she might be keeping when a ragged cry broke out behind her.

The three vampires who'd followed Vein down the alley lunged from behind, one for each of her arms, and one straight at her throat. Amethyst shook her hair down off her shoulders, and a blinding flash of light erupted from a glittering web of crystals woven in among her lustrous locks. The light was brilliant yellow, and the alley lit as if the night had passed in an instant and the sun had peeked her head in over the wall.

The vampires scattered. Vein crouched by the wall, his eyes very wide and his once well-groomed hair and clothing in complete disarray. There was a ragged tear at the elbow of one sleeve of his jacket, and his sunglasses were nowhere to be seen. Still, he didn't look beaten – just angry.

"I wouldn't do it," Donovan said. He stood and brushed

dust from his arms. He eyed his jacket, still lying in the middle of the alley, and sighed. "I'm going to have to pay a fortune to get that thing cleaned."

Amethyst turned to glance at the trampled jacket, and as she did so, Vein sprang. Donovan was already whirling the green crystal again, but Amethyst had anticipated the move. In fact, Donovan decided with amazement, she'd invited it by turning her head. She flicked her hair again, and Vein took the blast of light full in the face. He cried out, unable to stop his forward progress. He clawed at the air, and smoke rolled out from the sleeves of his jacket and up through his collar to wind about his hair. Amethyst held out her hand, and he smacked into it with a thud. He crumpled to the ground, then, screaming in pain and fear, he tore at his jacket, ripped it from his back, and turned to follow his friends back down the alley. He scuttled up the back wall like a spider, moving so quickly he was over wall and out of sight before Donovan's crystal stopped it's now lazy, pointless circle and dangled limply on its chain.

"Wow," he said. "You never told me Hercules was your brother. Where did you get that strength?" She met his gaze, stepped forward to offer him her hand, and promptly collapsed forward into his arms. Donovan, surprised, barely managed to catch her and hold her upright.

"I could use a drink, cowboy," she said. "Buy me one and maybe I'll show you how I did it."

She shook in his arms, and he all but carried her back to the phone booth. He pushed the numbers 3, 6 and 0 again, and they rotated inward. The alley stood quiet, and empty. All that remained were the empty booth, three pairs of battered sunglasses, and a half-burned sports coat. It was turning out to be a hell of a night.

NINE

Once Donovan got her seated at one of the small tables and a glass of rich red wine into her hand, Amethyst recovered somewhat. She still looked pale, but her hands no longer trembled. Donovan sat for a while, watched her in silence and admired the glitter of the crystals woven into her hair.

"You make quite the lovely cavalry," he said at last. "I don't know what my next move was going to be, but it wasn't going to be pretty."

"You get yourself into more scrapes than a pat of butter," she said. Her eyes sparkled as she glanced at him over her wine, and he very suddenly felt more kinship with melting butter than was comfortable. "What would you do without me, anyway?"

"I could have handled it," he said defensively. "I was just – regrouping."

"From where I stood when I joined you," she said, "you were regrouping with your back turned. Didn't I teach you how to use that shield?"

"I haven't had much time to practice," he said. "I'll tell you, I might have been more prepared, but the very last thing I expected tonight was trouble with vamps. Birds, maybe, some sort of charm or spell, but, these clowns? I'm working for their damned elders, and believe me, the minute I get a chance to report them its going to happen.

Besides, I've been holding off on practicing with the shield. I prefer private lessons, and you've been pretty unavailable since I got back."

"I have *commitments*," she said. "Just because you find time between running around the world and sorting books to spend a day or two with me doesn't mean I'll drop what I'm doing. Not every time, anyway…" She laughed and winked at him. "What were you doing with those idiots anyway?"

"They don't have anything to do with it," he said wearily. "They just don't think I'll do a very good job, and wanted me to hand the job over and run home."

Amethyst perked up a little. "So, you're working for the council of elders? It's been a long time since you did that, hasn't it? I remember something about some teenage kung-fu artist who thought he was a vampire slayer, but that was years ago."

"Yeah, he's all grown up now. I had a chat with him and he only works for hire now, and only with good reason. Turns out he was right, though. He's a damned fine slayer – took everything I had to get him to put an end to his 'quest' and look to his future."

Amethyst snorted. "Never saw that coming," she admitted. "Who could have imagined a vampire slayer working for the council of elders? I've never been able to figure out how you kept them from killing him; and why didn't they go to him, if they have trouble?"

"It isn't vampire trouble," Donovan said. "It's much worse. I guess Cleo found you?"

Amethyst sipped her wine, and then nodded. "About an hour ago. I wasn't at home, or I might have been here sooner."

"Your timing, as usual, was perfect," he told her. "That was some trick with the hair; what are those crystals?"

She laughed and shook her head, sending a ripple of light through her long wavy hair and shimmering down over her shoulders.

"You like them?" she asked. "They're particularly fine quartz. I had them cut and faceted, then carefully strung – like beads – so they could be worn."

"I have plenty of quartz," Donovan replied skeptically. "None of it has shown the slightest propensity toward flashing like sunlight and scaring vampires."

"Well, that's my own touch, of course. They had to be stored in bright sunlight for a very long time. There's a ritual that must be repeated daily to maintain their strength, and they have to be stored in a specially prepared elixir that preserves the energy from the sunlight."

"How did you know to wear them tonight?" he asked her.

"A girl has to have *some* secrets, Donovan DeChance. Why in the world would men remain so intrigued if we started giving them away?"

It was Donovan's turn to laugh, and it felt good, particularly since only a few short minutes before he hadn't been certain he'd ever laugh again. One thing was true beyond a doubt; he'd been cooped up in his own little world for far too long. He'd made a serious error, and if the danger confronting him was even a fraction as intense as he believed it to be, that put him one mistake beyond his limit. He couldn't count on being rescued, and the young vampires, for all their bravado, shouldn't have been much of a challenge. He'd been careless.

"When I get a chance," he said, "I'll stop by and see how you did it. That was the most effective defense against the undead I've ever encountered."

"I try," she said. "And when you 'stop by' you'd better bring chocolate, flowers, and something pretty. I'm going to start thinking you have someone else hidden away if you keep ignoring me. Now, what's this all about? Cleo seemed pretty disturbed, but for all her talkative ways, I've never been able to get more than weak impressions from her."

Donovan smiled, then grew serious and told her everything. He started with the break-in at Johndrow's party, Vanessa's abduction, and Kline's death. She stopped him and questioned him thoroughly at this point. They both knew the implications of such a death. Kline had been powerful, cautious, and very good at what he did. Neither of them would have wanted to try and figure a way past his defenses, though both had done so once or twice in the past, and they knew that to have done so put their enemy in an elite and fairly small pool of possible suspects. Removing themselves from that pool made it smaller still.

"You said his familiar was a crow?" she asked thoughtfully.

"A crow, or a raven," Donovan agreed. "It was big, and it

was black, but it was in and out very quickly, and I wasn't really able to concentrate on it. I had problems of my own with the face in the fireplace. Cleo got a better look than I did, but I left almost the second the thief was gone, so I haven't been over this with her at any length. She nearly got the thing on the bookshelf. I got a couple of feathers. One was mangled, but I was able to use the other to search for trace. I need to go over it all more thoroughly."

Amethyst nodded. "Then you contacted Johndrow?"

"Not immediately," Donovan said, watching her face to gauge her reaction. "I was concerned about the particular book that was stolen."

"Le Duc's journal?" she asked. Her brow creased in a slight frown. "Why? What is it?"

"You may be hell with crystals," he laughed softly, "but I see history isn't your forte. Le Duc was an odd one. The journal he left is very thin, and concerns only a single spell – the Perpetuum Vitae Potion."

"The Perpet…eternal life?"

Donovan nodded. "Le Duc never tested the potion, and because of certain tenets of the ritual, it's now forbidden magic. Apparently someone has decided that the rules don't apply to them.

"I remember now," she said thoughtfully. "Le Duc was killed by a vampire, wasn't he?"

"Yes. He was trying to acquire the final ingredient for his formula – the vampire's blood."

"Then Vanessa…" Amethyst's words trailed off, and Donovan nodded.

"Yes, she's going to be part of the potion."

"But, why her?" Amethyst asked. "I mean, there were plenty of others at that party, older and more powerful. Why would he choose Johndrow's lover?"

"I don't know for sure," Donovan replied. "She's beautiful. Maybe our thief is something of a romantic? Maybe he likes the idea of having a beautiful, ancient, powerful prisoner to gloat over."

"But, won't he hurry to finish this? Surely he knows that you, or someone like you, will be on his trail? There are protections to prevent detection, but they can only work so well, and for so long. It's just a matter of time until we find him..."

"Not we," Donovan said. "I will do it. I've been hired to do it, and, as I told Johndrow, I'd have done it anyway. I don't like having my things taken."

Amethyst's eyes sparkled again. "Yeah, you certainly had it all under control tonight. What was I thinking, offering my help to a big, strong cowboy like you?"

Amethyst looked up at him then, wide-eyed, and batted her lashes. If Donovan had had a drink he'd have tossed it at her. As it was, all he could do was laugh.

"You missed all the best parts," he told her. "I don't believe they'd ever seen an elemental summoned, for one thing."

"You summoned an elemental in an alley?"

"Under it," he corrected. "It was *Pachacama*,"

"Incan," she commented, sipping her wine and watching him over the rim. He knew she was flirting, and he wished he had time to let her know how well it was working.

"Yeah – not the most powerful available," he said, "but I didn't have much time."

"Why didn't you have the elemental take *them* and then banish it?" she asked. "They'd have been stuck pretty well, I think, and they'd have had plenty of time to think on the error of their ways while they waited for the sun to rise high enough to hit the alley."

Donovan stared at her. It was a use for the spell he'd never even considered, and the simplicity of it felt like a smack in the middle of his forehead. His surprise must have shown, because she laughed again and drained her wine, gesturing to the barman for a refill.

"Yeah, you have it all under control," she teased. "I told you men were no good at this sort of thing."

Donovan shook his head bemusedly. "Whoever took the book, and Vanessa, is going to more than he has so far to complete the ritual. There are ingredients he's going to need. That's why I wanted to see you. One of the things he'll need is a matched pair of Timeline crystals, and they have to be very special. They have to be a perfect harmonic pair."

Amethyst put down her glass and stared at him. All trace of humor had left her expression.

"There is only one matched set like that on this continent," she said. "It's mine, and it's securely locked in my vault."

"'I know," he said softly. "Like I said, that's why I needed to talk to you. I know your security is flawless, but I'd have said that about mine, as well…couldn't hurt to take some extra precautions. I know how rare it is to find both a timeline crystal and to have it flawless. How much less likely is it to find a matched pair?" He shrugged.

Amethyst was no longer paying the slightest attention to her wine. Her specialty was stone, crystals, and talismans. She had the finest collection in existence of all three of these specialties, and she was very protective of both the collection, and her secrets. Donovan has asked too much more than once and run into the stone wall of her stubborn streak, and he saw it boiling to the surface now.

"You think he can get them from me?" It wasn't a question, but more of an accusation, and Donovan sighed.

"I'm not saying that, and I think you know it. I'm saying that he wants them, and that I know you may be the only source that exists in the world. He must have a plan for how he intends to get his hands on them when the time comes, or why go to the trouble to gather the other ingredients and get the dogs on his trail?"

She didn't look impressed with his logic, but Donovan saw she was at least considering it.

"What else does he need?" she asked.

Donovan gratefully changed the subject. "He needs bone marrow dust from a particularly difficult to find Priest. There's only one grave in the area – I did some research."

He told her about his meeting with the collector, Windham, and what he'd learned from that exchange.

"So, no one has tried to collect it for him yet?" Amethyst asked.

"I don't think so," Donovan said. "I'm going after it myself."

She stared at him in shock. "Why? Donovan, if you think that's the only source locally, why not just destroy it, or secure it somehow? Why go out into the open like that and put yourself at risk?"

"Because," Donovan replied, "I don't just want to stop him from creating this potion, I want to catch him. I want my book back, and I'd like to collect the fee for bringing Vanessa back as well. I know she can take care of herself, but even the best of us gets in over their head now and then."

This brought another quick snort of laughter from Amethyst, and with a sigh Donovan picked up her glass and took a drink of her wine.

"Laugh it up," he said, returning her glass. "But promise me you'll keep an eye out for this guy? I wish I could figure out who it is. I can't imagine any of the major players involving themselves in something so risky, and I don't remember anyone with a crow. That bothers me more than anything. I thought I knew everyone in the craft that called this city home, so either I was wrong, or it's an outsider. Either way, it's bad."

"The crystals are safe, Donovan. When I'm not home, my apprentice Lance handles the wards. It's part of the fee he pays for instruction, and he's very meticulous. As for your rogue magician, I have a thought on that."

Donovan wanted to ask more about her apprentice, but he remained silent as she continued. He remembered Lance Ezzel, a tall, powerful young man with bright, piercing eyes and hair that was an odd, platinum blonde – almost white. He'd been with Amethyst for several years, and seemed bright enough to go the distance. She wasn't a patient teacher, and she was reluctant to part with her secrets at the best of times – the price for apprenticeship must have been tantamount to becoming her live-in cabana boy.

"You remember that guy Cornwell? Alistair Cornwell?"

Yanked from his thoughts of Ezzel, which were wandering toward jealousy, Donovan blinked.

"Cornwell? Vaguely. Wasn't he sort of a 'poseur' with delusions of personal grandeur?"

Amethyst laughed again.

"You've been spending too much time in the louder part of this club. You're beginning to talk like the kids over there; you need to spend more time in adult company."

Donovan met her gaze levelly, and this time it was Amethyst who looked away. He smiled. They both needed some time, and when this business was over, he intended to make a point of finding it.

"Anyway," she said, blushing slightly, "Cornwell had a little power, but not much sense. He came to me several times demanding that I share things with him, or loan him crystals for his experiments. He always wore crazy robes, like he'd stepped out of some King Arthur movie and though he was Merlin."

"Yeah, I remember him," Donovan said.

"Well," Amethyst continued, "don't you remember his familiar then? It was a ratty old crow named Asmodeus."

Donovan started.

"Yes! I remember now. The thing looked like it should have taken its last flight a few decades back, but I do remember it. He came to me once wanting a charm that would split the bird's tongue so it could be taught to mimic speech. As I recall, he wanted to teach it to say 'Nevermore.' He used to carry it around on his shoulder, even out on the streets. I warned him against it, but people just saw a crazy old man in ragged clothes and a half-dead bird. In California, who's going to notice something like that?"

"I haven't heard anything from, or about him in years," Amethyst said. "I suppose he might have studied...gained some power here and there? Maybe you and I aren't the only two he pestered. He's been out of the local scene long enough to turn his life around and actually learn something. He did have the gift, just not the patience, or the personality, you know?"

Donovan nodded. It made sense. All the times he'd spoken to Cornwell, the man had seemed harmless enough, but he'd always been seeking. First one spell, then another, then just ingredients, and always with questions about this and that book. Donovan was known as the leading expert in the area on ancient texts, so he'd never thought twice about the queries, but had he ever given away the existence of Le Duc's journal? Could he be responsible for this whole mess, just because he couldn't keep his mouth shut about old books?

"I don't suppose you have any idea where I might find Mr. Cornwell?" Donovan asked.

"Nope," she said, finishing her second glass of wine. "I'll ask around. I have to be going. I want to go check the wards on my vault, and to let Lance know there might be a new threat."

She hesitated, then stepped around the table and leaned close. She let her hair drape down over his head and teased her tongue across his earlobe. "You be careful, cowboy," she whispered.

Donovan took a deep breath, fought the sudden rise of heat that flushed through his nervous system, and sate very still.

"I really don't think there's any danger of a break in at my place," she added, "but I'll put some extra effort into security, just in case. I'm sure if Lance and I put our minds to it, we can design something new that will surprise anyone who thinks they have a plan for getting in. I almost hope he tries."

Donovan thought about Kline and the description of how he'd lain broken and battered on the floor. He hoped that their thief stayed far away from Amethyst and her crystals, but if not – he hoped it was Lance who was on duty when the visit took place.

"I'll see you soon then," he said, giving her a hug. Amethyst turned and disappeared into the phone booth in a flash of sun-drenched quartz, and Donovan glanced at the bar a final time. He eyed the bartender, took in the stolid, uninterested expression and the noncommittal tilt of the man's jaw, and then shrugged. Who else was he going to ask?

"Excuse me," Donovan said, taking a seat at the bar, "I was wondering if you'd seen a friend of mine in here recently?"

"Depends," the bartender said, still polishing the glass in his hand carefully. "I've seen you with several people today, but it's hard to tell if they're your friends from back here."

"Fair enough," Donovan said. "I was thinking of one person in particular. I think I've seen him here before, but I can't remember when. His name is Cornwell, Alistair Cornwell. I've been trying to find him all day, but he seems to have disappeared."

The bartender didn't look up from his work at all.

"No one is friends with that one," he said. "He isn't welcome here."

"Then you've seen him?" Donovan asked, trying not to sound eager.

"About a week ago was the last time," the bartender said. "Had to have him eighty-sixed."

"I don't suppose you have any idea where he'd be staying, then," Donovan asked.

"I never talked to the guy except to mix his drinks," the bartender said, glancing up at last, "but I hear things. I always hear things. Most of those things I keep to myself. It's bad for business to get a reputation for telling secrets."

Donovan sensed that no response was expected, so he waited in silence.

"This guy, though," the bartender shook his head. "Good riddance, I say. If you're trying to find him, I hope he isn't really your friend."

Donovan continued to hold his silence.

"He has that old church on the east side," the bartender said with a shrug of his own. "Out near *The Barrio*? It's been vacant for years; he bought it and fixed it up some. That's what he said when he came in; anyway, you can take it for what it's worth."

"I know the place," Donovan said, nodding. "I thought it would have fallen down or been demolished by now."

"The city won't do it," the barman growled. "Some kind of historic monument or something. They won't tear it down, and now that your buddy owns it, I suppose it will never be fixed up either. Just an eyesore."

"Maybe I'll see if I can do my civic duty," Donovan said, leaving a ten on the bar and rising. "I think I'll go pay old Alistair a visit."

The barman slid the bill off the bar and into a pocket without seeming to move.

"Give him my regards," he said. "He was a lousy tipper."

Donovan grinned, winked, and for the second time headed through the phone booth and into the alley. This time it was empty, and he made his way to the streets without meeting a soul. Things were looking up.

TEN

There is a line that divides the city of San Valencez cleanly, though it isn't marked on any legitimate map. Though there is no clear indicator that you have passed from one part of the city and into the other, there are rules and borders, and the citizens of both halves of the whole abide by the former and remain on the proper side of the latter.

The barrio begins at the 42nd St. overpass, caked in dust and decorated in neon spray paint and a wide array of gang colors. The Dragons, and Los Escorpiones, Comancheros and the East Side Kings, all have left their mark at one time or another. No one gang owns the gateway, but they all guard it.

One building stands directly on the line, half on one side, and half on the other, as it has always stood. The Cathedral of St. Elian stares out over *The Barrio* on one side with blank, sightless windows for eyes. The walls are unmarked by graffiti, but ill-treated by time. On the other side the sunlight glares off grimy glass so brightly it reflects a grimy parody of the outside world back at itself.

In earlier times this Cathedral was neutral ground. Every Sunday families from either side of the odd, cultural line of demarcation that marked entrance to the "other side of the tracks" came to worship. They sang hymns and harmonized. They tithed and raised funds to buy a larger bell to be housed in the steeple, and funded missionary work. Then, slowly, as the "good" side of the city drew back, leaving empty streets and vacant homes, and the "other" side grew thick with families and children, overpopulated and angry like a swarming hive of humanity, the church faltered.

Without the funding provided by more well-to-do parishioners, the upkeep of the massive building became a burden on the community, and on The Church in Rome. Typically, The Church backed out first. For years the building was home to a parade of faith- healers and evangelists, spiritualists and charlatans, and all that time the rot seeped deeper. The walls crumbled a little further, and the brass bell, once so magnificent in its tower, pealing its call to worship through the lower east side of the city, hung corroded and silent.

Eventually even the street preachers avoided the Cathedral. An air of decay and rot permeated the air near the building. Rats and stray animals took up residence, and transients peered from the lower level windows in search of prey. Anyone who thinks a city isn't a jungle needs to spend more time in the darker parts later at night. There are hunters, there are predators, and anyone and anything can become the prey, given the right moment.

Then, after the cathedral had stood empty for months, thing shifted again. Inside the cathedral the aisles had been swept, though haphazardly. Some of the pews had been wiped clean, though only to store stacked books and rolled manuscripts. The inside of the glass on the windows had been spray-painted black, blocking out the world. The rectory had been cleared, and a thin, wild-eyed man slipped in and out from time to time, barely visible in his passing as if something blocked him from sight, or distracted anyone trying to watch him.

Grandmothers whispered that he was a priest. They believed that Mother Church was coming home to the cathedral, and that the bell would sing one Sunday morning, calling them back to worship. The men whispered, spat and made the sign to ward them against the evil eye – and they watched, wondering who was moving in on what, and whether they should be angry, frightened, or trying to form allegiances.

The gangs rolled past in silence. Sometimes Los Escorpiones slouched on the street corner, or dangled from the windows of other abandoned buildings nearby to keep a watch on the doors, and the man who used them. It was noted by both the men, and the grandmothers, that the gangs stayed clear of the cathedral itself, and this caused further speculation, but no one ventured near enough to get a clear answer.

Late at night, strange lights flickered behind the darkened windows. Smoke rose from the ancient chimney, and it was oddly scented. No one knew exactly what the smell was, but it made them uneasy. The smoke dropped to ground level and whirled around their ankles, slipped under their doors and found its way through the cracks in shutters and cracked panes of glass.

There was a voice, too. At first it seemed like many voices, because it was never the same. The language changed. The intonation changed. Sometimes there was rhythm, and sometimes it might have been the mad cackling of a crazy man. The more they listened, though, the more certain all became that all the sounds and all the voices were really only one, and though they knew it must be the thin, wild-eyed man with disheveled hair – the guy who looked at first glance like a homeless crazy man, and then like some kind of angry spirit, it was hard to believe such a small man could make that God-awful racket. Harder still to understand why the sight of him made their blood run cold, or why they couldn't sleep peacefully if they saw the lights dancing in that old stone building, or heard the sounds.

Inside, seated cross-legged on one of the half-cleared pews, Alistair Cornwell glared at the book in his hand and concentrated. It was an incomplete copy of a very old grimoire, and he was doing his best to re-create what was missing from other sources. He knew that complete copies of the incantation existed, but they were expensive, and there were only a few places they could be obtained, none of which would have welcomed his business.

He'd gotten this partial tome from one of the collectors, a grubby little worm of a man known only as Chance. It was an apt name, because when you bought things from him, you were certainly taking a chance on quality. The book had been described as "almost complete," but the last three pages of the most important incantation it held were missing, and Chance had no idea what happened to them. In fact, he wasn't willing to divulge his source for the part of the manuscript he *did* possess. Cornwell had concluded that it was stolen, and that the pages were lost.

Worse still, with his own shaky reputation, and the fact he'd bought a probable "hot" grimoire, he couldn't ask anyone about the incantation, or even mention he intended to try it. Doing so could implicate him in whatever theft had brought him the book in the first place, and admission that he was going to attempt magic beyond anything he'd ever pulled off in the past, without proper safeguards, would result in ... unpleasantness.

He'd already scraped up the matted, half rotted carpet from the large, flat bit of floor behind the altar. It was no easy task. The rug was ancient, and it had been rained on, urinated on, and pounded into place by the passing of thousands of feet. The circle Cornwell cut was large, nearly twice the circumference he needed to work with. He'd brushed dry dust over the expanse of wood and swept it away, and then cleaned it thoroughly. He treated the wood with scented oil and, following the detailed instructions at the beginning of the incantation, he polished the surface until it gleamed, covering every inch of it in slow circles with a soft rag. He repeated this for seventeen nights straight, one night in a clockwise motion, and the next in a counter clockwise pattern. He hoped that the number was actually 17. It appeared to be the European digit with the slash through the center of the upright stroke, but the paper was old, and the text was smudged. It could have been a 19.

This was the kind of imprecision that had landed Alistair in such dire circumstances, working on the edge of *The Barrio* by candle light. He knew he should have verified the number. He knew, in fact, that he should have an innate understanding of the ritual itself, which would have rendered him capable of figuring out on his own which number was more significant to the operation at hand, and why the patterns followed one upon the next as they did. It was too late for that. It had been too late for many years.

He'd spent time as an apprentice, and for many years he'd progressed rapidly. It hadn't been enough, of course. There were restrictions, things he wasn't allowed to try, powers he wasn't "ready" to wield, secrets that were barred from him and locked away behind walls and wards and charms he could never break. Shortcuts had presented themselves, and Alistair, invariably, took them. He couldn't stand the thought of waiting, year after year, to be found worthy of things he knew he was ready for now. The title of "apprentice" didn't sit well on his heart…he was destined to greater things. That's how he saw it, anyway. Others disagreed, and he'd been banished.

Now he worked in solitude, disgraced and avoided by others who understood the arts he practiced. He didn't know if they were aware of his efforts or if, as far as that dark world was concerned, he'd dropped off the face of the earth. He also didn't care. Alistair Cornwell had one purpose in his life, and he intended to fulfill that purpose with, or without the assistance or approval of his so-called peers.

There was a raucous cry from the rafters overhead, and a bit of debris dropped to the floor, just to the right of his cleared circle. Alistair started from his seat as if he'd been bitten and scrambled forward. He leaned in close and peered at the circle, but it appeared to be clean. Whatever had dropped hadn't invalidated his monotonous efforts at purification. He swallowed hard, took a deep breath, and then whirled to glare upward.

"Damn you, Asmodeus," he cried, shaking his fist.

There was a flutter of wings. Another trickle of dirt and dust filtered down through the dense air, and Cornwell drew himself up quickly. He spread the ragged cloak he wore out like the wings of some sort of giant bat, using the material to block the fall of debris from the circle behind him. Moments later there was a louder rustle of wings, and a huge old crow landed on the corner of a nearby pew. The bird glared back at Alistair balefully. Cornwell snorted in disgust, which proved to be a mistake. He breathed in some of the falling dust, and moments later sneezed loudly. He wiped his nose on his cloak and returned to the book.

"We're ready," he announced.

The bird didn't answer, but it eyed him dubiously and looked ready to take off at any moment. Cornwell paid no attention; he was focused. He had everything he would need, or the closest substitute he could find for each item, laid out on the very front pew. He had colored chalk. He had small, charred braziers. He had incense sticks, candles, several pouches of dust gathered from different sources, a vial of murky brown liquid, and a small test tube of blood. Asmodeus had obtained the tube for him from a local clinic, flying in an open window in a rush of wings and dark feathers. It was a close call, nearly ending the bird's existence on the tip of a nurse's umbrella, but Asmodeus cleared the window sill at the last moment, the vial clutched tightly, and managed somehow not to crush it, drop it, or step on it during his landing when he returned to the cathedral. It was not an approved method of obtaining ingredients, but then, if Alistair had approached this through normal channels he not only would not have gotten the blood, but very likely someone would have come through and stripped away the other things he'd worked so hard to gather.

He could have purchased the blood, of course, but stealing it had been so much easier, and it had drawn less attention. Sure, it made a small splash in the news. It wasn't every day that a crow made off with medical supplies, even if they were shiny, but not all the news in the outside, mundane world made it to those who might figure out the significance. He'd been very careful to gather his materials slowly and from a variety of sources. The summoning he planned hadn't been attempted in many years, and was considered extremely dangerous. If he were part of the "inner circle" of the city he would have safeguards from a dozen others in place, and even if he failed, the damage would be contained.

Here he was not only on his own, but so were those in the surrounding streets. If he managed to summon the demon he sought, he would gain everything he'd been denied by his failed apprenticeship, as well as enough riches and power to insure he could no longer be ignored. If he failed, it was impossible to tell what might happen. The worst that could happen, the most humiliating failure, would be if nothing happened at all. With the substitutions he'd been forced to make in his choice of ingredients, and the incomplete incantation, fleshed out through his own research and intuition to its full length, it was impossible to judge with any certainty what might happen.

Cornwell was willing to take the risk. He was sensitive enough to the powers surrounding him to know that the ritual was only the face of the procedure. The concentration of ingredients, rhythm, proper intonation and form were a focus used to draw on powers one already possessed. He knew he could perform this summoning, and he knew that if he could make the ritual real to himself, it would become self-fulfilling, in a way.

This did nothing to relieve the pressure. With a last careful glance at Asmodeus to make sure the bird had no further notions of creating whirlwinds or contaminating the circle, Alistair began.

He placed the articles he needed to complete the ritual dead center in the cleared area. These included a small altar, a brass chalice, which according to the incomplete ritual should be gold, a ceremonial dagger with glass stones where the jewels should have been inset, a wand made of several oak branches twined together and tipped by a very clear, nearly perfect quartz crystal. In the weave of the branches, crystals of other colors glittered. Not all of them were what the book called for, but they were substituted by color, red glass for the ruby, and various types of quartz for other gems.

Each and every shortcut had required its own lengthy justification. He had to convince himself that the color was all that mattered in the crystals, that the gold chalice was just an affectation of a well-to-do magician, and that it was the symbol of the cup that mattered. As long as he could convince himself, he knew it would be fine. The nagging doubt at the back of his mind threatened to topple this flawed fortress of illogic, but he kept it under wraps and silenced it any time it became too loud by imagining the things he would have once he succeeded.

Asmodeus was less convinced than his master, and not too shy to squawk warnings in arcane bird-tongue. Cornwell's failure to train the bird to mimic human speech was one of the creature's most irritating defeats. It was such a simple trick that even normal, everyday humans had managed it. Of course, they surgically split the bird's tongues, which allowed the animals to create sounds that were otherwise beyond them, but with his abilities and insights, not to mention the bond between himself and his familiar; Cornwell should have been able to pull off the task easily.

He knew there were charms that would do the trick. He'd known a witch with a frog familiar, one of the odder combinations he'd encountered, and much too comical to be taken seriously, but even that woman had managed it. When her frog croaked, the small amulet it wore on a gilded collar transformed the words to passable English. Alistair had never been able to manage it. He had changed Asmodeus' voice many times, once to that of a pig, and twice to different breeds of dog, but he'd never been able to make the words comprehensible, and over time the old crow had grown weary of his efforts and refused to take part in the ritual again. If Cornwell attempted to bewitch him, the bird took off with a squawk and a flurry of wings that left the air heavy with dark, ratty feathers.

Alistair wasn't thinking about Asmodeus as he prepared his circle. There would be plenty of time to right the mundane wrongs of his life once the ritual was complete. With his instruments carefully placed in the very center of the open space, he took a large, thick chunk of white chalk and very slowly, very carefully, drew a circle around himself. He had left small marks just outside the range of the outer circle to guide his hand, and he knew that the first circle he drew was exactly ten feet in diameter, five feet to any given point on the outer rim from the center.

Once this was complete, he drew a second circle two hand-spans shorter in radius, leaving about ten inches to a foot of space between the two concentric borders. He didn't have to make it so large, but he knew the more space he gave himself to properly draw the angelic symbols and names, the better chance he'd do it without some bizarre spelling error sending him spiraling off into the pits of hell. It was a possibility, after all; that's where the door he intended to open led to.

He worked feverishly. Now that he'd begun, he knew he would have to remain with the ritual, safe within his circle, until everything was complete. He needed to get the formula written, the braziers lit, and the initial invocations completed as soon as possible to allow as many hours of darkness as possible for the main ritual. A sneeze at the wrong time, or some weakness of body or mind intruding, and disaster was certain.

He placed the braziers and candles, lit each in turn, and spoke the angelic names, invoking the spirits of north, south, east and west, air, wind, fire and earth, all in their turn. His voice was steady, and he felt remarkably calm. He'd been very careful, and very thorough. Anything that he did not have, he'd replaced with something suitable, and something in the way the air in the old cathedral, normally stagnant and void of energy, crackled along the short hairs on his arms and at his scalp told him he'd been correct. It was the pattern that mattered, the colors and the layout, the *focus* on his goal.

When all preliminaries were out of the way, he knelt before the small altar. He placed the cup in the center of this, and began, slowly, to add the other ingredients he'd gathered. Particular grave dust, herbs, a few spices that he'd actually gone out to the supermarket and bought, then purified. He mixed slowly, and as he did so, he glanced to his left and read from the text of the old book. He wouldn't reach the point where he ran out of original pages and began speaking his own version of the ritual for some time.

The final ingredient was the tube of blood. He'd removed the name and information on the donor and purified the test tube as well as he could under the circumstances. It was risky having blood from a relatively unknown source. There was no way to be certain of its purity, not to mention other qualities or chemical additives it might possess. Again, Alistair believed most of what he'd been told, and what he'd read, was there to confuse the issue and prevent more people from attempting the ritual. Blood was blood, after all, and it certainly came from a human donor. Probably it was better not to know whose blood it was – it removed any chance of getting caught up worrying over specific details. He could spend time on vague concerns, but he had no basis for any of it, and thus he found it simple to put the issue aside. Either it would work, or it would not, but whatever was going to happen was going to happen soon.

And it was happening – something, that is. A thick, cloying mist rose from the moldy carpet surrounding his cleared circle. The foggy cloud was drawn to him, but at the same time it was repelled by the protections he'd set. Within a very short time the church was no longer visible. He knelt in a whirling white vortex, cut off from the world beyond, and even from the pew where Asmodeus had been sitting when the ritual started.

Alistair would have kept the familiar with him in the circle, but the damn bird wasn't to be trusted. There was no way to be certain of his control, and if the old crow picked the wrong moment to lift off and go flying into the rafters he'd break the circle – and the protection. Better to let the feathered rodent deal with things on its own and hope that it had sense to become scarce until the ritual was complete, and things had calmed. There hadn't been a squawk since the ritual began, and that was a good sign.

There were only a couple of pages to go before he would need to tilt his head to the other side of the altar and begin reading from his own book. He wondered fleetingly if he should release the ritual – his ritual – in a more permanent text, once he'd succeeded. Certainly there was room for a new voice in the magical texts, particularly if that voice could debunk so much of the old melodramatic nonsense and replace it with something more practical. For one thing – if you could perform the same magic with a bit of red glass that you could with a ruby; certain suppliers of magical items were not going to be as popular once Alistair ratted them out. It would serve them right for not selling him what he needed.

The flames on the candles rose suddenly, first an inch, then a foot. They blazed, though the wax seemed not to diminish. Alistair grinned fiercely. It was the sign that the first portion of the ritual had been completed, and that it was working. His protections were complete. The next step was the easiest, and he had the entire original text for its completion. It was time to open the door between dimensions – not all the way, but far enough that he could send his summons through into that other realm. At the same time it was the easiest to accomplish, it was the most difficult to control. If he wavered, or if he misspoke a word, he was lost.

Sweat trickled down the back of his collar, but he ignored it. Despite the danger, things were going so well that it was difficult for him to worry. He would get through this, and when he had done so, everything would be different. With the proper otherworldly allies, he could accomplish anything.

He didn't notice the wavering in the smoke surrounding him at first. His gaze was fixed on the book at his left; his lips moved slowly, and though he didn't speak loudly, the words rang out strong and sure. When he lifted his gaze to shift it from one book to the other and take up the words he'd scribed so carefully into his own grimoire, he saw the figure standing outside his circle.

Alistair tried not to look. He needed to shift his gaze back to the ritual, and to continue. It didn't matter who it was; they couldn't break through the protective circle. If it was someone sent to stop him, or to prevent him from completing his ritual, they were too late. The wards were set and the spirits had been invoked; only he could break the circle as long as he maintained his concentration.

Something caught his eye, though, and he couldn't look away. The cup sat, forgotten on the altar, the final ingredient still sealed in its tube and the intricately woven oak sapling wand remained untouched.

A tall slender figure in a very dark hooded robe stood outside the circle. Alistair saw eyes in the shadowed depth of the hood, but could make out no features. There was no attempt to enter the circle, no movement, and no sound. The figure stood and stared in at him as if he were some sort of caged animal.

None of this bothered Alistair in the slightest. He'd half expected to be discovered at some point in the ritual, but once he'd passed a certain stage, he knew that there was nothing anyone could do but to wait and to see what would happen. They could set wards and confining spells around the church. They could contain what happened, but they could not enter his circle without his willing it, and no way was he letting any of them in. Not until he had what he was after.

But it wasn't just the robed figure. There was something sitting on its shoulder, something big and black, sleek and feathered. Dark eyes gazed coldly in at him, and he froze.

Without thinking, he dropped the small pouch he held in his hand and spoke a single word – a word that was no part of the ritual, not what had been written originally, or what he'd added himself.

"Asmodeus?" he whispered.

He saw his error too late. It wasn't his familiar seated on that shoulder, but a much larger, much younger bird. It spread its wings as he spoke, taking flight. This dislodged the hood from the intruder's features, but Alistair never saw them. The smoky mist stopped circling him and hung motionless in the air. He dropped his gaze to the second book and searched for the point that he needed to recapture the rhythm, but as he spun, his hand caught the rim of the cup and toppled, it. The thick, murky contents splashed over the page and obscured the words. He reeled back, and as he moved, the stranger outside the circle reached out with the toe of one boot and scraped a small break in the circle.

The smoke billowed and rushed in through that breach so rapidly that all sound and most of the air were sucked from the cathedral. In that instant, the robed figure reached back and flipped his cowl forward. Without air to hold it aloft, the raven tumbled, but his master stepped toward the door, held out an arm, and the bird thudded to a landing, gripping tightly. Without a word the intruder spun and sprinted toward the back of the cathedral toward the rectory and the street beyond.

The circle had become a white pillar, stretching from floor to ceiling. The interior was completely obscured, and the air hummed with energy. It built, like the rising screech of a siren, until in a burst of intense sound and bright light, the circle exploded. Air and sound raced outward, pounding the windows from the old cathedral outward and sending a shower of broken wood frame and glass shards in a long arc, pummeling the street and homes beyond. The sound was deafening, half scream, and half roar. A cloud rolled out, low to the ground, billowed, and rose until the entire structure of the cathedral was cloaked in cloying fog.

Inside, still standing, Alistair clutched his throat and tried to stagger forward. The breath had been ripped from his lungs in the explosion, and he was blind, but somehow he had the presence of mind to try and move away. Above him he heard Asmodeus cry out, loud and long. He heard the flutter of the old bird's wings, but he saw nothing.

Near his ankle the air shimmered. At first it was just a darker patch against the polished wood floor, but it widened, and as it did so, something moved in the space beyond – something that glowed sickly green. Alistair staggered in a circle, and his foot came into contact with that dark patch. There was a great cry, and Asmodeus dove from the rafters, riding the thin air in a long, slow arc toward his master. The bird flew all out, making no attempt to land on a shoulder or minimize its own risk - the goal was clearly to knock Alistair clear, but it failed.

As the great old bird soared closer, something reached through that dark patch, touched Alistair's ankle and groped its way upward. Whatever it was sank into Cornwell's flesh and dug deep. The crow hit its master hard, knocking him back, but as the body fell, something inside ripped free – something bright white and glowing. The taloned claw that had stretched up out of that darker place gripped it tightly and yanked. It disappeared, and the portal closed with a bright snap of energy. Cornwell's body toppled to the floor, and Asmodeus soared back toward the rafters, wings flapping madly.

At the door to the passage leading to the rectory, the cowled figure re-appeared. The old church was silent as a tomb. Dust still rose from where the windows had blown out; moonlight and the artificial illumination of streetlights filtered in through the haze. The cleared bit of floor and its broken, arcane circle stood out stark in that void, empty props. Cornwell's body lay limp and unmoving.

The figure glanced up, spotted Asmodeus clinging to a rafter above, and raised his arm, as if to send his own familiar in pursuit. Then he hesitated, cocked his head, and stood very still. Someone was coming – not the men and women of the neighborhood, or the police, but someone with power. The figure whispered something to his bird, scuttled forward, plucked the oak wand from Alistair's altar, and then spun on his heel and was gone. Far above, Asmodeus let loose a fierce cry that echoed through the rafters and shot out the windows and open doors into the night.

ELEVEN

Donovan had traveled the streets of the city for many years, and he was no stranger to *The Barrio*. A wide variety of practitioners of strange arts called that area home. There was Martinez, for one, and though Donovan respected the old man's abilities, he had no wish to renew that particular acquaintance. There was something in the white haired old guy's gaze that didn't sit well on the heart, and rumor had it that he was fond of leaving certain dimensional doorways open a bit too wide. He also played a lot of games with the gangs and other parts of the everyday city, and Donovan liked to remain as clear of that world as possible.

Donovan didn't have the sight, though he knew several others who did, but he could occasionally sense something in another's aura, a taint of odd coloration, or a hint of impending doom. Martinez gave him that sensation, and since he had no way to express what he could not quite bring to the surface of his mind, Donovan preferred avoidance.

There were others as well, some respected, some feared, and a few to be avoided at all costs. The Latin wings of the arts were varied, and tended toward darkness. Santeria, various forms of voodoo, and gris-gris flourished on the vermin infested streets. Their symbols lurked in the colorful graffiti and the tiny altars sprouting around street corners.

It didn't surprise him to find that Cornwell had chosen this area of the city to call home. There was less chance of someone stumbling in on him and interrupting his experiments. There were ways to find ingredients and objects of power in the lower east side that existed nowhere else, and that were less likely to draw unwanted attention.

Donovan stood for a while on the corner of 42nd Street and watched the old cathedral. There was no doubt that something was wrong. Several windows were shattered, and he saw from the larger shards that remained they had been blackened from the inside. Whether this was something Cornwell had done on purpose, prior to the breakage, or whether it had happened as the result of some out-of-control arcane explosion was impossible to tell from where he stood.

Energy crackled in the air. Something was happening, or had happened very recently, and it shivered over Donovan's scalp and down his spine in an electric tingle. Before advancing, he turned seven times in place and muttered a charm of protection. He had no idea what he'd be walking into, but he had no intention of finding out unprotected. He didn't fear Cornwell, but there were things Cornwell could have unleashed. Also, there was something not quite right about the entire scene. Donovan didn't know the renegade from any close association, so it was difficult to sort out the energies that rippled around him. He thought he sensed two distinct patterns.

There was no sense in lingering on the street. From the look of things, something had happened in the church, and it hadn't been very much before Donovan's arrival. If that were true, and whatever had happened had been loud or intrusive, there could be others arriving any moment. There would be police, and there would be locals. Even if they feared the place, they would come, and some of them, followers of Martinez, and others, wouldn't fear the place at all.

Donovan crossed the street to the front of the church. There were wards in place, glamours and cheap charms meant to cause ripples of fear and to start shadows dancing at the periphery of any intruder's vision. It was meant to frighten mundane visitors, or to distract those of incidental power. Donovan's protection charm deflected these easily, and he frowned.

The amount of energy he sensed in the cathedral wasn't in line with the level of magic he was encountering on the street. Whoever had set these protections was not particularly talented. In fact, he was downright sloppy. If Cornwell was behind them, then there was no telling what Donovan might face inside.

Either someone else was involved, or Cornwell had gotten in way over his head. If he had, there was no way to gauge at what point things had gone south on him, or what forces might lurk within the shadowy cathedral.

Donovan hesitated at the door. He wished he had Cleo with him, or had thought to ask Amethyst to accompany him. He took a deep breath and crossed the threshold, quickly dodging to one side as he stepped through the door. As his eyes adjusted, he noted that there was still dust in the air from whatever had broken the windows. The light was dim, but adequate, and after a moment he was certain that no one was moving. Drawing the green crystal pendant from around his neck, he clutched it in one hand and inched forward slowly.

The carpet down the center aisle was worn, and the dust on it wasn't as thick. Someone had walked that way often. Most of the pews were clotted with debris and there was a musky, animal scent in the air that tasted of rot when he breathed. Most of the windows had blown out, and a light breeze wafted across the cathedral. It helped. Donovan wondered briefly how Cornwell, or anyone else, could have breathed in the place when the windows were still sealed.

In the rear, a hallway led back to what must have been the rectory. As Donovan approached the front row of pews, he noted that there were supplies stacked to either side of the center aisle. There were books, scrolls, vials and crates. Most of it had already gathered a light coat of dust, but there were signs that some of it had been used recently.

He snorted as he saw a pile of what looked like everyday Tupperware. With a glance at the back wall to be sure no one watched from the shadowed hall, he stepped closer. The plastic containers were labeled with the names of various common roots and powders. Donovan shook his head.

"Tupperware?" he asked no one in particular.

Turning from the supplies in the pews, he stepped forward and stood before the kneeling rail at the altar. Cobwebs dangled between the once polished wooden slats. The carpet had been scarlet, he thought, but had faded from moisture and ground in dirt to the color of dried blood.

Something lay sprawled on the floor beyond the altar, and Donovan was about to mount the short steps and have a look when the air above him exploded with sound. A high-pitched, keening cry rang out, accompanied by a rush of heavy wings. Donovan ducked left, spun, felt the wooden altar rail crumble under his weight and toppled to the side. Something sliced the air cleanly where his face had been, and without thought he etched a symbol in the air with the forefinger of his right hand and breathed a word through it.

There was a screech, a second flurry of sound, and then a heavy thump. Donovan braced himself on the floor with one hand, felt the damp, rotted carpet seep between his fingers and recoiled in disgust. He staggered upright and looked down at his attacker. It was a crow. It wasn't as large as the bird that had invaded his office, or as young. There were feathers missing here and there, and it was scrawny. It was either very old, hadn't eaten regularly, or both.

"Asmodeus," he said. He remembered what Amethyst had told him about Cornwell's familiar. If this was it, then Cornwell wasn't his man. No way was this the bird that had invaded his home and made off with Le Duc's journal.

He let his gaze slide up from the bird to the floor beyond the altar, and he stopped, standing very still. There was a body on the floor. It lay across the lines of a large circle of protection, arms stretched out to either side, and one leg bent at a nearly impossible angle.

Donovan stepped over the stunned bird. He was careful not to touch the body, or to cross the lines of the circle. The body had broken the plane those concentric lines represented, but the circle itself might still be active. He needed to study it and be sure. If he stepped in and whatever had been summoned was trapped on the other side, he might not be able to escape with his life.

There was something odd about the inert form, and Donovan frowned. He stepped closer and reached out with the toe of his boot to turn the face upward. What should have been a light enough tap to show him the fallen man's face sent the body sliding sideways and flipped it. Donovan stared.

Skin wrapped tightly around a framework of bone was all that remained of Alistair Cornwell. The empty sockets that had held the man's eyes glared up at Donovan sightlessly. Within moments, as if the stress of being moved was too much for it, the body began crumbling in on itself. First the flesh fell away, then, with a jittery vibration that might have been the wind catching something very dry and very light, the bones shifted and fell away to dust.

The bird fluttered weakly on the floor. The tiny gust of wind its wings stirred up caught the dust and sent it swirling up in a tiny spiral. It should not have been enough of a breeze for this; Donovan stepped back and watched carefully. The whirling cloud glinted in the illumination from a streetlight peeking in through one broken window, and then, with a sound like one of the tiny pockets of air in bubble wrap being popped, it disappeared into the shadows. Nothing remained but the circle.

Donovan examined this, and found that his fears had been unwarranted. Whatever had been contained by this circle, or kept at bay, was gone. There was a clean break in the white chalk like, as though something had been dragged across it. He frowned. Such a breach of another's protections was unthinkable. Even if the ritual had been a particularly dangerous one, the thing to do would have been to set up a second circle and contain the possible damage.

There was a small altar in the circle, and Donovan knelt to examine it. He took in the toppled brass cup, the colorful and worthless blade, and the two books, one on either side. One was older, and he picked this up first. When he realized what it was, he frowned. He thumbed through it to the point where the text ended.

He glanced down at the other book, where the cup had spilled its contents. He reached down gripped the tome gingerly by one corner and shook off the excess moisture. Walking back down to the first pew, he laid it out and glanced through it quickly. Most of the first part of the text had been obscured by a dark, blotchy stain, but he was able to make out enough to see what it was. Cornwell had tried to recreate the ritual in his own hand. Donovan read a few lines, shuddered, and glanced back at the circle. Had he done it? This was a powerful ritual. Had it just backfired, allowing the demon to drag its summoner back through the portal that was created, or was there a more sinister answer?

Donovan quickly inventoried what lay closest to the circle, and within it. Almost everything was there, the braziers, the candles, a variety of powders and the symbolic sacrificial cup and sword. There should have been more though. He turned back to the older book, flipped through the pages, and found what he wanted.

The wand was clearly pictured and not difficult to assemble. Assuming that Cornwell had gathered the proper crystals, and the three flexible oak saplings, it would have been simple to create the instrument that was called for. Even a rank amateur would understand that there was a huge distinction between substituting one item for another and leaving something out altogether. And if something were left out, it would not be the wand.

He turned back to the circle and began a search, moving in a spiral pattern, starting in the center and working outward. He was careful to check the corners, and the shadows. Whatever had blown the windows out of the cathedral had probably originated in or near the circle, and the wand could have been blown free. He found nothing, and after a quick look down and through the pews, he concluded that if the wand had existed, it had either been taken, or destroyed.

He turned to the rear of the cathedral and the hallway leading out and back. As he approached this, something in the aura of energy shifted. He stood very still for a moment, and then drew a flat piece of colored crystal from his pocket. He held this up to his eye, and studied the floor.

Small lines, like gossamer, floated in the air and trailed off down the hallway. Someone had passed through there recently – someone with a great deal more talent and power than Cornwell had possessed. There was no way to tell what this other might have carried with them. Donovan stepped into the hall and something along the wall caught his eye.

He leaned down and plucked a single black feather from

the dust. It gleamed blue-black, and he knew that, despite how it would look to the casual observer, this feather had not come from the ragged, decrepit old crow in the next room.

Donovan thought back to the winged intruder in his study, and his frown deepened. He could not imagine why, but he knew now that the wand had been taken. He'd have to look for a connection in Le Duc's journal when he returned to his office. For now, he had some quick cleanup to take care of, and not much time to do it.

He heard the distant wail of a siren. It could be that the locals had finally broken through their innate dislike and fear of the police and made the call the authorities. If the windows had just blown out, the sound might have alerted someone on patrol. It was possible that the sirens might not be headed his way at all. In any case, Donovan didn't want to be caught in the old cathedral. It would be awkward trying to talk his way out of such a situation, and even more awkward trying to charm them long enough to escape. Better not to be seen at all.

He walked quickly back inside and headed toward the pews. He couldn't leave all of Cornwell's supplies lying about. Some of what he'd gathered was dangerous in the wrong hands, and it was going to look damned strange to the police as it was.

He quickly sorted through the books and scrolls. Most of it was garbage, things that could be purchased in any mundane used bookstore, but there were bits and pieces of genuine material in the lot, and he wished he had enough time to go through it all carefully.

The powders and ingredients were easier. These he dumped on the floor and kicked away beneath the pews. Without the proper ritual and words to transform them, they were nothing more than herbs, dust and powder. No one would think twice about a homeless person leaving behind an empty pile of Tupperware.

The sirens grew louder, and he hurried. He gathered up all the crystals, books, parchments and odds and ends he could carry and hurried toward the rear of the church. When they arrived, they'd come to the front. If he hurried, he could be off and down the street before then. They wouldn't figure out what it was that had caused the explosion. They also wouldn't find any trace of the inhabitant. They'd get vague stories from the locals, but none that would help. They wouldn't be looking for a pile of dust, so there was no concern that they'd stumble across something important.

As he worked, the old crow tottered to its feet and glared at him. Donovan ignored it. The bird was a familiar, and though it looked ratty and time-worn, it would possess the intelligence to understand he wasn't the threat. Whoever had entered the cathedral and put an end to its master, that someone wasn't Donovan.

It watched balefully as he tied the parchments and books together into a bundle and wrapped them in an old cloak. There was no time to sort through it, so he packed anything and everything into the bundle that seemed potentially harmful, working quickly.

The sirens were just down the street, and there was no time left. He'd done what he could. With a last glance around the cathedral, he slung the bundled package over his shoulder and hurried toward the rear hall. Blue and white lights flashed on the street outside. A door slammed. Donovan ducked into the back hall. He saw dim light ahead, and knew it was the rear door. If the earlier intruder had been able to make it out that way, there was no reason to believe he couldn't follow.

There was a fluttering sound behind him, and he cursed. The bundle hampered his movements, and he was unable to turn before the bird reached him. It didn't attack this time, however. With a soft, forlorn caw, the battered creature landed on the bundle Donovan carried and hunkered down, digging in with its talons.

"Shoo!" Donovan said, trying not to raise his voice. "Get off there. Go on back. I don't have time for this."

He heard voices. The sound of radio static shattered the near silence, and the screech of tires on pavement announced the arrival of a second police cruiser. Donovan cursed again and ran the last few yards to the rear door. He stepped out into a shadowed parking lot. It was overgrown with vines and surrounded on three sides by a broken down fence. There were holes in this where others had crawled through before, and he studied them hurriedly, trying to choose which would best suit his needs.

A dark figure stepped from the shadows, and Donovan spun on him.

"Martinez says you should give that package to me." The voice was low and menacing. There was a trace of a Hispanic accent, but Donovan had no time to place it.

"Tell Martinez I'm sorry I couldn't stop by to chat," he replied, circling warily toward the nearest break in the fence.

There were voices audible in the cathedral, and a third cruiser had screeched to a halt out front. The flashing lights blinked off the cloudy, overcast sky and gave the parking lot an eerie, otherworldly aspect.

The shadowy figure lunged. Something glittered brightly in his right hand, and Donovan dodged left. With the bundle over his shoulder he couldn't get off a proper charm, but if he dropped it he'd never get it back together and get out of the lot with it before the police found their way through the hall and out the back door.

Something shifted on his shoulder, and he stumbled. He started to topple, and then righted himself. He reached into his pocket with his free hand, but before he could sift through his pocket for what he needed, something dark dove through the air and caught his attacker full in the face. The man was fast. He whipped the blade he held up in a lightning arc, but he sliced only air.

The old crow dropped on him again, this time from one side, scoring the man's face and slicing a deep cut in his ear. He cried out. Donovan dove for the fence, ducked through a hole in the old rotten boards, and was gone. He heard the man cry out a third time. The bird cried out, as well, and for a second Donovan thought it had been hit, but moments later he heard the steady beat of wings overhead and knew it had escaped to fight another day.

He smiled, right up until the heavy weight of the thing thumped down hard on his bundle again. As he wound his way through the dark streets and out of *The Barrio,* he shook his head and frowned.

"Cleo," he informed Asmodeus darkly, "is not going to like this."

TWELVE

Donovan wasted little time on the streets. If you knew where to step, and when to turn, there were back roads and alleys in San Valencez that could take you a great distance, even on foot, in a very short time. Most of the citizens of the city never found these shortcuts, and when they did, they did their best to explain them away, or forget them entirely. If they stumbled into a dark corner, or through the mouth of an alley in one part of the city, and stepped out into another, they attributed it to kidnapping, or someone having slipped them something in a drink.

Donovan stepped into an alley three blocks from *The Barrio* on 43rd Street and the blue and white flashing lights of the police gathered at the abandoned cathedral winked out. It was a strange sensation, like floating in an ocean of gelatin, or walking through very heavy rain. It passed quickly, but it never failed to unnerve him slightly.

At the other end of the alley, he hesitated for just a moment and scanned the street in either direction. His neighbors were used to seeing him in strange company, but he didn't see any reason to give them more of an eyeful than was necessary. The sight of him trundling along with a hand-made knapsack of occult bric-a-brac with an old flea-bitten crow perched on top might be enough to get them talking, and if there was too much talk he'd either have to do something about it...or move. He also didn't want to draw attention to the alley. You could only tell it was there if you stood at the correct angle. If you looked directly at it, you saw nothing but a continuation of the wall on either side. It was the closest portal to his home, and Donovan counted on it for quick, silent getaways.

His luck held. It was early, and there was no traffic. In a couple of hours the street would be alive with early morning commuters and delivery trucks, but for the moment, nothing moved on the street but a sheet of newspaper that blew down the sidewalk and plastered itself against the brick base of his apartment building. Donovan took a deep breath and stepped out of the alley.

Before he'd taken more than a few steps, there was an audible snap of energy, and the dim light of the streetlights was replaced by a bright, blue-white radiance. He spun, and there, striding toward him, her eyes blazing and her hair lit by dozens of tiny blue crystals, was Amethyst. Her fists were clenched at her sides, and she moved with the speed and purpose of a bulldozer. Without the radiance in her hair, she'd blended in with the wall behind her, and he hadn't seen her. He cursed his own laziness for not checking more carefully.

"Wha...?" Donovan backed toward the apartment wall. He flailed for his pocket, but knew he had no time to reach it.

Amethyst stopped directly in front of him, hands on her hips and chin tilted defiantly. She started to speak, but at that precise moment, Asmodeus decided to act. He didn't attack this time, not having reached his advanced age through foolish acts, but exploded straight up in a flurry of black feathers and angry squawks that caught her by surprise.

Lights came on in several windows above the street, and Donovan cursed softly. So much for a quick, quiet entrance. Taking matters into his own hands, he stepped forward and put a hand on Amethyst's shoulder and shifted the awkward bundle to his other hand.

"What is it?" he asked her. "What happened?"

She wasn't listening. She'd watched the bird take off from his bundle and instantly understood the implications. As Donovan eyed the windows of the buildings surrounding them warily, Asmodeus settled reluctantly back onto his shoulder and eyed Amethyst with distrust. The glitter of the crystals in her hair had faded to a soft shimmer.

After another moment of silence, he turned toward his

building. "Inside," he said. "We have to talk, but let's get off the street before someone comes out to see what's wrong and sees you glittering like a Christmas tree."

She glanced away from the crow and met his gaze. She followed him inside, and moments later they were in the small lobby of his building. They stepped into the third elevator from the left, and when the door had closed behind them, Donovan keyed an intricate set of digits into the number pad on the wall. They ascended rapidly, and in silence.

Amethyst hadn't said a word, but the tension in the air between them was palpable. Something was very wrong, and Donovan willed the lift to hurry them upward. He needed to get to his own space, to his books, his computer, and to Cleo. Then he needed to sort out what he'd just been through, figure out why their mystery thief would want a haphazard, half-baked magician's home-made wand, and, by the way, just what in hell was wrong with Amethyst, and was any of her anger directed at him?

This possibility had occurred to him the moment he saw the flare of crystals she wore. She wasn't dressed for vampires this time. The blue crystals were intended as protection against enchantment. He knew she wore them only when she expected trouble, and she'd worn them to visit him. It wasn't a good sign.

Once they were inside his suite, he felt better. He set the wards behind them and tossed the bundle of Cornwell's possessions onto his dining room table. He'd momentarily forgotten the crow, and when the bundle struck the table, Asmodeus leaped up in a cawing, outraged rush of wings. He landed on one of the bookshelves, and at that precise moment, Cleo leaped.

The bird hadn't yet seen the cat, and was glaring down at Donovan, who leaped forward, ignoring the impending crash with his bookshelf, and snagged Cleo out of the air with one hand. Turning his back to take the brunt of impact, he curled the clawing, spitting animal to his chest. He hit hard and slid down the shelves, his spine catching on every shelf as he dropped. Cleo struggled wildly, but he clung to her and called out to Amethyst for help.

She stood, stunned, watching him until he came to rest

hard on the floor. He'd hit hard, and the impact nearly knocked the breath from him. Cleo gave another burst of energy, and this galvanized Amethyst, who reached down and grabbed her from Donovan's groping hands before she could squirm free and launch another assault on the bookshelf. The cat still struggled, but by now the crow had seen her. It glided across the room and came to rest near the very peak of the tall, ornate mantle that fronted the fireplace. It would be difficult, even for the large, agile Cleo, to reach him there.

Amethyst dropped the cat and held out her hand to Donovan, who watched it in confusion for a moment before reaching out, taking hold, and allowing himself to be pulled upright. His tailbone ached and his spine felt as though he'd been flogged. It did nothing for his mood.

"Christ," he said, pressing his fist into his lower back and arching.

His words brought his guest back to the moment.

"They're gone," she said.

He stared at her. "Who is gone? What are you talking about?"

"The time line crystals – the matched pair. They're gone."

He stared at her and straightened. For the moment the pain in his back, and Cleo's slowly stalking form moving toward the fireplace were blanked from his mind.

"How is that possible? Where was Lance?"

Amethyst shook her head, and he stepped closer, put an arm around her shoulder, and led her to his couch. He helped her sit down, stepped to the wet bar on the far side of the fireplace, and made them both a drink. On his way past, he swept his arm across his desk and dislodged Cleo, who yowled at him angrily and hissed up at Asmodeus. He wasn't really worried that she could reach the bird, but he wanted her to know he didn't approve. The crow looked ruffled, but unperturbed.

When she'd had a sip of strong brandy, Amethyst spoke.

"I'm sorry. I came here the moment I was certain Lance was going to be fine. He was attacked. Somehow this … thief … broke into my place. He overpowered Lance and made off with the crystals."

"But, what about your protections?" he asked.

"Intact," she said softly. He watched her take another drink, and frowned.

"What do you mean, 'intact,'" he asked. "I thought you said that the crystals were taken?"

"They were. They are gone, but the wards that protected them were left in place. Nothing has been disturbed, including the entrance charms. Whoever we're dealing with is very powerful, and very clever. Somehow they entered without setting off the security, took the crystals without breaking the wards, and left Lance unconscious on the floor with a lump the size of a crystal ball on his head. I found him that way, unconscious and stunned. He may have a concussion, but I gave him something for the pain, and he's resting."

"And there was no sign of forced entry?" he asked. "Lance saw nothing, heard nothing?"

Amethyst glanced around at his computer, and at some of the other electronic devices in the room, and shook her head. "I don't keep video surveillance, as you know. I don't have a computer, or a television. Still, there are other ways.

"I have a series of crystals imbedded in the walls that act as repositories of events. When someone moves in front of them, or when someone speaks, vibrations record themselves, for a time, in the crystal. It doesn't last very long – but long enough.

"I checked the crystals after I saw to Lance. There is something there, but I can't make it out. Just prior to my arrival there was a shadowy image flickering about the room. It moved too quickly for its image to be fully captured. For a few minutes that's all there was to see. When the image cleared, all I could see was Lance, sprawled on the floor. Otherwise, the room was empty."

"If there was no clear sign of a break-in," he asked, "and the wards that protected the crystals are still in place, how did you find out that they were missing?"

"I didn't, at first," she admitted. "I don't know why, but with all that's been going on, I felt as though I needed to get an inventory – just to be certain. I expected to see that everything was in its proper place. It was, except for the crystals. Their case was there, just as always, but when I opened it, it was empty."

He stared at her.

"That isn't possible," he said at last. "There are a number of ways those crystals could have been taken; but none of them could have worked without leaving some sort of trace. You're sure that it's the same case, that there's no sign of a transference spell?"

"I'm not an amateur," she said, taking a longer deeper pull on the brandy. "Don't you think I know what I saw? I'm telling you I have no idea how the crystals were taken."

Donovan stared into his brandy and concentrated. He ran over the details she'd presented him slowly, shifted them one way, and then another. Something was bothering him, but he couldn't nail it down.

"You have the crow," she said, breaking his train of thought.

He glanced up, saw that, for the moment, the bird was safe on its mantel top perch, and he nodded.

"It's not the bird that was here before," he said. "Cornwell is dead. Whoever killed him broke a magic circle in the middle of a summoning."

Amethyst stared at him incredulously.

"In the middle? You're sure?"

He nodded.

"There was a break in both the inner and outer circles, as if someone drew their foot across it deliberately. The church was all but destroyed. I took what I could, and I got out of there."

"What about Martinez?" she asked. "I can't imagine something like this happening right under his nose."

"One of his people showed up as I was leaving," Donovan said. "If it weren't for my new feathered friend up there," he nodded at Asmodeus, "I might not have gotten off so easily. I think all they were after was Cornwell's possessions. I'm pretty sure that Martinez wouldn't have broken that circle, and if he did, why send someone else back later for the things he wanted from the church? Why not just take them?

"And there's more. I found this."

He reached into his pocket and pulled out the blue-black

raven feather. He held it out to her, and she took it, holding it carefully as if it posed some odd threat of its own. She glanced up at Asmodeus, but Donovan shook his head.

"Different bird altogether," he said. "The other was much larger, and younger."

Asmodeus let out a caw at this, and for the first time since arriving home, Donovan smiled.

"You're no spring chicken," he said, glancing up.

"Chicken." The bird repeated.

Donovan blinked.

"You talk?"

"Talk." The bird agreed.

Amethyst started to laugh.

"It seems that Cornwell managed that spell after all. I guess ol' Moldy up there just didn't want to talk to him."

Donovan heard her, but his mind had drifted again. He kept thinking about the closed case, and the missing crystals. Time was running out for Vanessa much more quickly than he'd thought, and he needed answers. He looked at it from every angle he could conceive, but came up with nothing. Still, something about it bothered him; something was there, just out of reach, something important.

"That only leaves the bone marrow dust," he said at last. "If whoever is behind all of this manages to retrieve that, or find someone else to do it, then we may be too late to stop him."

"If he has something that can snatch those crystals from me, despite, my precautions, what makes you think he needs anyone to retrieve the bone marrow powder? Isn't it possible he can just snatch it from the casket without opening it?"

He looked at her, and then shook his head, frowning.

"I don't think so. I don't know what it is, exactly, but there is something in your theft we're overlooking. It's itching at the back of my mind, but I can't seem to pry it free. We are both familiar with what is, and is not possible. This is ritual magic, and there are no spells for transportation of objects that I know of. Look around. I think it's more likely that whoever it is *wants* us to believe he can perform acts we know are impossible. The more off-balance he keeps us, the more chance he has of finishing his ritual. If he does, and it works, nothing we do will make much difference."

He swept his arm in the direction of the books on his shelf.

"I have nearly every occult text known to exist in the last three centuries, in one form or another. I don't' claim to be familiar with all of it, but I can tell you this – if that sort of magic had ever existed, it would still exist. Someone would have found the record of it, recorded it, and reproduced the effect, and then someone else would have found a way to guard against it. Fewer and fewer new secrets are discovered, because to get beyond all that's been tried in the past takes so much time."

"I'd like to believe that's true," she replied, "but I wouldn't bet my life on it. That's what you're doing, you know. You're betting Vanessa's life on it." She frowned, thought about what she'd just said, "Well, her existence, anyway. I guess life is the wrong term in this case?"

Donovan shrugged, and she continued. "If you're wrong? If someone has figured out something new, something we aren't prepared to defend against, then we may be too late already. Whoever it is has been at least one step ahead of us all along – snatching a vampire out from under Kline's security – not to mention breaking Kline himself like a rag doll, then breaking in here, killing Cornwell, and stealing my crystals. I wouldn't want to be responsible for completing any one of those tasks, but whoever this is took them all on, and so far he hasn't left a trace."

Donovan sighed. He was about to rise and refill his drink when the phone rang. He walked to the desk and answered it. He frowned, and then answered.

"Tonight? You've talked with him? Good. Get back in contact and tell him you have someone to do it."

He listened a moment longer, then hung up the phone.

"That was Windham," he said. "He's gotten me the information on the buyer for the bone marrow dust. The offer is still open, and so far, no one has taken up the challenge."

"Maybe there's still time," she replied. "Maybe he's just hoping to send you off on a wild goose chase that will take long enough to keep you out of his hair until he finishes Le Duc's ritual."

"I don't have a choice," Donovan replied. "If I don't go after this dust, someone else will. If I manage to get out of the graveyard with it, I'll have something he needs, and he'll have to deal with me. Without going out of state, he won't find what he needs anywhere else, and he doesn't have time for that. Eventually we'll find him; if he waits too long, we'll catch him. When we catch him, I would not want to get between him and Johndrow.

"I'm going tonight. He won't know it's me, of course, I'll be going through Windham, but it should get me close enough to either figure out who it is we're up against, or where he's holed up. I can't go after him if I can't find him."

She didn't look convinced.

"I suppose," she said. "In any case, I have to get back. There are still some things I need to check, and I want to make sure Lance is okay. I don't think we'll have any more trouble now that those crystals are gone, but you never know. Whoever it was might think Lance can identify him and come back to prevent it."

"Are you going to question him?" Donovan asked.

She looked startled. "I...yes. I suppose I am. I didn't think about it, but even if he doesn't remember what happened, there might be imprints of some of it that I could read. I was in such a hurry to get over here and tell you about the missing crystals that I wasn't thorough."

"Let me know what you find," he said. "I'll keep thinking about it, too. There's still something not quite right about the whole situation; if it occurs to me, I'll contact you. I can send Cleo."

"Or your new buddy," she laughed, tossing her head and grinning up to where Asmodeus sat, glaring smugly down at Cleo.

"Buddy," he said, flapping his wings and nearly toppling from the mantle.

"Thanks for reminding me," he muttered. "I'll have to find a way to make a truce between these two, or I'll come back to find the building reduced to a pile of rubble."

Amethyst laughed, and turned toward the door. Donovan walked her to the hall, leaned in, and gave her a quick kiss.

"Don't worry," he said. "We'll get through this, and when we do, we'll have a reason to celebrate."

"I hope you're right," she said, ducking into the elevator.

As the door slid shut behind her, he stepped back into his apartment. There wasn't much time. He had to get a message into Windham's hand so the collector could pass on the intention to fill the order for the bone marrow dust. He also had to gather the materials he'd need, do what he could to map his way through the graves, and get a report out to Johndrow. The old vampire would be worried sick, and after the first encounter with the hotheaded young Vein and his cronies, Donovan was in no mood for further interruptions.

When he was ready, he glanced over at Cleo, who stood poised on his desk. She'd been like that, watching every movement Asmodeus made, waiting for him to make the mistake of flying too low.

"You have to let it go," Donovan said.

Cleo ignored him.

He sighed. Stepping forward, he drew the cat into his arms. She squirmed, but not like she'd done when he caught her earlier. He cleared his mind of thought, pressed his hand to her forehead, and thought about the cathedral. He relived the image of Cornwell's dried, husk of a body crumbling to dust around the toe of his boot, his escape through the rear of the church, and the subsequent attack, where Asmodeus had come to his aid. Cleo grew very stiff in his grasp, but he held her until the images subsided, and when he placed her gently back on top of the desk, she had calmed.

From his perch, as if on cue, Asmodeus croaked "Cleo."

The cat started to wash her face, and Donovan breathed easier. At least it seemed both animals might live to see his return. He double checked the items in his bag, folded the note he'd prepared into his inside jacket pocket and turned for the door. He glanced longingly at his bedroom, then stepped into the hall, and closed the door behind him with a snap.

THIRTEEN

Johndrow sat and watched as Vein paced the room. There was nothing left to be said about the fiasco at Club Chaos, but there were still things to be settled between the two of them. For all his anger, Johndrow understood Vein's anguish. Vanessa had brought the young one to the blood, after all. They were tied together in ways that Vanessa and Johndrow would never be. Johndrow and Vanessa were blood-bonded, but that bond had been a choice, something cultivated over many years of shared intimacy. What Vein felt was primal, like the protective instinct of a young man toward his mother.

"There has to be something we can do," Vein said. He spun to face Johndrow and dropped his palms flat on the desk between them, meeting the elder's eyes. "We can't just sit back and hope the magic man pulls her through this."

"What would you have us do?" Johndrow asked, keeping his voice neutral. "We don't know where she is, and we don't know who her captor is. Even if we managed to locate her, we don't know what we'd be facing; so how would we prepare? We must wait."

"I can find her," Vein said. It wasn't a boast; Johndrow saw this in the young one's eyes. "I feel her. The bond is weak, but it's there. I could follow it. You know I could, you've done so yourself, in other places, and other times. I know the stories as well as any."

Johndrow nodded. It was true. He'd spent an entire winter tracking the one who'd made him, but that was a different matter altogether from this. That had been a journey fueled by hatred, and vengeance, and there had been only one end possible.   That bond had itched at Johndrow's thoughts and clawed at his mind. That other's eyes had mocked him and the dry, lilting voice behind that gaze called out to him in tones that broke like brittle crystals.

"I had no choice," Johndrow said. "When I chose to walk that road, I walked it alone, and I knew that it was likely I would never return. Vanessa brought you to us, but you came willingly enough. I was taken, toyed with, and cast aside. That is what I thought about each night, when I woke to the darkness, and that is what I thought about when I fed. There was no time for pleasure, and no room for forgiveness. This is different."

"It is not." Vein said flatly. "You are right in saying that what she gave me is a gift that I cherish, but how does that weaken the bond? I know she's held against her will. I know that she's great danger, and that the bond could be severed permanently. As much as you loathed the tie that bound you to the one you killed, I cherish mine. I have to do something."

"Ah, but there is a difference," Johndrow said, rising slowly. "There are two differences, in fact, distinct and important. The first is that, when I tracked and killed the one who made me, there was no council in place to stop me, or to help me. I was on my own, and I was going mad. You, on the other hand, are not alone. You have those you call friends, and you have the council."

"What is the second difference?" Vein asked.

"DeChance," Johndrow said, stepping around the desk to stand beside the younger vampire. "You have DeChance on your side. I know you don't understand it – that you probably don't believe it – but that one is strong, and he is smart. He can go places we cannot, and he can do things for us that no one else might accomplish. He has a personal stake in this, as well, so there is no fear of treachery."

"As long as the blood in his veins flows hot and red, and it is his own, he cannot be trusted," Vein said. "You yourself taught me that rule, and I have never forgotten it. He may help us for the money. He may even help us out of friendship. It changes nothing. He is what he is, and we are…something altogether different. There is no way he can change the instinct that makes his kind fear our kind, and with that fragile bond in the center of your bargain, I can't trust her to him. I want to, believe me. I want to believe she will be here with us any moment, asking for a glass of your precious brandy and wrapping around you like a cat in heat. I don't believe it, though, and that's why I have to do something – anything – other than sitting here and waiting."

"The Council will not sanction any rash action," Johndrow said softly. "I want you to understand that. I know you believe you are doing the right thing, but your attack on DeChance might have cost Vanessa her life, if it had been less ill-conceived. Don't believe he'll be unprepared a second time."

"I have no further interest in the magic man," Vein said, glancing away toward the dark, obsidian surface of Johndrow's window shield. Beyond it the afternoon shadows lengthened and stretched out dark fingers to clasp in the center and banish the light of day.

"But you will go?" Johndrow asked softly.

Vein nodded.

"I have to go."

"If you find her," Johndrow said, "tell DeChance where she is. Don't try to get in alone. Don't try to do it by yourself. I know you want to, but that's your pride speaking, and pride speaks only for fools. Don't let thoughts of revenge, or heroism, cloud your judgment. Whoever took Vanessa is no fool, and he will know you are coming – you or someone like you. He will be aware of the blood bond, and he will use it to his advantage."

Vein turned to the door with a shrug. "If he has blood, I will make it mine. You can count on that."

He stepped through the door and pulled it closed behind him. Johndrow stood in silence and watched him go. When he was sure Vein was out of sight, and hearing, he whispered.

"Bring her back to me, Vein. Bring back my life."

Vein took the private elevator down to the garage level. His car waited for him, as he had known it would. The others were already in the back, and the trunk was loaded with the equipment they expected to need. He'd only visited Johndrow out of a sensation of grudging respect. If Vanessa saw something in this man to look up to, the least Vein could do was to acknowledge it. That was as far as he was willing to go, however.

He had lied to the elder on several counts, or, at the very least he hadn't been fully forthcoming. Foremost among the things he'd left out of their conversation was the fact that he was pretty certain he already knew where Vanessa was being kept. He'd followed the weak thread of the blood bond since the night of her capture, and after countless weaving, spiraling drives up and down the streets of the city, he'd managed to pinpoint where that bond was strongest.

Since the meeting with DeChance, Vein had been obsessed with two things. He needed to find and free Vanessa from whomever, or whatever had taken her so easily, and he wanted revenge on the magic man and the woman. Vein had worked long years to earn the respect of his small band of followers. They weren't old in the blood, and there wasn't a very bright bulb among them, but they were loyal. Seeing him bested publicly, and with such indifference, had been a blow to his ego, and to the loyalty and courage of his small posse. For the moment it was on the back burner, but it was an insult that couldn't be ignored. That's how Vein saw it, anyway.

He stepped off the curb as the sleek limo pulled out of its assigned spot and drew up beside him. The rear door opened and Vein slid inside. The others waited, all dressed in the long dark overcoats and dark sunglasses they preferred. It was an affectation, and Vein knew it. The world around them changed every few decades. Styles came and went, and with each transformation of that outer world, a more subtle shift ran through Vein's own. This new wave was born of bad movies, old westerns, cheesy gothic novels and a simple desire to be "cool" that had not faded with the years. Vein was young enough to have clear memories of the time before he'd met Vanessa, and even in those early days of America, the long coat and gruff demeanor was in style. It hadn't changed that much over the years, and for the first time in the history of humanity, vampires were "cool" just by existing. It was a good time to be undead, and Vein intended to make the most of it, regardless of the edicts and warnings of the elders. It was his time.

"Did you find everything?" he asked.

A blonde man in the front seat nodded. His hair was cut in a flat top, and his collar was turned up, shielding his face from view. This was Bruno, who was the youngest in the blood, but had been the oldest at the time of his transformation. He appeared to be in his mid forties, and it bothered him that he didn't fit in well with the others, all of whom had given up the breathing life in their twenties. More than once he'd been mistaken for their father, or some sort of teacher with his class on a field trip. He was tall, broad, and a half-notch smarter than the others. Vein counted on him when there was anything more than the simplest of planning involved.

"Right here," Bruno said, patting the seat between himself and the driver, who paid no attention to him at all. Kali had been eighteen when she was taken, and beautiful. She, like Johndrow, had been taken against her will, and her attitude had never improved. She hung with Vein and his crew because they paid little attention to the rules, and because Vein had promised her that eventually he would help her hunt down the one who had changed her. She didn't speak unless spoken to, and most of the others steered clear of her when Vein wasn't present. She liked that just fine.

Vein watched her for a moment as she pulled out of the private garage and onto the streets. He felt a special kinship with Kali that he lacked with the others, and he knew he'd have to pursue it eventually. Everything in its time.

"We had a little trouble with some of it," Bruno said, breaking the silence. "That was expected, though, and we handled it."

"We'll deal with that when it's over," Vein said, dismissing the matter. "If we succeed, no one is going to begrudge us the few things we took, and if we don't?"

He shrugged, and none of his companions felt compelled to fill in the blanks. If they failed they weren't likely to be coming back at all – at least not in any condition for immediate punishment. All of them had issues with the elders in one way or another, and this was put up or shut up time. They'd been saying for years, at least since they linked their various cars to the "Vein train," that they knew how to handle themselves, now it was time to prove it.

The sun had dropped the final few feet below the horizon and the city was drenched in twilight. Some street lights flickered on, others awaited more complete darkness. Businesses were caught in that dead zone between daylight and fluorescent splendor. Neon kicked in here and there, but was mostly silent, that gaseous, humming incandescence saved for the darker shadows. Bright lights to keep the city safe, dark, beautiful colored neon to lure them back into shadows. Vein loved the twilight.

They saw their goal long before they reached it. The Tefft Complex was a huge, gleaming structure of reflective glass windows, steel, and concrete. Lights winked out of offices up and down the north, east, and west face of the building, visible from anywhere in the downtown area. It wasn't the tallest building in San Valencez, but it was one of the most imposing, and, as Vein had discovered, it had a secret. Like a giant, metallic bone stretching up into the darkening sky, he knew it had a core that wasn't visible to the casual observer. The Tefft Complex had a hollow core, and it was in that central, sealed section he knew Vanessa was being held.

There were several businesses housed in the complex. There was a small, foreign bank, a jewelry importing firm, an insurance company, and even a small coffee shop on the first floor. Banks of elevators rode smoothly up and down the walls of the skyscraper, and if you walked in through any of the main entrances, you'd see that they ran in a tight circle near the center of the rear wall. The southern face of the complex had no windows, and the elevator shafts did not actually run across that back facing wall – and they were not all visible.

It had taken some doing, but once Vein had determined he had the right building, he'd started digging. When it came to the darker side of the city, what seemed apparent on the surface was almost always deceiving. The Tefft Complex proved no exception to the rule. There were at least two elevators in that structure that could not be accessed through the lobby. There was also a large section of the building itself that was accessible by no obvious means, but that certainly existed.

A little more digging, and he was certain he'd found the flaw in the façade. While the elevators didn't open into the main lobby of the building, there were maintenance halls between the shafts, and they extended to the hidden shafts, as well as the others. Private elevators weren't uncommon, and they required the same types of maintenance and service that public elevators did. Vein and his crew were very adept at climbing, and it didn't seem likely that an elevator shaft would cause them much trouble.

What they might find once they entered that closed level he could only guess, and the guesswork was what made him nervous. Johndrow was right about one thing – they were less equipped than DeChance against most magical attacks. Strength and speed were on their side, but the innate weaknesses of undeath were too widely known and easy to emulate by magical means.

It was a problem. Vein had sent his followers crawling through all the darker pits of the city in search of charms, protections, and weapons that might give them an edge, or, barring that keep them from being destroyed. The haul was a small one, but surprisingly potent. He grinned, thinking about it.

On the corner of Oak and Vine, there was a small gift shop that specialized in occult items. Though she wasn't always there, it was known that this shop was run by the woman called Amethyst, the one who'd humiliated Vein so easily in the alley. Her specialty was amulets, charms, and crystals, and though most of what she sold in the shop was powerless, meaningless junk, you could find the better items if you knew where, and how, to look. As it turned out, Vein wasn't the only one in the city attracted to Kali. Amethyst had an apprentice.

Kali had talked the guy out of five amulets that would protect them from magical detection, and one larger crystal meant to deflect spells. In addition, Vein had purchased a blood crystal. There was little magic available to the undead, but magic didn't always reside in the practitioner. Often it was imbedded in an object – a talisman, or a scroll where the words were enchanted to act of their own volition once the bearer spoke them aloud. Blood crystals were among the only enchantments unique to the undead, and Vein had gone to a lot of expense to acquire the one he wore around his neck.

The crystal had only one purpose. Once he placed a drop of his own blood on it, the stone would swing out to the length of the thong that held it around his neck, and it would stretch in the direction of the strongest blood bond. In this case, he intended to use it, once they'd managed to break through the security of the inner building, to find Vanessa as quickly as possible. He wasn't bonded to any other, not among the elders, and certainly not among this crew. The only one with promise was Kali, and as he'd told himself earlier, that was for another time.

They pulled to the curb several blocks away from the Tefft Complex and sat with the motor running for few moments. Bruno handed out the amulets, and they slipped them over their necks in silence. Vein stared down at his, an almost solid black crystal.

"You sure these things will work?" he asked.

Kali shrugged. "How would I know? He said they would. Why would he lie?"

Vein shrugged and opened his door, stepping out onto the sidewalk. It didn't matter. They were committed, and he, for one, was going to see it through to the end, even if the damned amulets didn't work. He'd been sitting long enough; it was time for some action. He slipped his sunglasses on, and a moment later the others had gathered around him. They stood and stared up at the huge, looming structure, then started walking toward it as a group.

Vein and Kali took the lead. Behind them the other three lined up. Pierce had been unable to join them – he'd been the in the alley with Vein, and had not been back around since the attack. His absence was another thing to be dealt with at a later time. Kali more than made up the difference. Bruno walked directly behind Vein, and beside him was a thin kid they called Shade. On the far side, tall and lanky, walked the oldest of them next to Vein. His name was Robert, but they called him bones.

Vein didn't like using the names they'd been born with. They were so much more than they'd been, why cheapen that with an outdated label? Of course, the elders disapproved, but they generally disapproved of everything Vein and his friends attempted or suggested, so the names stuck, and none of them answered to anything else. Vein wondered if Pierce had gone back to being "Darren Pierce" already, or if they could drag him back into the fold.

They entered the lobby of the Tefft Complex and headed straight for the elevators. There were security guards, but Vein gave them no chance to act. They stepped into the first elevator and Kali pushed the up arrow. The doors were closing before the first of the guards got the courage to press off the wall he was leaning on. Too late.

Once they'd left the first floor behind, Vein wasted no time. He nodded, and Kali poked the STOP button. There was a trap door in the top of the elevator car, and Bruno had it open in seconds.

"Up, and to the right," Vein said. There should be a short tunnel, and on the far side of that there's a maintenance ladder leading down between the shafts."

Bruno nodded, levered himself up and through the hole, and was gone. Bones and Shade followed. Kali met Vein's gaze for a moment, searched his cold features for something, found it, and disappeared upward like a wraith. Vein pushed the up button, leaped, and was through the door before the machinery ground into motion. He found the small maintenance tunnel, pulled himself inside, and crawled quickly through. The ladder was right where he'd expected it to be, and he dropped the six feet to the floor of the darkened passage without a sound. They stood in the darkness and glanced both directions down the corridor. The walls thrummed as the elevators rose and fell steadily; gears caught smoothly, cables spun on huge, greased pulleys.

"Come on," Vein said, heading off to the right. "We were in the first public shaft, so the next one over should be one of the two private lifts."

They moved quickly. The darkness was no hindrance, but

the further they moved from that public elevator shaft, the more the awareness of what they were about to attempt hit home. They had no way to know what kind of security awaited them, or how effective the charms they'd purchased might prove. There was no time to worry over it now, if they'd been detected, there was no sign of it.

They came to another wall, and Bruno heaved himself up the side.

"There's another short shaft," he reported, "like the other one."

He disappeared into it without waiting for the others, and they scaled the wall and followed. The far side opened into another elevator shaft, and a quick glance up and down showed that the elevator, currently, was on the ground floor. It was impossible to tell where the exit might lead without crossing the shaft and looking for another way out, but Vein wasn't interested.

He pulled the blood crystal out from beneath his shift.

"Kali, would you do the honors?" he held out his arm to her, wrist up. She didn't glance down at it. Instead, she met his gaze steadily. As she did so, her hand shot out and her nail opened a small cut in the skin of his forearm. She missed the vein by less than an inch. He didn't flinch. Quickly, he held the cut over the crystal. Vein shook his arm; a single drop of blood seeped out before his skin could close and heal over it. The blood fell across the surface of the crystal and spread.

The effect was instantaneous, and eerie. None of them had ever seen one used before, though all of them were familiar with the concept. The crystals were rare, and expensive, and usually they were only employed in the "Blood Hunt," the quest to find the one who'd brought you to the blood and kill him or her for the act. Kali watched with particular interest.

The blood spread out in a smoky haze. Though they had clearly seen the drop fall onto the crystal, it didn't seem to have actually touched the surface. It formed a coating, iridescent and pulsing, and when the coating was complete, Vein released it. Instead of dropping to his chest, hit hung very still, floating in the air, then, almost lazily, the tip rose, pointing almost straight up the shaft of the elevator.

"Let's go," Vein said. He grabbed the wall of the elevator shaft and began his ascent, climbing in quick, graceful bursts like some sort of human spider. The others fanned out and followed, ringing the shaft and coming up level so that they climbed as a unit. None of them wanted to slip, or to be left behind, and if there was an attack, they had a better chance in a group where they couldn't be picked off individually.

It became clear early on that there was a significant difference between this shaft and the public elevators. Though they climbed for what seemed an eternity, they passed only two doors. Each time they came level with one, Vein hesitated, and glanced down at the crystal, but it never wavered. It was pointed up, and he knew they were going to have to go all the way, nearly forty stories up, before they found what they sought.

They climbed in silence, and in a remarkably short time, the group of them clung in a tight semi-circle by the final door. The blood crystal stretched out from Vein's neck, pointing not quite straight ahead, but almost. It angled to the left a little, and Vein noted this, then turned to Bruno and nodded.

Bruno climbed a bit higher, found two support beams to lodge his booted feet in, and dangled in front of the door. He slid his fingers into the crack in the center of that door, and with a single swift motion, he dragged it open. There was no time to hesitate. Vein swung through, and the others followed in a dark cloud. When all but Bruno had entered, Bones knelt and held the door, Bruno swung in over his head. Bones let the doors close with a soft snick, and they stood very still.

They were in a corridor that curved out and around in both directions, stretching back toward the outer south wall. The crystal swung to the left at about a forty-five degree angle, pointing off through the wall in front of them.

Vein turned left and followed the direction the crystal pointed, moving swiftly and keeping low. The others spread out, making as many separate targets as possible. Bones watched behind them for anyone, or thing, that might be following or trying to sneak up on them. They were out of sight of the elevator before they saw the first door.

Vein held up a hand to caution the others and watched the

crystal carefully. It still pointed further around the curving hallway. It was possible they could go through the room ahead to get to where Vanessa was held, but it seemed more likely there was another door. Vein slipped past the first silently, and the others followed. He rounded another bend. There were two remaining doorways. One was at the very end of the hall, flat against the wall, and the other, like the first they'd encountered, was on the right hand wall. Vein stepped up to this one, and the crystal tugged him closer, pointing dead center at the wooden door.

He glanced at Kali, then at the others.

"This is it," he said.

He tried the knob. It was unlocked, and he turned it slowly. They waited. When there was no sound, he pushed gently, and the door swung open. The hinges were well-oiled, and there was no sound. The room was almost bare. They stepped inside and stopped at the sight that met their eyes.

Vanessa hung from the wall. Her wrists and ankles were chained, and the chains disappeared into recesses in the stone face behind her, holding her tightly. Her eyes were wild, and despite the futility of it, she struggled crazily. Vein took a step forward and she tried to scream, but she was gagged, and they heard only a muffled shriek. Too late, Vein caught the angle of her gaze, and realized she wasn't staring at him.

He whirled and cried out. The others spread, but it was too late. There was a blinding flare of light, like what they'd experienced in the alleyway, but intensified. Vein tried to dive forward but was driven back hard. He crashed into the wall beside where Vanessa hung, and the light pinned him there. He clawed at it feebly, the strength melting from his limbs as heat rose so quickly, and so intensely, that it threatened to consume him in a sudden blaze.

He could not see their attacker. He tried to reach for Vanessa, but could barely lift his leaden arms. Then, with a soft, futile snarl, he fell forward on the cold stone and passed from thought.

Vein woke to pain, but he shrugged it off. He was in a small room of some sort, and he stood carefully. Nothing was broken, or, if anything had broken, he had healed. He didn't have any idea how long he'd been out. The others lay in jumbled heaps around him. Only Kali was on her feet, gazing at him levelly, and waiting.

"Where are we," he asked.

Kali shrugged. "Wherever he put us."

The others began to stir. Vein glanced down and saw that the blood crystal was still hanging about his neck. There was a soft laugh, and Vein spun, trying to find the source. A moment later he realized he wasn't in a room at all. It was an elevator. He slammed up to the ceiling, but found no trap door. He tried the walls, one after the other, but despite several attempts, each harder than the last, he was unable to bend, break, or open them.

"You won't get out that easily," a voice said softly.

Vein stilled himself, fought back the panic that threatened to rise, and stood in the center of the elevator.

"Who are you? What do you want?"

"I didn't want anything from you," the voice replied, "though I'll admit it was entertaining. Vanessa is quite concerned for your welfare. It's very touching, and it gives me an edge, don't you think?"

Vein quelled the urge to smack into one of the walls again.

"This is a very unique elevator," the voice continued. "It's built into the back wall of the building. Most of the time I keep it hidden from the world, but sometimes, well, I'm a bit romantic, I suppose. The wall behind you opens to a very solid window – about two feet thick, I believe, and reinforced with a silver mesh. It's not quite as effective as if it were the east side of the building, but eventually the sun touches everything, doesn't it Vein?"

The wall slid slowly open, and they had a clear view of the dark, star-studded sky beyond the complex.

"How long do you think it will take," the voice asked with a soft, insane chuckle, "for all of you to become ash? I have a theory. I'm betting that it will take less time than it takes for that elevator to reach the ground, with the noon-time sun beating down on it. Not that it matters. The doors are charmed, and you won't be able to open them, so if you manage to survive to reach the bottom, you'll be dust before anyone gets you out. You can rest assured on that point."

Vein wasn't really listening. He was studying the window. He saw the tiny silver threads woven into the glass. He thought about those slicing skin as the glass shattered, shredding his flesh like a cheese grater from hell.

"What do you want?" he repeated.

"I have everything I want, Vein. Now I don't have to worry about you taking it."

There was another whir, and the wall opposite the window slid aside to reveal another glass partition. This one looked out into the passageway they'd walked through moments before. On the other side, a man stood, gazing in at them with a lopsided grin on his face.

Kali slammed into the door with such sudden force and anger that Vein was sure it would shatter, and she would be shredded, but the glass held.

"You!" she screamed.

Their captor laughed, turned, and walked away.

FOURTEEN

It was just growing dark when Donovan slipped back into the alley outside Club Chaos and entered the phone booth. He dialed the code and moments later stepped into The Crossroads, glancing to his right, and to his left as he entered. He didn't really fear trouble inside the bar, but he didn't want any more surprises.

He'd come equipped for just about anything. Charms and pendants dangled beneath his dark shirt, and he had several objects of power tucked into the various folds and pockets of his jacket. It really wasn't cold enough for a jacket – it was warm most of the year in San Valencez – but unless he intended to play super hero and wear a utility belt, he needed the extra storage. Many of the patrons of Club Chaos wore jackets, trench coats, or cloaks, so no one paid any attention as he stepped to the bar and took a seat.

There was only one other customer along the length of polished wood. The seer seemed to have found somewhere more interesting to ply her trade. Jasper Windham sat hunched over the polished bar with his long, cadaverous fingers wrapped around the base of a large glass tumbler. Amber liquid glinted through the glass, and when he turned to acknowledge Donovan's arrival, glass clinked.

Donovan didn't speak immediately. Though it was not going to slip past prying eyes that he was meeting with a collector, he didn't see any reason to be more obvious than necessary. He sat down, caught the bartender's attention, and ordered a brandy. When he had his drink, he took a sip, and then turned to Windham.

"The offer is still open?" he asked. "You're sure?"

Windham nodded. Then he turned and met Donovan's gaze. "There are others in the game now. That's what he told me, anyway. He wouldn't give out names, and I think he's just telling tales to convince me to hurry and get what he wants, but he's spreading the rumor that at least three others are considering his offer. If he's telling the truth, and one of them gets to that grave first..."

"I understand," Donovan said. "Do you know who these others are?"

"I'm not sure I believe any others are involved," Windham replied. "If they are, then locally we have Craven and Gavin. Besides me, they are the only two I'm aware of who would have the necessary equipment and talent to pull it off. There are others who might try, but they'd either destroy the item in question, or get themselves destroyed in the process. It doesn't seem likely this would be trusted to anyone less than reliable."

"Have you contacted them?" Donovan asked.

"We aren't in the habit of sharing information among ourselves," Windham said. He laughed then, a cold, thin, raspy sound that rattled in his throat and reminded Donovan of dried leaves blowing in a frigid wind.

"I should have guessed," he said, taking another sip of his drink.

Windham glanced at him again. "You sure you're up to this? Maybe that dust is safer right where it is, if you know what I mean."

"I have an assignment," Donovan replied. "It's important."

"Rumor has it," Windham continued, returning his gaze to his drink and twirling the nearly empty glass in slow circles, "that you're after Johndrow's woman. Are you working for the Elders again, DeChance?"

"Don't believe everything you hear," Donovan replied, wondering if Vein and his cronies had been nosing about and giving away too much information.

"Makes no difference to me, either way," Windham replied. "It's just this; I don't think it would be good for any of us if that bone marrow dust gets into the wrong hands. I told you there are three of us who could get it, but none of us has. There are other rumors. I hear things about journals, and formulas that should never have been written down in the first place, and I worry."

"I'll get the dust," Donovan said, taking a longer drink. "Don't worry about that. "I won't lose it once I have it, either. I've already had something of mine taken, and I intend to get that back as well. Did you bring what I asked?"

The collector nodded. He took another sip of his drink, hesitated, and then he reached into a deep pocket and pulled out a small amulet dangling from a silver chain. He held it out to Donovan as if reluctant to release it.

"What is it?" Donovan asked.

"It's charmed," Windham answered. Then he shrugged. "I don't know exactly what it does. The only way to contact the buyer once you have what he's looking for is for that amulet to touch the dust. Once the object is verified, the information on delivery and payment will be made available."

Donovan stared at the small pendant. He considered taking it back to his apartment and testing it to see if he could break the charm. If the information he needed was already in his hand, it seemed foolish to take the added risk of breaking into a graveyard.

"I don't think I'd try that, if I were you," Windham said, guessing his thoughts. "I've seen one of these before, or something very much like it. It was a different time and place, but a similar charm. A collector that I knew tried to have the charm broken because he wanted to know who he was working for. He took it to a man trained in such things. When they broke the charm, they found a curse beneath it. Very nasty, that was."

Windham didn't have to go on. In such an instance, there would be no time to protect one's self, or, even if you did find a way to do so, no way to prevent whatever other action the curse might entail. It wasn't a chance Donovan wanted to take.

"Just touch that to the dust," Windham repeated. "You'll know what to do next."

Donovan nodded. He tucked the amulet away in an inside

pocket, and stood, draining his glass and wishing suddenly he had time for more than one. A bottle, maybe.

He pulled out his wallet and laid a bill on the table. In that same motion, he deposited an envelope in Windham's lap. Again, no one was watching, and if they had been watching, they would have expected to see money change hands. Donovan had been known to use collectors in the past, and everyone was familiar with Windham. Still, Donovan erred on the side of caution. He turned and exited the bar without another word. He reached the street and headed east. The Shady Grove cemetery was outside of town at the halfway point between San Valencez and Lavender, California. It was several miles, and he had no time to make it on foot, but there were other ways.

He checked the street for prying eyes, found it vacant, and stopped in front of a dark stairway leading down from street level toward a brick wall. There was no apparent reason for this stairway, but he knew it well. He turned three times, took three steps down, climbed back two, and then descended. At the wall he stopped, and a door shimmered into view. He etched a symbol into the dust clotted on the glass pane that centered this door, and it opened with a mechanical sound reminiscent of large tumblers sliding into place – very large. The sound echoed. Donovan stepped through the doorway, and was gone. Where he'd passed, the brick wall stood solid, and grimy.

Johndrow listened as the phone rang for the tenth time, and then slowly lowered the receiver back into its cradle. It was his third attempt in as many minutes to reach DeChance. He wanted an update on Vanessa's abduction, and he wanted to warn DeChance about Vein. Ever since the hotheaded young one had left, Johndrow had grown more and more certain he'd made a mistake in allowing it. He wanted to believe that all parties involved would keep Vanessa's welfare in the forefront of their minds, but it was growing harder to believe it as true. He also wanted to feel as if he was a part of it all, as if he were doing more than sitting back on his heels and waiting while others fought his fight.

He knew Vein hadn't been swayed by their talk, and in

reality, he was glad the young ones had gone on the hunt; just sorry they'd gone alone. Maybe they were right. Maybe he was just getting old and complacent, and they didn't need outside assistance to settle a matter like this. The blood bond was strong enough that Vein could probably track it to its source, and they were not without resources of their own, albeit darker and less magical in most cases than what DeChance offered.

He thought about calling Joel, but decided against it. There was nothing either of them could do, and if he got started talking about Vanessa he might never stop. He needed to keep his head clear, and he needed to be ready to act if the need arose. Until then, he needed to be able to do something much more difficult. He needed to wait.

A knock sounded lightly on his door.

"Enter," he called out.

A thin young man stepped through the door. He kept his eyes downcast, but his voice was firm.

"There is a message for you, sir," he said.

"Send them in," Johndrow said.

"There is no messenger," the young man replied. "Only this."

He held out a dark bundle, and Johndrow, frowning, nodded toward his desk.

"Open it on there," he said.

The young man complied, and they both stared. What hope Johndrow had faded, and he drew in his breath so sharply it sounded like a hiss.

On his desk, wrapped in a long, dark jacket, were five pairs of very dark sunglasses. Johndrow stepped forward, reached out, and then pulled his hand back. He didn't need to touch them; he knew who had worn them last.

"Who brought these?" he asked sharply.

"It wasn't a man, or a woman," the boy replied. "The bundle was dropped from the eaves by a bird. A raven, I believe. When we retrieved it, it was tied with a red ribbon, and this note was attached."

He held out a white note-card sized piece of paper, and Johndrow took it, flipping it over so that he could read the single word lettered across its back.

"Johndrow."

"There was nothing more?" he asked.

The young one shook his head. "Nothing, sir. What shall we do?"

"There is nothing we *can* do," Johndrow said. He swore under his breath and crushed the card in his hand. "Nothing but wait."

The young man's eyes glittered, but he held his silence, and a moment later he turned on his heel and left the room. Johndrow watched his retreating back for a moment, then glanced down at the sunglasses and shuddered.

"Where are you, DeChance?" he asked the night. "Where in hell have you gone?"

FIFTEEN

Mist swirled about the base of the tall, wrought iron gates of the Shady Grove Cemetery. Donovan approached from the rear, not out of any fear of being seen, but because the particular doorway he'd chosen to use opened into an abandoned barn nearby. In any case, if he'd come in through the front gates he'd have needed to make his way to the rear of the graveyard eventually – that was where the priest was buried. All of the oldest graves were in a lightly wooded, semi-overgrown section of Shady Grove that few visited. Most of the graves were so old the markers had begun to crumble, or had fallen. Most of the families of the deceased were long gone themselves, or had married and moved on beyond any blood ties that might have bound them to their history. The world moved on, but Shady Grove remained.

A trail led from the barn up to a point where it joined with the old back road into the cemetery, and it was at this crossroad Donovan stopped to consider his options. The gates were tall, stretching nearly twenty feet into the air. The fence wound around to either side and was formed of iron spikes similar to those on the gates, though a bit shorter – perhaps ten feet. They were joined near their base, and again near their top, by a poured concrete frame. It was a solid, imposing wall. Nothing human could slip through those bars, and it would take a superhuman effort to climb either wall or gate – that and the luck not to slip at the wrong moment and be impaled on one of the spikes.

Donovan thought back to a time not too far in the past when just such a thing had happened, then dismissed it from his mind. He had to keep his mind on the task at hand. The graveyard, and its past, was interesting, but not relevant, and he had plenty of work ahead of him before he'd have leisure to dwell on either.

He watched the shadows beyond the gate for a few moments, but nothing stirred. He knew there were two guards on duty at all times. Earlier disturbances had prompted the city of San Valencez, and the neighboring town of Lavender, to combine funding for twenty-four hour surveillance on the cemetery. Kids had used it in the past for late-night gatherings, but that wasn't the worst of it. The graveyard had a history of murder, dark ritual, and unexplained mystery that made daylight citizens uneasy. The result was a constant patrol, and though the guards themselves had quickly begun to grow lax as day after day passed with nothing more interesting than leaves blowing across the trail and an occasional teenager turned away at the gates, the San Valencez and Lavender Police Departments still cruised by regularly, flashing spotlights between the gravestones and watching.

The locked gate didn't trouble Donovan. He stepped up quickly, gripped the heavy padlock in one hand and pressed a small circular charm to the back. The lock opened with a soft pop, and the chains snaked down to pool at the base of the gate. Donovan opened one half very slightly, cringing at the loud creak, and slipped inside. Once inside, he wrapped the chain back around the gate, slid the hook of the padlock through the links on both sides, but left it open. A casual glance would not show that it had been tampered with, and on his way out he didn't want to be bothered with stopping to open it again. He didn't expect to be in any more of a hurry when he left, but you never knew.

When he was clear of the gate, he stepped immediately into the shadows. He didn't believe the guard would actually patrol this far back so late at night, even though it was part of the job. Still, if anyone had been close the sound of the gate creaking, and the clanking of the chains would have been unmistakable. No one came, and Donovan set to work.

He brought out the charm that Windham had given him and let it dangle from its chain. He knew that if it was created to react on contact with the bone marrow dust he sought, that he could magnify that reaction and use it to track the proper grave. He'd narrowed it to an area by quick research, but records from that far back were sketchy at best, and not too reliable. The ground that had comprised the cemetery had been a much smaller plot when Father Vargas had served the congregation at the Cathedral of San Marcos, and the maps of the area and of the grave plots were not set in any perspective that made sense in the modern layout.

It didn't matter. There was only one older area of the graveyard, and of that section a very small portion was reserved for the use of The Church. Using the charm like a dowsing rod, Donovan carefully crept between trees and around low-slung, ornate monuments. He moved steadily toward the center of the older section, and before long he knew he was on the trail. The pendant hung at a forty-five degree angle, defying gravity, and led him onward.

Windham had been right on at least one count. If there were other suitable graves, the pendant would not have reacted so strongly and the search might have taken much longer. It would have shifted from side to side, catching the essence of other possible targets; it did not. The pull of Vargas' grave was strong and steady.

As he proceeded, he kept a close eye out for any glimmer of approaching light. He didn't want to be disturbed as he strolled through the garden of the dead, but he also didn't want to expend any energy that might attract less-earthly attention before it was absolutely necessary. The walls between worlds in Shady Grove were exceptionally thin; he sensed motion just out of the periphery of his sight, but ignored it.

It took nearly twenty minutes, but at last he came to a grave marked by a squat, heavy cross. The cross was ornate; there were some chips missing from the edges, and green mold grew up one side of it and dangled from beneath the arm, but for all of that it was impressive. The ground near the grave was permeated with energy that pulsed with Donovan's heartbeat. The pendant pulled against the thong holding it out away from his skin, as if it wanted to fly to the stone and become a part of the design. He quietly removed the enhancement he'd added to the charm's attractive qualities, and tucked it away.

Donovan didn't hurry. There were mistakes to be avoided, and he intended to steer clear of them all. He walked around the grave in a circle, and began to clear his mind. He measured his steps carefully, and when he finished the first circuit, he immediately began another, carefully walking the same line, placing his feet one in front of the other precisely as he had the first time around. As he continued this, he slowly picked up speed. He drew a small pouch from his pocket. Being certain not to violate the precision of his steps, he opened the pouch. He dangled his hand before him at an angle and very carefully sprinkled the powder on the ground. Where he passed, a thin wall of mist rose. He completed the circuit, stepped within the circle, and closed the pouch.

Donovan didn't move for several moments. He watched carefully, letting his gaze slide along the base of the mist wall he'd created, but there were no breaks. It was solid, and complete. He placed the powder carefully back in his pocket and drew out another bag. This one was slightly larger. From within he quickly unpacked four small braziers for the compass points, which he placed, filled with scented powder, and lit, each with a short invocation to the archangels, Earth, Fire, Air and Water. The last was spirit, but he would not invoke that name until he was ready to open the grave.

A rustle in the air caught his attention. He glanced up and saw that the crow, Asmodeus, slowly circled within the perimeter. He hadn't realized the creature had bonded with him so closely in such a short time, but it was good to see him there. It meant the ward was complete, and he could begin; there was no way the crow could have found him unless it had traveled dimensions. The spell he'd just woven cut him off from Shady Grove, and the other graves, but it did considerably more than that. It removed the small plot of ground within the circle from the dimension it normally inhabited and placed it in a sort of limbo, where he could do what he needed to do. The crow had come to him in this other place, and was trapped as surely as those beyond the mist were impeded as long as the circle held. When he was done, he would seal the grave, break the circle and the dimensions would snap back into place.

If someone stood in Shady Grove and stared at the spot where Father Vargas' grave had been moments before, they would see a mist that clung low and heavy on the ground, and grass. Leaves would blow across the space, and if they stepped on that patch of ground, it would be solid and unmarked. It might be bad if they were still standing there when Donovan released the ward, but it was a chance he had to take. The spell insured privacy, and if he was going to act quickly, he'd need all of that he could manage.

He drew a dagger from his pocket next. It had a large, carved obsidian hilt. This was in the form of a Celtic equal-armed cross. The grip was inside a circular hand guard and required the insertion of one finger through a round gap in the arm of the cross nearest the blade. Donovan plunged it into the earth to one side of the grave and began to slowly draw the blade in a rectangular pattern around the exterior of the space where the coffin rested, presumably six feet down and rotting. He had no way of knowing how large Father Vargas had been, so he allowed for a very large, ornate coffin. It took another ten minutes, but eventually he slid the blade back across the first point where he'd jammed it into the soil.

He lifted it free, held it up before him so that he gazed at the surrounding mist through the circle and the cross, and closed his eyes.

"Father Antoine Vargas," he said in a firm voice. "Rise and face me. Release the earth, as the earth releases you in turn. "

Donovan leaned in, slammed the blade dead center in the rectangle he'd drawn, and then stepped back quickly. Asmodeus sensed the shift in energies and dove from the air to land with a heavy thump on Donovan's shoulder.

At first all that happened was a gentle vibration in the ground beneath his feet. He watched intently, and the hilt of the dagger shook slowly, and then faster, as if some unseen hand gripped it beneath the soil and was flailing back and forth with increasing violence. The dagger shimmered as its motion picked up speed, and in only a few moments it reached an odd, thrumming harmonic that matched the vibration from below. Donovan stood very still, though he felt the frequency of the shivering, pulsing energy battering at his thoughts and his heartbeat.

The sod split at the point where the dagger pierced it. The ground rippled outward in four directions, toward the corners of the rectangular pattern he'd drawn. Soil and the grass curled back and something long and dark rose, very slowly, cresting the break in the earth like a huge spacecraft hovering just beyond the curve of the horizon. Where the ground peeled back, it hardened and remained very still.

The casket was worn. Whatever finish had protected it was long eaten away by moisture and worms. For all that, it was amazingly intact. Donovan stepped closer and placed his palms flat on the lid. He spoke softly and curled his thumbs under the lip. With a quick motion he lifted, and the wood parted. There was a groan, and the sound of rotted planks tearing free from one another as ancient glue cracked and the wooden pegs binding the joints of the casket parted with a snap. The lid flipped up and back and Donovan leaned in.

There wasn't much time. He knew that his opening of the ground in this "between" spot – dragging the bit of earth and the casket out of their own dimension – would attract attention. Any large release of magical force caused ripples and waves, and this was a larger than normal shift. There were plenty of dangers other than human guards and thieving collectors, and most of them were deadly.

He leaned in over the casket and nearly fell back in shock. There were no bones. There was no body. Instead, placed near the middle of the casket, and supported on all sides by ragged velvet, a large ceramic urn rested. It was sealed by red wax along the seam of its lid, and the sides were decorated in very complex and well-rendered patterns, depicting the lives of the saints. He hadn't expected the body to have been burned – it wasn't something The Church did, particularly not back in the days of Vargas' death. There must have been more to the story that Windham had failed to discover, or that he'd kept to himself for his own reasons.

In any case, there was no time to worry over it. The dust he needed could be extracted from the ashes, and this actually made his task simpler. He'd intended to remove the dust and seal it away immediately, but now things had changed. He could simply take the urn, replace the empty casket, and be on his way.

He gripped the urn and lifted. At first it resisted. The cloth was very old, and had grown moist, despite the sealed casket. It had expanded and begun to rot around the base of the urn, forming a sort of gluey substance. He yanked again, and it came free. There was a stench of wet, rotten cloth and damp earth. Donovan placed the urn on the ground. He stepped around the hole in the ground, gripped the lid, which hung precariously from its ancient hinges, and heaved it up and over so that it fell back across the casket with a dull thud.

The dagger remained imbedded in the ground. There was no hesitation in the descent. The coffin snapped back to where it belonged as if held on some great elastic strap that had just been released. The earth rolled back over the top with a roar. In less than the span of time it takes to draw in a quick breath, the ground was smooth and unbroken. The implosion of force left Donovan momentarily stunned, but he recovered quickly. When the earth folded back to allow the coffin to rise, it had curled over, and he was able to grasp the blade firmly and slide it free.

As he did so, he took half a step back. He didn't want to risk stepping through the circle and breaking the ward. He sensed forces moving about him. Voices whispered just beyond the ring of mist, dark sibilant voices speaking in a myriad of forgotten tongues. Something sizzled and snapped, like the strike of a bolt of lightning. He dove across the re-sealed grave and reached for the urn, already forming the words in his mind that would protect him as he burst through the mist and broke the circle.

He reached down and his fingers brushed the surface of the urn, but another pair of hands was a fraction quicker. They were sheathed in dark, skin-tight gloves. Donovan cried out and tried to snatch the urn, but at that moment another dark gloved hand shot through the mist. This one connected solidly with Donovan's chin, and he staggered back. There was a hiss like the release of steam from an iron, and the mist surrounding him was sucked suddenly from the air. Donovan called out the words of protection and prayed they weren't too late.

The mist cleared, and he turned to see dark shapes hurrying away toward the back gate of the cemetery. One of them held the urn clutched tightly to his chest. They moved with eerie speed. He poised himself to follow, recovering his balance quickly. The crow, which had remained on his shoulder throughout this encounter, took off with a screech and flurry of wings. Donovan cursed, came up against the stone cross that marked Vargas' now empty grave with one knee and dropped to the ground in pain.

He staggered to his feet and started to limp away from the grave, forgetting the braziers, still burning with incense and all the evidence of his presence. He'd intended to be very certain there was nothing new to draw attention to the cemetery, but the sharp sound of a round being chambered drew him up short. He raised his hands and turned, very slowly.

An old man stood, watching him across two graves marked only by stones set into the earth, his hand steadied on the outstretched wing of a marble angel. The barrel of the gun was leveled at Donovan's chest. The old man's hand shook slightly. He was as frightened as his captive was irritated.

"You just stand there, real still," the man said. "I'm going to pull the radio off my belt and call my partner over here, and he's going to call the police. You're going to stay right where you are until they get here. This is private property, and you're trespassing."

The man glanced down at the still smoking braziers.

"What did you think you were going to do? Raise the dead?"

Under other circumstances, Donovan would have laughed. He kept his hands up over his head, and met the man's gaze levelly.

"You don't want to shoot me, friend," he said softly. "You don't want to shoot anyone. I'm not hurting anything here."

"I was here a few years back," the guard replied, not

lowering his weapon. "I saw what folks who deal with this kind of thing," he reached out with one booted foot and kicked over the brazier closest to him, "can do. Don't tell me there's no harm in it, I know better. Don't give me a reason to pull this trigger."

Donovan cursed under his breath. There was no time for this. It was probably already too late to catch whoever had stolen the urn, but he might still be able to follow their back trail. He still had the amulet necessary to complete the deal – unless they had one of their own.

There was a sudden rush of sound. Something cried out, very close, and very loud, and instinctively Donovan hit the dirt. The .45 fired, and the bullet whipped just above him. There was a grunt, and a cry of surprise, but Donovan didn't stop to see what had happened. He knew Asmodeus had returned, but he didn't know how much the bird had disrupted the guard's concentration. He rolled to the side, leaped to his feet, and took off at a dead run for the back gate. A few moments later he heard a feeble call to stop, but he ignored it. The guard had apparently come to his senses and realized he'd probably better not shoot someone for the crime of trespassing, particularly not in the back.

It was only a matter of moments until the man's partner showed up, but it didn't matter. The gate was not only still unlocked, but the others who'd passed through had tossed the chain and lock aside and left one half of the huge gates hanging open. Donovan cut through the gap and headed back down the path toward the old barn. The crow flew just above his head and a couple of feet behind. It cried out to him, but for the moment he ignored it. He knew it was there, just as he'd known, when the guard was struck. Twice now Asmodeus had come to his aid. Donovan would have preferred Cleo's company – he was more familiar with her, and she'd been with him for so long the two of them often acted as a single entity, but the crow had a way of growing on a person.

In the barn, Donovan pulled out the crystal lens he'd used in the old church where Cornwell had died. He glanced through it, holding it to either side of the gateway he'd used to reach the place. There was nothing. No trace of any passing but his own. He stood there for a moment, his mind racing, trying to decide what to do next.

Asmodeus settled on his shoulder, and dug in suddenly with taloned claws. Donovan cried out and turned to stare at the creature. Their eyes locked in a steady gaze, and a wave of vertigo hit that nearly knocked him to his knees.

He flew. He swerved to avoid trees, but the motion wasn't his own. Donovan rode Asmodeus' mind through the broken wall of mist. Two figures fled through the graves, dancing around trees and sprinting with uncanny quickness toward the back gate of the cemetery. They slipped the chain free without hesitation and dashed off down the trail. He thought they would turn off toward the barn, following the old trail, but they didn't.

The two turned, glanced once over their shoulders, and then turned off the old deserted road on the far side from where Donovan had entered it. The ground dropped away quickly into a ditch, and they followed this, though the earth was damp, and their feet left deep, squishy imprints in passing. Ahead a large culvert loomed. The two ducked their heads and disappeared inside without a pause.

The crow dove after them, dizzying Donovan with the rush of air and the impossibly swift passage of images. They dove past the entrance to the huge concrete pipe, whirled in the air, dove back and plunged into darkness. Donovan wanted to scream, but before he could even regain his breath, they soared out the far side. It only cut under a secondary road, a drainage pipe for water. There was no sign of the two, and he knew in that instant it was another gateway.

Asmodeus released Donovan's shoulder and took flight again. Shaking his head, he turned to follow the crow back out the door of the barn. He heard voices, and saw bobbing lights down the trail, but he avoided the guards easily as he wound his way up to the abandoned road. By the time he reached it, slipping from tree to tree as swiftly as he could without breaking into the open, they had already turned onto the side road toward the barn. He heard them discussing what to do next, but he didn't wait around to find out if they had the courage to visit the barn on their own, or if they planned to call the police.

Donovan crossed the road and slid down into the ditch. He slowed himself, carefully turning seven times before entering the pipe. He held the colored crystal lens out and caught immediate traces. The wispy remnant of two travelers hung in the air, and without hesitation, he followed.

When he came out on the other side in an unfamiliar alley, he hesitated, but only for a moment. He tugged the talisman free of his pocket, and held it out. It swung to the right, and he took off at a run. They couldn't be too far ahead. He was sure they thought they'd lost him, and they couldn't realize he would use the talisman to trail the urn they carried.

The trail led onto the darkened streets. There was no traffic, and Donovan saw no one on the sidewalks. He followed the lean of the pendant's chain for five blocks, turned into another alley, and followed this to its end. He came to a chain link fence. It was locked, and a sign proclaimed "NO TRESPASSING – SERVICE ENTRANCE ONLY" in large, bold letters.

At the far end of a service drive, double doors stared back at him. They were also posted, and he didn't need the talisman to tell him the urn had been taken inside. The building hummed with energy. Donovan pulled back to the alley's entrance, and gazed up at the side of the building. He knew the place; it was the Tefft Complex. He didn't know much about it, but he'd heard rumors.

Footsteps crunched loose gravel in the alley, and Donovan froze. Someone was coming, and he had no time to try and figure out who it was. Drawing in a deep breath and holding it, he pressed himself against the wall and waited. High above, a crow cried.

SIXTEEN

The tower room was very dark, and Vanessa was weak. She sat on the edge of the bed and stared at the walls around her listlessly. There had been no further visits from her captor, and other than the short blast of hope she'd felt when Vein and the others had rushed in, there had been no break in the utter solitude. She thought about Johndrow and wondered where he was. She wondered if he, too, would come crashing through the door eventually. She thought not. More likely he and the council had hired someone to do the work. It was their way to hold back in the shadows and act only when all other avenues were closed to them. It was her way too – or had been.

She wondered briefly what had happened to the others. She had no doubt it was bad. She tried not to think of all the ways they could have been destroyed, but there was no other game to occupy her mind. She had several lifetimes of memories, but none of them comforted her. She still felt the bond with Vein, so they were close by, but it seemed unlikely any of them would last much longer.

The silence was broken by a grinding whirr that came from the wall at her back. She felt a vibration deep in the stone, and she shivered. She'd heard it once before, and a glance to the side confirmed that the chains binding her had begun to retract slowly into the wall. She rose quickly. She knew she couldn't break the chains, but she had to try, and there was no time to waste. If she let them grow too short she'd have no leverage.

Vanessa pressed herself to the wall, leaned down, and kicked her feet hard against the stone. She launched forward, hit the floor running, and shot to the end of the chains with incredible speed. She hit the end of the restraints and pushed harder. It was like slamming into a wall, but she threw herself into it. She heard a groan of machinery from somewhere below, and thought, just for an instant that she might do it. The chains were so taut they thrummed. Then she slid back half an inch, and another. She strained against the inexorable pull, but it was no use. Within moments the chains had fully retracted, and she hung helplessly, spread eagled against the wall.

The outer door opened again, and her captor stepped inside. He carried a leather bag in one hand, and he placed this on the floor, closed the door, and then turned to smile at her.

"Bravo," he said, clapping his hands mockingly. "That was an astonishing display of speed and strength; and yet, at the same time it was a waste of time. You must have known the chains were enchanted. I took very special precautions with you, studied your kind for years before I set the spells. I assure you, the restraints are more than adequate."

Vanessa continued to struggle, but she was weak from the lack of fresh blood, and it was difficult to fight back the rage that threatened to consume rational thought. He was so close she could smell him. She tasted the tang of his blood through his clothing and his skin, and she remembered that taste. It was powerful blood, old and rich, and despite her captivity and impending final death, she craved it.

He stepped closer and examined her carefully, as if she were a horse, or an animal he intended to purchase. Vanessa shook with fury, and as he leaned in close she snapped at the air, closing her fangs on nothing but his scent.

He laughed. Stepping around her, he pulled a small control box from his pocket. He pressed a button. The wall behind her made another sound, and before she was fully aware of what had happened, a steel collar slid out of the wall on either side of her throat and clamped in front. Now her head was all but immobile. He reached out and stroked her hair. He ran his hand down her cheek and teased one long, manicured fingernail over her chin, then slid it back along the top edge of the collar. She trembled at the touch and tried to shift her jaws nearer to his flesh, but the collar held her easily

"That should do," he said at last. "Our time together has grown short, and I can't afford to have you whipping around and making a nuisance of yourself. I'm sure you understand. This isn't about you, after all, lovely as you are. It's about life. My life, to be precise. I intend to make it last a long time, you see, and you are going to help. I need something that you have, and once I have it, the formula I create will make me immortal."

Vanessa's eyes flashed with anger and he laughed again.

"Oh, not like what you possess," he said. "What you have is a great gift, there's no doubt of it. To live forever, as long as you are able to borrow the blood of others to keep you young; it's a concept worthy of hours of debate and certainly better than the mortal alternative.   You do have your weaknesses, though, don't you, Vanessa? You miss out on all that fine sunlight, for one thing. You can't appreciate a good steak or a cold beer without flavoring it with fresh blood. There is so much more to life as I know it; why would I willingly give it up when there is an alternative?"

Vanessa tried to shake her head in negation, but she was held still and helpless. He smiled at her again.

"Aren't you curious?" he asked. "I'd have thought you'd spend your last few moments asking questions. For instance, what happened to your friends who tried to break in and save you so valiantly, or, what are you going to do with me? I know I'd be thinking about those things if it was me chained to the wall.

"We have a little time," he continued, "so I'll go ahead and tell you. It will pass the time."

As he spoke, he turned away from her and walked back to where he'd left the leather bag. He retrieved it and placed it on the bed where she'd been sitting moments before. He unsnapped the top and began to remove the contents one item at a time. As he pulled each free, he examined it carefully.

From where she hung bound to the wall, Vanessa couldn't see what he did clearly. In the periphery of her sight she saw him pull something long and flexible free of the bag. She heard a sharp clinking sound as something made contact with glass. He worked steadily, paying no attention to her at all as he organized and manipulated the items on the bed. When he had finished, he turned to her again, and the smile was back on his face. It was not a pleasant expression, but had the slick, oily aspect of a serpent.

Vanessa closed her eyes. She had no idea what he was planning, and she didn't believe there was any chance she could do anything to stop him, but if she lost her mind, he would win without a struggle. If she let him frighten her to the point where her mind snapped, there would be no return from it. She also needed to get free of his scent. She knew, now, that the blood he'd fed her was not his own. It hadn't been fresh, and with the weakness of her captivity dulling her senses, she'd just assumed that it was. Now she felt the draw of his lifeblood and knew she'd never tasted it – never would taste it – and its proximity drove sharp talons into her concentration, shredding it.

With a great effort, she spoke.

"What have you done with the young ones?"

His oily smile became a toothy grin.

"Oh, they're still around," he said. "I have them very close by, in fact. You'd think I'd be angry with them after breaking in here unannounced and trying to disrupt my plans, but I'm a generous man. I have a surprise for them, a treat they wouldn't get anywhere else. I'm going to share some of what I was just talking about with them."

Vanessa thought hard, trying to remember what he'd said.

"The sunlight," he said casually. "I'm going to give them the first sight of the morning sun they've had in quite some time. I can't imagine when the last time you saw that was – what are you, three, four centuries old? But these others...they remember. It hasn't been so long since all the pleasures of life were ripped away from them and dangled like carrots on a string, just out of reach. I haven't spoken with them about it, but I would be willing to bet they remember what it's like to greet the sunrise. I bet they even remember well enough to miss it. "

"Where..." She couldn't finish the question. She'd felt the touch of dawn once since her transformation. It had burned much hotter than any fire she recalled from life, and had nearly ended her existence. She remembered, and she hoped with sudden clarity that her memory, and her sudden flash of terror, wouldn't transfer to Vein across their bond. Better that he not know what awaited.

Her captor stepped close to her again, placed his hands on her cheeks and gazed into her eyes.

"They will only get to see it once, of course," he said softly. "I'm certain I'll have to have a cleaning crew in for the elevator once it's done."

Vanessa gritted her teeth and strained against her bonds in frustration. He stroked her cheeks, and then his hands slid down to the metal band around her throat. She tried to glance down at his hands, but she couldn't see what he was doing.

"Don't worry, "he said, leaning in to whisper in her ear. "It won't take long. I'm sure they'll be brave and not cower in the back of that elevator. I'm sure they won't try to cling to the ceiling like bats, clawing their way over one another to the back corners, out of the light. I'm sure they'll stand and face the light like warriors."

Vanessa began to tremble, but she fought it. She didn't want him to see her lose control, not in anger, and certainly not in fear.

"What are you doing?" she asked.

"I wondered when you'd get to that," he replied. "This is a very special day for you. I put a lot of time and effort into this room, and into your restraints. This collar, for instance, is more than it appears to be."

He fumbled with something in the center of the metal band, but she still couldn't see what he was doing. There was a soft click, like a button being depressed, or a spring releasing. He saw that she didn't understand, so he leaned in again. This time he lowered his head so his lips were even with the metal band.

Vanessa felt a cool breeze on the skin of her throat. It should not have been possible, circled as she was in steel, but she felt it all the same. Her eyes widened.

He raised his head and met her gaze. She tried desperately in that second to reach out to him with her mind. She could do it, had done it a thousand times. She found some nerve; some cord buried deep in a man's thoughts, twisted it, and used it to draw him to her. She reached out and, just for a second, as their eyes locked, she felt something. She concentrated her will, but he shook his head, as if to clear cobwebs, and stepped back.

"Amazing," he said. "I would have thought you were too weak for that, and that I was too well blocked. You are strong."

He returned to the bed and picked something up. Vanessa squirmed in her bonds and tried to see what it was, but he kept it blocked from her view with his body until he stood before her once more.

"I'm going to enjoy this very much," he told her. He held up a long, slender tube. It was made of metal, and apparently coated in silver. Vanessa shuddered and drew back. He paid no attention to her. Instead, he returned to the bed again, and this time he brought back a length of plastic tubing, and a flask. A final trip to the bed, and he was ready.

He held up the silver tube again, and as she watched he slid the end of the plastic tubing over one end of the metal. Next he placed the other end in the neck of the large flask and placed this on the floor beneath Vanessa's manacled feet. He straightened, slid his hand into his pocket, and retrieved a round, black piece of rubber. Vanessa didn't know what it was, but the fear had built within her once more, and her mind thoughts dove inward, seeking some place deep, safe place to hide.

He tapped a finger on the center of the tube.

"It's really a very simple device," he said. "There's a hole at both ends and a third opening here in the center. When I slide this pump over the center," he poked the tube into one end of the black rubber circle and it slid through, protruding now from either end, "it forms a primitive siphon."

He squeezed the rubber ball. The plastic tube jumped as air, drawn through the tube, was forced down toward the flask below. It was then that she noticed the tip of the tube. It was hollow, like the end that had been inserted into the plastic tube, but it was also cut at a wicked, forty-five degree angle. It came to a sharp point at the tip, and then angled back.

"Who are you?" she asked.

"That isn't important anymore," he said softly. "Very soon all that you are will be a part of me. Very soon your blood – or should I say, the blood you have borrowed for so long – will be mine. All of it. You will cease to exist, and your worries over the "young ones" as you call them, and over old Johndrow, will be at an end. You will no longer hunger, and you will no longer lust. You will be mine in the truest sense those words have ever been spoken."

He slid the end of the tube into the hole in the center of the band of steel. Vanessa screamed then. She screamed and she spat, and she tried desperately to struggle, but it made no difference. The cold, hard silver tube slid through the collar neatly and pressed against the soft skin of her throat – then pierced her cleanly. Transfixed, she tried to catch his gaze and make him pull it out, but she could not. He stood very still, watching her as she hung there, back arched against the stone wall, eyes rolling back like those of a mad animal. Then, without another word, he began to very slowly squeeze the rubber ball.

He didn't hurry. At first the blood flowed erratically, but the even pumping motion of his hand squeezing that black rubber ball took on the mesmerizing rhythm of a heartbeat. She heard it as her thoughts grew fuzzy. She recognized it, though it had been more than three centuries since she'd felt such a pulse through her own veins. She tried to scream again. She fought up through the thickening darkness that engulfed her mind, but it was too hard. Her limbs were heavy and hung limp in their bonds. Her eyelids fluttered, drooped, snapped open, and then finally closed.

She felt his fingers on her cheek again, stroking her. He played with her hair, and she thought he was whispering something. She tried to hear it, and to understand the words, but she couldn't wrap her tired mind around the task. The words had the same rhythm as the pulse she felt, and that grew weaker each second. She felt cold as she had never felt. Ice seemed to coat her skin, which was suddenly very thin and brittle.

She thought about Johndrow. For a moment, with her eyes closed, she imagined it was his touch on her cheek, though she knew it was not. She knew what was happening to her, but no longer had the strength to even think about it. The irony of it struck her, though. She knew how Preston Johndrow would have coveted a drop or two of the blood flowing so freely from her – something he could preserve in a bottle of Merlot, or perhaps a smooth cognac, to be shared at some point, far in the future.

Then even these thoughts faded, and she grew very still.

On the wall, across the room, a colored crystal glowed brightly, then faded, and then glowed again. Looking up from his work, Vanessa's captor caught the signal, and smiled. He watched the end of the plastic tube carefully. The flow had slowed to a very thin trickle. He gave a last squeeze, and then let the rubber expand in his hand. There was a last dribble, and he heard a soft hiss.

He turned to the wall. What hung from the manacles and the collar was a husk. Dry, paper-thin skin coated brittle bones. Where Vanessa's beautiful eyes had reached out to snare him, black pits gaped. A quick swipe of his hand would have reduced her remnant to a pile of ash, but there was no time.

He quickly stoppered the bottle and stowed his equipment in the bag. The vial he wrapped carefully in two layers of satin before placing it in the bag, as well. Then he turned toward the doorway, and exited the room, leaving it open behind him.

Once in the hall, he didn't go far. He rounded the corner and pressed a button on the wall when he reached the end. The wall slid aside, and he stared into the elevator compartment. Vein and the others were crouched near him, staring at the far wall, where the glass window overlooked the city. The night was fading, and they must have sensed the approach of dawn. When they heard the panel slide open, they whirled. He watched them with detached curiosity.

Vein stepped up to the window. He didn't try to break through – it was pointless, and the silver mesh imbedded in the glass would have sliced him to ribbons if, by some impossible chance, he found a way to fracture the glass.

"Where is Vanessa?" Vein asked. There was a tremble in his voice, not exactly fear, but close. "I felt…something. Where have you taken her?"

Their captor didn't answer them. He set the bag he carried

on the ground at his feet.   He opened it carefully and pulled out the satin-wrapped flask. Without a word he unwound the satin and held it up so that the blood glistened in the dim light of the hallway.

Vein's features melted through emotions, starting with shock and ending in rage. All pretenses at calm forgotten, he slammed into the glass. The elevator shook from the force, and he reared back, slamming into it again. The others gripped his arms, but he flung them aside, crashing into the barrier with more and more force. All the while his tormenter stood very still, holding the flask of blood in his hand reverently. Finally, with a supreme effort, Bruno and Shade managed to pin Vein's arms, and Kali wrapped her arms around him from behind, holding him away from the glass. It was smeared with his blood, and though the cuts were healing fast, the gory remnant remained.

Cradling the flask carefully, their tormentor laughed softly. "Very touching," he said. "Such a moment we're having. Say goodbye to her. I wish I could tell you she was going to a better place or that her spirit would rest, but I don't know that for certain. I know where this is going," he held up the blood, "but that won't matter to you for very long. Can you feel it? The sun? It will rise in less than an hour, and it won't be much longer after that when it reaches this side of the building.

"You might find a way to break out the glass, but I doubt you can survive the fall, and even if you could, you'd be sliced up by the silver mesh. I think I've thought of just about everything, but if you find your way out and down somehow, please, by all means sneak back in and we'll do this again.

"One thing," he wrapped the flask of blood carefully and stowed it back in the bag. "When you come back, I won't be quite like I am now. I'll even be a little bit more like you, I think, except for that whole undead thing. I'll be as alive as I am now, and a thousand years from now, I'll be able to say the same."

He turned, glanced over his shoulder, and added. "You know, I'm really going to *miss* you guys."

Vein saw the man press a button on the wall, and the panel slid back into place, hiding the interior of the building from view. He spun in his follower's grasp and would have made a dive for the window on the far side, but they'd had a chance to adjust their grips, and they held him back.

"No," Kali whispered in his ear. "There may be a way, but that isn't it."

Vein shook with anger. His sight had glazed with the red, killing bloodlust that threatened just below the surface of his mind, dormant by day and very close to the surface by night. He knew she was right, but he didn't want to listen. He wanted to bash himself against that window, again and again, until it either shattered, or the force of his blows shook the entire elevator free of the building and sent it plummeting to the earth. They could survive that, if the glass held, and they didn't slam through the silver mesh on impact.

In the East, still far below the skyline, but rising, the sun began its slow transit. They all felt it, and they knew, even if they managed to calm Vein's rage, that they would burn, caged like rats, unless they found a way to break out. Far below headlights began rolling down the streets. Lights flickered on, and horns blew. As they hung, awaiting death, San Valencez came to life, unaware of the drama playing out far above – oblivious to the world of night.

SEVENTEEN

Donovan remained pressed to the wall, out of sight. The footsteps drew closer, and then a furtive figure slipped from the alley, staring up at the huge building, as if studying it. He couldn't help himself; he gasped.

"Amethyst," he said softly.

She spun, saw him leaning against the wall but didn't immediately recognize him, and drew something from her pocket. Instinct took over, and Donovan pushed off from the wall, diving and rolling to the side. At the same time, he prepared his defense, cursing himself under his breath. The first thing that came to his hand was the green crystal pendant – a gift from the woman he was preparing himself to defend against. Perfect.

Amethyst drew back her arm, breathed something into the air, and was about to bat it toward him when she stopped. She let out a startled gasp of recognition and pulled back. The cloud spun lazily in the air, and Donovan saw what was about to happen.

He drew the pendant, held it in his palm, breathed a short incantation over its surface, and then, with a flip of his wrist, he let it fly straight toward Amethyst's face. She wasn't watching him any longer. Once she'd realized who she was attacking, and stopped her charm, things had gone south for her very quickly. She stared at the hovering cloud, which seemed to be made up of flitting, buzzing insects. She spoke, too low for Donovan to hear, and the cloud wavered, but did not disperse. Instead it spun, coalescing into a solid point at one end and stretching back in a tornado-shaped funnel. The tip of that deadly whirling mass took aim on her face and dove.

Donovan watched, frozen in place by a combination of fascination and horror. There was nothing more that he could do from where he stood, and probably nothing he could have done if he'd been closer on such short notice.

Before the whirling plague could strike, the crystal he'd thrown whipped across the gap separating that whirling darkness from Amethyst's face. The pendant was an emerald blur. The black gnat-cloud struck it, spread out, whirled together again as if it might burst through, and then – miraculously, dispersed. Amethyst had recovered her senses when the crystal spun into place, and she took control of it without hesitation. Using it as both shield and weapon, she shredded her own backfiring curse until nothing remained but the psychic echo of expended energy.

It was very quiet on the street. Donovan stared at Amethyst, who stared right back. She held the crystal loosely in her hand and he wished, suddenly, that he'd taken the moment's opportunity the short battle had presented him to reach for something else to defend himself with. He knew the thought was foolish, but he couldn't understand why she was here, and there were still nagging doubts in his mind about the theft of her crystals.

His mind raced. He had no idea what she might be doing here, but it occurred to him that he'd been very trusting. Over the past several years he'd grown to know her pretty well, but trust was another matter. He really had nothing concrete upon which to base that trust, just intuition, and intuition had failed him in the past.

He thought about the crystals. All the security she'd claimed to have, and yet they'd been stolen easily. No record that could be seen in her crystals. No indication of how the case had been opened or the crystals themselves removed. Was it possible, or had he just bought into her story and been duped? He didn't have much time to consider all of this before she started walking toward him. The green crystal dangled from her hand, and he thought about how it had dispersed that cloud. He was pleased to know, at least, that when he'd chosen to defend himself with it, it would have worked, but that was small consolation. Amethyst hadn't been any more aware of who she was attacking than he'd initially been aware of who he was defending against.

"Kind of late for a lady to be out walking the streets," he said, standing very still.

She must have seen something in his stance. She drew nearer, and she slowed her steps. She didn't smile. Donovan's heart slammed in his chest. His thought whirled with incantations and wards, but none of them made it to his lips. She stood about a foot away from him, her head cocked, and her hand balled into a fist and pressed into one hip.

Then she smiled, and she held out the crystal to him.

"What's the matter, Donovan," she asked. "Trying to decide if I came here to make a deal with the devil?"

He started to answer, then clapped his mouth shut guiltily and took the crystal pendant. He didn't fully let down his guard, but he found he could breathe again, and it was a start.

"It occurred to me," he said.

Amethyst glanced up at the Tefft Complex, soaring high above them into the low hanging clouds. She frowned.

"I was a fool," she said, turning back to him. "It's Lance, my apprentice. Here I was thinking myself an amazing teacher, proud of his accomplishments and leaving him in charge of things I should never have relinquished control of for a moment. He was there under my nose all that time, even after the crystals were stolen, and I still didn't see it."

"Lance?" Donovan said. He turned and followed her gaze up the outside of the huge skyscraper. "Lance Ezzel? Who is he? I mean…"

"You mean," She replied, "that no apprentice could have engineered all of this. You mean that someone who was still learning the arts wouldn't have a fortress like this to hide away in, or the knowledge to put together a ritual like the one he's about to perform. I wish I knew the answer to that. When he came to me, he showed some talent, but he must have dampened it for my benefit. I didn't check – why would I? Someone with this sort of …"

"He wouldn't have needed to sneak in," Donovan finished.

She nodded. "He must have been planning this for a very long time, Donovan. He played me from the start, and he'd met you – through me – and well as others. All the connections he'd need, in fact, if he were a very powerful magician moving into our territory from…somewhere else. We handed it to him and shook his hand as he took it."

"There isn't much time," Donovan said. He shook his head to clear the confusion of thoughts. "Whoever he is, he's got Vanessa in there, and he's got everything else he needs too."

"The bone marrow dust?" she asked. Her voice sharpened. "How?"

"It was a setup," Donovan replied. "I think the collector, Windham, was in on it, but there's no time to worry over him now. They got the dust, and they think they got away. In fact, they would have gotten away, except for that damned crow, Asmodeus."

Questions danced in Amethyst's eyes, but he waved them away.

"All of that can wait. How do we get into this place?"

"Well, we could hang around out here and wait for an invitation," she said, "But I've always preferred a more direct approach. There's the front door, but somehow I can't imagine that the main elevators reach the floor we're after."

"Back down the alley," Donovan said, and started off at a trot. Amethyst followed quickly, and in moments they were back at the chain link gate. Donovan opened the lock the same way he'd opened the padlock at Shady Grove, pressing the small, round pendant to the rear of the lock. It snapped open without protest.

"That was easy," Amethyst commented, staring down at the lock dubiously.

Donovan shrugged.

"He may not be expecting intrusion from this direction. Maybe he thinks we can't find him. Who knows?"

Amethyst didn't look convinced, but she followed him through the gates and up to the door marked *Service Entrance Only*. Donovan stared at it for a long moment, but he didn't touch it.

"Won't that amulet work on a door lock?" she asked him.

"It will," he said, "but there's something...wrong...about this door. I can't explain it, but I have the feeling that opening it is exactly what he hopes we'll do."

They stood and stared at the door a moment longer.

"This isn't getting us anywhere," she said at last. "Step back."

Donovan started to protest, thought better of it, and flattened himself against the wall on the opposite side of the door from where Amethyst stood. She reached into the front of her blouse, an act that on any other occasion would have gotten an interested stare from Donovan, and pulled out a dark blue crystal that protruded from the center of a gold sphere. Staying against the wall herself, she held the amulet out in front of the door and spoke a single word.

The door exploded from its hinges and flew off down the service drive. It slammed into the fence with a nerve-jarring clang. Smoke rose from the point where it had been ripped from the wall, but otherwise, there as no indication of a threat.

Donovan saw Amethyst push off from the wall, and he moved.

"Not yet!" he cried. Before she could step in front of the door, or peek around the corner, he was moving. He launched himself in a headlong dive, and that single, quick motion saved her life.

Amethyst stepped toward the now open doorway, and Donovan collided with her, wrapping his arms around her legs and dropping her back heavily. As he passed the entrance, a stream of sound and color rushed out, growing wider and brighter and louder with each passing second. It cleared his back by inches, riffling his jacket in passing. Loud, angry cries filled the air. They heard the beat of heavy wings.

Donovan rolled over out of the direct line of fire. Amethyst stared upward for a second, gasped, and then reached for the amulet she'd used on the door. Without pretense at careful aim, she fired a blast into the air over their heads.

Dragons peeled off in either direction with a loud screech. When they'd cleared the door, they couldn't have been more than a foot tall and a couple long, but they grew with astonishing quickness until they filled the sky. Amethyst's blast missed the first two, but when they split, it smashed into the pair following and drove them back into the final creature with a crunch of bone and the hot smell of burned flesh and sulfur. Donovan reached to his boots, drew forth two odd, half-moon-shaped blades, and leaped to his feet. He didn't look up at the dragons as they rolled majestically and plummeted back to the attack.

He drew back his left arm, let the first blade fly, whispering a short charm under his breath. It whipped through the air, curved to the right, straightened out, and just as one of the dragons gave a loud roaring cry and dove for his throat, the blade passed cleanly through, like a flashing guillotine. Donovan didn't stop to check his handiwork. He threw the other blade and dove to the side. He caught the second dragon as cleanly as the first, but it was only a few feet from the ground when it died, and the impact of its collision with the concrete drive shook the foundation of the building.

Amethyst had taken out two with her initial blast and was sighting in on the last.

"Get in there," she cried. "I'll take care of his pets. Get in and stop him."

He didn't hesitate. He slipped through the door into the passage beyond, hit the ground again and rolled in case something else waited there, but he saw nothing. The corridor he stood in had several doors leading off from it. At the far end of the passage, on his right was the door to an elevator. He ran for it.

When he reached the sliding doors, he saw that they were closed tightly. Two crystals were imbedded in the wall, one on each side of the door. One was dimly lit and glowed rose red in the semi-darkness. The other was clear and unlit. Donovan considered the two for only a moment, then reached out and touched the unlit crystal. It glowed immediately. There was a grinding sound, and then it stopped. The glow dimmed, and the rose-red crystal remained lit.

He considered breaking through the doors and climbing. There were ways he could ease and speed the ascent, but it was too risky. The fact that Ezzel had locked the elevator in place on the top floor seemed to indicate he either knew he had company, or had expected it. If Donovan allowed himself to be found out while in that shaft, it would be a simple matter to lower the elevator and crush him.

He turned and ran back to the door to the alley. Amethyst stood outside the door. She leaned heavily on the wall. There was no sign of the dragons...nothing moved, and the carcasses that had steamed and released their foul order moments before had dissolved into pools of a black, sticky substance Donovan didn't recognize.

"The elevator is sealed," he said.

She glanced up, and he followed her gaze. Near the top of the building something glinted, and he frowned. He glanced back into the darkened doorway, then back up the wall.

"Whatever that is," he said, "is directly above the elevator. Could the elevator car be stuck up there?"

Amethyst reached into her pocket, pulled out a green satin bag. She untied it and shook a small, clear globe into her hand. As Donovan watched, she breathed on the ball, closed it between her palms and closed her eyes. She said something under her breath and opened her hands.

The crystal globe had gone smoky, and as they watched, it slowly cleared. When the last of the mist had disappeared from its depths, an image shimmered into view. At first it wasn't clear, but Amethyst whispered something, and it came into focus.

They saw the top of the Tefft complex. The moon had dropped nearly off the edge of the skyline. Dawn was approaching fast. They looked closer, and saw that the glint they'd caught before. It was a window of some kind, a single glass pane on the stone face of the building. It was near the top. Amethyst spoke again, and the image shifted closer.

"Damn them," Donovan said. He saw Vein and the others, staring out defiantly at a sky that would soon fill with sunlight and incinerate them.

"It's a trap," Amethyst said.

"Of course it is," he sighed. "And I still can't leave them

there. I'm being paid by their council to save one of their own...I doubt if they'd consider it much of a service if I let that whole group of idiots die in the process."

"There's not much time," she said softly.

"How do you know?" he asked.

"The crystals," she said simply. "He took my crystals, but I still feel them. He's set them in place. The ritual is beginning now, and once he's started, he can't stop. They can only be used once every cycle of the moon. If he tried it again before that, the crystals would shatter. It's one of the reasons they are so rare."

He stared at her, then back up the wall of the building.

"How long?" he asked. "How long before it's too late and he'd have to wait?"

She closed her eyes. Something her skin shimmered for a moment, as if encased in a sheath of light. Then she opened her eyes and met his gaze.

"An hour, maybe two, but it won't be any more than that. If he waits longer, the ritual will fail, and the crystals will be destroyed."

She fell silent, and Donovan turned away toward the building. She reached out and gripped his arm. He turned back.

"If that happens," she said, "if he destroys the crystals? You don't want to be in the building. You probably don't want to be on this block, but you definitely don't want to be in there. It won't exist."

"They'll explode?" he asked, frowning.

"No," she said. "They are timeline crystals. If they are destroyed, whatever they have the strongest link to will draw them along with everything and anything near them through time, space, and dimensions – whatever is between them and their source. Donovan, whatever is too close to them may not be destroyed, but it won't be here, and there won't be any way to get back."

"Then I'd better hurry," he said.

"What are you going to do?" she asked.

"If I can't go up the inside," he replied, I'll have to go up the outside. If I can blow the outer door off of that elevator, they'll have a chance, and they'll have to take it. I'll be going in that way and going after our boy Lance."

"I'm going in the front," she said. "I think I can trace your friends up there," she pointed at the trapped elevator. "They must have found a way in. If you make enough of a disturbance blowing the side off the wall, maybe I can slip in under his guard. One of us has to get through."

Donovan nodded. He stepped forward impulsively, and she almost stepped back, but he was too quick. He pulled her close and slid his fingers into her hair, feeling crystals slide over his fingers. She pressed against him, and they kissed. He let the moment linger for a heartbeat, and then stepped back.

"Be careful," he said.

"I'll try, she replied, grinning at him, "but I'm kind of pissed off right now."

He stared at her, glanced up at the building, and then laughed. "I bet you are at that," he said.

She winked at him, turned, and was gone, running back around to the front of the building. He watched her go until she was out of sight, and then turned back to the wall. It wasn't going to be easy, but he'd come prepared to climb the inside of the elevator shaft, and the exterior wall wouldn't be that much different. There would be wind to contend with, but he thought he could manage, as long as he reached them before the sun crested the horizon.

The charm was simple, but he took his time. This was one tall building, and though he might find a way to survive a fall, he'd never make it up the side twice in the time allotted to him. He drew a leather bag from his jacket pocket. It bore a beaded design in the shape of a thunderbird, and the top was tied closed with drawstring straps. The bag was old and slightly brittle, and he handled it carefully.

As his fingers brushed the old hide, images floated through his mind. He saw an old man with gray hair. Feathers and bones were woven into that hair, and the eyes that stared at him over a hawk-like nose were slate gray and piercing. Across time and death, he felt the old shaman's presence, and he breathed a prayer of thanks. The images dispersed, and he continued.

He opened the bag and drew out two feathers and a beaded necklace. The necklace was a string of claws, more feathers, painted beads, and stones. Donovan slipped it over his neck. He quickly removed his boots and placed one feather in each, then laced them back up.

Working quickly, he shuffled in a slow circle and recited the incantation he'd learned so long ago. He closed his eyes and pictured the old Lakota's face once more. He felt the rhythm shiver through his bones, and felt the familiar lightening, as if the air around him had permeated his skin, soaked in and drained back out, taking his weight and his mass with it. He continued until he actually felt a breeze through his heart.

"One with the wind," he whispered. He didn't hesitate. He turned, and like a large insect, he scuttled up the side of the wall. The cracks and niches he used for steps and grips were narrow. They shouldn't have held his weight; but they did.

As the sunrise seeped closer to the horizon, he climbed, repeating a soft prayer to the thunderbird as he went and wishing the ancient god could grant him its wings.

EIGHTEEN

Deep in the secret heart of the Tefft Complex, beneath the chamber where Vanessa had been held captive, but far above the ground floor lobby, a larger space had been created. The elevator appeared not to stop on this floor, and the only other access was by certain passages not obvious to the average eye. There were other safeguards. Ezzel knew that the wards he'd placed weren't going to stop anyone truly determined to get in, but at this point it didn't matter. He didn't need them to be stopped, only slowed. When he stepped from the elevator, he sent it upward, and with a short phrase, he locked it in place. This elevator was a mechanical device, but it responded to other controls as well, and it was these less mundane methods he now employed.

The center of his private floor was another round chamber, and it was there that he gathered the items he'd spent such time and effort gathering. They were spread over the top of a long altar table, which itself sat in the center of a wide circle that had been first carved, and then burned into the floor. The braziers that would have to be placed at the compass points in a less permanent circle were imbedded in the stone floor. The room was designed with a single purpose in mind.

The inner circle was also cut into the floor, but it was narrow, and shallow. Ezzel stood within, pouring white powder from a vial around this smaller circle. As he passed each of the braziers he lit it and spoke the invocation, then continued until he reached the final brazier. A ring of symbols had been carefully drawn between the concentric circles, and when he reached the southernmost point on the circle, he would close it, seal it, and light the powder. He'd run through this with meaningless elements a thousand times. He'd repeated the ritual, breaking it into pieces so that he set no random power loose on the room, nor created any anomaly accidentally, and he'd committed every motion, and every word to memory.

In the center of the altar, the ancient journal rested on a wooden stand. It was open to the first page of the ritual. Ezzel didn't need it. In fact, if he'd still needed to read the instructions or the words of the ritual from that book, he would not have been ready to complete the process at all. The timing of each segment was critical. He just felt it was proper that some portion of Le Duc join him at this penultimate moment – the culmination of something begun centuries earlier. Le Duc had met his untimely end trying to secure the vampire's blood necessary to complete the ritual. Ezzel had been more careful, and more patient.

The urn with Father Vargas' remains stood off to one side, beyond the circle. He had extracted the ashes he needed the moment it was in his possession. At the bottom of a chute he used to dispose of garbage, the corpse of the collector, Jasper Windham, had begun its long courtship with rot and maggots. Loose ends were not acceptable, and even though Ezzel knew he was no longer operating in secret, he saw no reason to change the rules of the game now. Windham couldn't be trusted – it was obvious in the way he'd betrayed DeChance, and with a very long lifetime ahead of him, Ezzel intended to surround himself only with those he could trust. The rest would be eliminated, or brought in line.

The room he'd prepared for his ritual was awash in color. Tapestries hung from the walls, depicting astrological signs, chemical formulas, arcane symbols and images from the Tarot. It was mostly an affectation – but it was one that he enjoyed. The entire room – the building surrounding it – the melodrama of the kidnapping and thefts – none of it had been specifically necessary. He could have spent the time and money to range further and find the ingredients he needed. He could have taken a different vampire, one with fewer connections and less beauty. He might even have found one whose people wouldn't have been sad to lose them. In some ways he wasn't so unlike the pretender he'd slain, Cornwell. He liked the idea of who, and what he was and saw no reason not to surround himself with the symbolic trappings.

Ezzel didn't want his triumph to be a secret. He didn't want anonymity, or silence. He was about to complete something that had never been completed. When the ritual was finished, he would be immortal. He would have lifetimes without end to enjoy every pleasure the world had to offer, and he didn't want that feat to go unnoticed. If he could have performed the ceremony on top of the most prominent building in town with an audience of his peers watching him become more than their peer, he would have done so.

For the moment, all of that was incidental. He concentrated carefully and made his way around to the final compass point. He lit the brazier, watched the white, scented smoke rise in curling tendrils to join that from the other braziers. With a quick flick of his wrist, he completed the inner circle and stepped back. He took a deep breath, and inventoried his equipment for the thousandth time. Everything was in place, and had been in place for a week, but there was no turning back once he lit the powder. He had cast the wards, but the circle remained open. He could step across that line, never speak the words, and walk away. He even thought he could get out without being caught, and disappear from San Valencez.

He glanced down at the ring. Between two of the carved characters the Timeline Crystals winked back at him with reflected brilliance. They were set into the stone of the floor, ready to form the portal. It would be the last point through which he would pass as a mortal. He thought of Amethyst, imagined the shocked, angry expression she must be wearing, and almost laughed. Yes, he could go now, take the crystals, and leave it all behind.

For a moment, he pretended to give the notion serious consideration. He remembered the desert near Cairo, and the years he'd spent studying scrolls and crawling the tunnels of pyramids. He thought of Jerusalem, the temples and the mosques, and the secrets still buried in caves from the Dead

Sea to the holy city itself. He thought of Asia and Europe, even the hills and mountains of California and Tennessee. Each held memories, and each held bits and pieces of the trail that led to this moment. None of those he'd met on the road had believed in the formula – not the way Ezzel believed in it. They knew legends. Some of them knew Le Duc's name. One even had a single page transcribed from the journal, enough to state the purpose of the ritual, and to name it, but not to reveal any of the necessary elements.

It had been a long, hard, intriguing journey. Even the gathering of the final elements had been entertaining. DeChance was not to be taken lightly, and walking into the den of one of the vampire council members, stealing his lover from under his nose, and draining her slowly had been Ezzel's gift to Le Duc. In his way, it was a tribute. Le Duc discovered the formula, but failed in the collection. He'd been a great alchemist, but not particularly powerful in other elements of the craft, and the vampire he'd chosen had bested him easily. Nothing more had ever been heard of him, but the journal survived.

Now it rested on the altar behind him, and the circle was complete. Ezzel closed his eyes, whispered a quick and meaningless charm for luck, and lit a large, sulfur match. He dropped it into the white powder, and the flames shot around the circle. They flashed to blue flame, leaped and danced, and then settled. Smoke rose in an even curtain that closed him from the rest of the room. At first it was thin and translucent. The colored tapestries and metaphysical paraphernalia he'd gathered were visible through the haze as vague lumps and dangling shadows.

Then the smoke thickened and he stood within a cylindrical white wall. He watched it for a moment, turning in a slow circle and examining the protective ring carefully, but he knew he'd find no weakness in it. It was perfect. He turned to the altar, stepped closer, and began.

It took Amethyst longer to find the maintenance passage that reached the two private elevators than it had taken Vein, but she was more careful. Once she was in the first floor passage she stopped and established a tight web of protection around herself before moving on. She reached the elevator shaft and began to climb. She didn't have the advantage of a Thunderbird bag, but she did have an amulet consecrated by rites sacred to air and wind, and she made good time.

Under other circumstances she might have worried that the elevator would descend, catch her between floors, and crush her, but she'd seen what Ezell planned. The one elevator would not leave the top floor by his hand, it was meant as a death chamber for the vampires, and it needed to remain in place to keep them trapped. Ezzel wouldn't be leaving until he'd finished what he started, and that meant he needed the second elevator for his escape. She saw the bottom of the car far above. She climbed as quickly as she could, and as she did, she thought about what to do when she reached the top.

Ezzel had posed as her apprentice, and during the time he'd spent with her, she'd shared a lot of her knowledge with him. There might be other things he'd taken, and there was no way to know what he might have stolen from her books and papers when her guard was down. It was infuriating, but she couldn't afford to take any chances with him. Whatever she used he might be ready to counter. She'd have to dig deep and be resourceful. Thankfully, everything she knew had not been shared, and not everything she owned that was powerful was stored in the single vault he'd stolen the timeline crystals from.

She stopped a floor below where the bottom of the elevator car hung over her head. Clinging to the maintenance ladder, she leaned out and breathed a handful of dust on to the crack in the center of the door in the side of the shaft. As that dust settled, she spoke a short charm. The doors slid open. She swung out on the ladder, away from the door, and then used the momentum of the return swing to flip in through the opening. She landed heavily, but without injury, and rolled to her feet. She pressed to the wall, slipped to the first corner, and then stood very still.

She didn't really expect to meet anyone in the hall, but she was in no mood for further mistakes. If Ezzel completed this ritual, part of the blame was hers, and if she couldn't stop him, she intended to let him know she was there. It wasn't so much the ritual, or his thievery, or even the deaths he took so lightly. It was the fact that he'd lied to her, fooled her, worked with her and gained her trust.

She rounded the corner and began checking doors. All were locked until she reached the last. It hung open, and she saw dim, flickering light in the dark opening. She moved very slowly up to the edge of the door frame and stopped. Then she took a deep breath and glanced inside.

At first she saw only shadows. The walls were stone, and the only light was from a couple of guttering candles that had nearly burned themselves out. There was very little furniture. She saw a cot along one wall. There was a small table. She saw and sensed no one.

Once inside, she moved along the wall carefully, searching the barren room for shadows and finding none. Then she reached the cot, and when she did, she noticed something dangling from the wall just beyond it. It wasn't very large, and at first she thought it might be empty chains, or a torn tapestry. She stepped closer, looked, and reeled away, gagging. What hung from the manacles on the wall and leaned precariously over the lip of the metal collar was barely recognizable as human. The skin was like leather worn so thin and brittle it could have been paper. The eye sockets were empty pits. Bones jutted and threatened to release their tenuous hold on one another.

"Vanessa." Amethyst whispered the name, but she didn't look back. She knew what the remains hanging on the wall meant. Caution was no longer a viable option. She needed to find Ezell immediately, and probably that wouldn't be soon enough.

She pulled a small yellow crystal from her pocket and tossed it in the air. Before it could fall she snapped a command and whipped her finger in an intricate spiral between herself and the door. The crystal fell about a foot, wobbled in the air, and then hovered. It pointed toward the center of the building, and down. She snatched the crystal and took off at a run.

She didn't bother to follow the hallway around to the end; that was where the other elevator would end, and that was where Donovan would enter. There was no way to know how he intended to get in, but since the wall was solid, and the elevator was apparently strong enough to hold adult vampires against their will, it was unlikely to be a good idea to be on this side of the wall when he decided to try it.

As she ran, she let the yellow crystal hover just above the palm of her hand, and a moment later she was back at the first elevator's shaft. There were no stairs. She leaned out through the still open doors, grabbed the maintenance ladder, and swung back into the shaft.

The crystal led her down two levels. There was a door, but it was not readily visible. She had to search, then close her mind and visualize it, before it shimmered into view. She wondered for just a moment why the car was all the way at the top. If she'd wondered another second, it would have been too long. She leaned out, blew the powder into the crack of the door and gripped the ladder. There was a grinding roar, and without thought she swung out and whipped herself through the air. As she moved, she screamed the opening charm and prayed it would work quickly enough. She launched herself at the doorway. Even as she slid through the opening, barely clearing the sides of the half-open door, hit the floor and rolled, the elevator ground to a halt. The inner door opened with a snick.

Amethyst glanced back, shuddered, and then turned to scan the hall. There was no one in sight, but she no longer needed the crystal to guide her. There was only one large, ornate doorway. A glow slipped out around the cracks. She stood still and closed her eyes. The shimmering vibration of the timeline crystals shivered through her pores. They were approaching resonance – the point when the radiance Ezzel had drawn from the depths of each would blend with that from the other until they formed a portal between them. At the final point of the ritual, he would step out between them, pass through that radiance, and the effects of the formula would become final and irreversible. In that small nexus of power, the past, present and future would be one single moment, and beyond that, the effects of the passage of minutes, hours, days and centuries would have no further affect. That was the theory.

She didn't want to see it tested. She cleared her mind, drew in what energy she could from the air, from the amulets and crystals she wore, and even from the vibration of the timeline stones themselves. They were her crystals, after all, and they had been hers for many years. She'd spent time with them, studied them; a part of her was imprinted in their depths, and in the frequency of their vibration. Ezzel might have cleansed them before putting them to use, but somehow she didn't believe he'd done it. He knew a lot, and he had talent, but no one knew everything, and crystals were her specialty, not his. These were very powerful, very delicate artifacts, and he'd have to travel a long way to find another pair their equal. If he cleansed them improperly, he could disturb the balance, and the repercussions wouldn't quiet for months. If he was smart, he'd left them alone and taken his chances. She hoped it would be enough.

She crossed the hall and tried the knob on the door. To her surprise, it wasn't locked. She turned it, peered through the crack, and gasped. The circle was immense, and it was active. The smoky cloud that obscured it was thick and dense. She couldn't' make out what was happening on the other side, and though she knew she was equally obscured, it did little to calm her nerves. This was powerful magic, and once the circle was in place, it was beyond foolish to try and cross it, or break it. The purpose of the circles of protection was to protect those inside the circle from what they summoned, and to protect those outside the circle from the energies contained within. Any sudden, unexpected break could destroy whoever stood inside the circle, or whoever stood outside. If it were powerful enough magic, it could be worse.

She took in the room at a glance. It was nothing like she'd expected. She'd known Ezzel for months, but as her apprentice, a quiet, soft-spoken man who was eager to do whatever she asked, and who might as well have been part of the wall when she wasn't working with him. This room, this explosion of wealth and power and ostentatious – nonsense – didn't equate with the man she'd thought she knew.

She approached the circle carefully. There were was

nothing to see from where she stood, but she caught the scent of the incense he'd used to set the wards, and she felt the crystals, warm and shimmering, beneath that curtain. He hadn't placed them inside the inner circle. They had to be mounted side by side in the center of the concentric rings to form the portal.

That was good. Amethyst wouldn't break the circle. She knew the danger, and she wasn't going to send the building and herself crashing into the pits of hell if she could help it. It was possible, though, that if she concentrated she could disrupt the vibrations in the crystal enough to prevent the formation of the portal. If she managed it, Ezzel would be trapped inside his own circle. It might not last, but it would buy them some time. It might be all that she could do.

She stalked around the outside of the circle. The more she thought about the theft of the crystals, and the quiet, handsome man who'd fooled her so completely and then taken advantage of her with such cold, unfeeling arrogance, the angrier she became. She pressed the palms of her hand as close as she dared to the whirling mist. She felt forces alive and powerful, just beyond her touch. Their aura shivered along the outer edge of the circle. She felt their awareness as well. Ezzel would have no concentration to spare for her, but the spirits he'd summoned were under no such constraints, and they wanted out. As long as they sensed that she might work to break the circle, they would only watch her. She knew that didn't give her much time.

On the far right of the circle she felt the direct presence of the crystals, and she stopped. She stood very still, willed her mind to seek the twin vibrations, and sought to match them. She felt the spirits within the cloud drawing near, hovering and watching. They knew she could break the circle by attacking the crystals. What they didn't yet know was her purpose, and she knew she'd have to act very quickly to succeed.

The vibrations rippled through her, and she willed one of the smaller crystals she wore around her throat to match that shivering warmth. She drew it in slowly and tried to keep the intrusion as inconspicuous as possible. She would have one moment to strike, and she waited for it as long as she dared.

With a lash of will she shifted the vibration of her smaller crystal, fighting to keep it bound to the larger, stronger timeline crystals. The spirits in the circle snatched her intentions from her thoughts and pounced with shrieks of anger and rage. Something dark rose behind her, but she didn't see it in time. She concentrated and forced her will into the aura of the combined crystals. The darkness folded over and bent double, and then struck like a snake. It wrapped around her and dragged her from her feet, driving the breath from her lungs in a savage wrench.

She screamed and clawed at the writhing shadow, but the link with the crystals was broken, and now she fought for her life. The thing that held her was dark, and the stench it released engulfed the room, blotting out even the hint of incense. She fought to breathe, but it squeezed inexorably, driving the air from her struggling lungs.

Within the circle, Ezzel sensed a shift in the rhythms of the circle. He could not react, but he was aware. If he let his concentration waver for even a moment, he would be destroyed. Still, the disturbance itched at the back of his mind. It was the crystals. Their vibration had shifted very slightly. If they shifted more, he might not be able to bring them back into alignment – he might never escape the circle with his life.

Then, as suddenly as the disturbance had intruded, it was gone. He saw nothing but the table before him, the elements of the ritual, and the inviolate white smoky ring surrounding him. As he worked, he smiled.

NINETEEN

Donovan reached the glass outer-wall of the elevator quickly. He leaned around the corner and caught the terrified stares of Vein and his companions, but he didn't have time to worry about their state of mind. The sunrise was only moments away, and if he didn't get them out and under cover soon, fright would be the least of their troubles.

He examined the intricate silver mesh worked into the glass, which was thick, maybe three inches and very solid. Donovan had to lean out from the wall to see this, and the wind buffeted him each time he did, threatening to blow him from his perch. The Thunderbird spirit lightened him, but every blessing has its curse. Each motion threatened to send him flying away in the grip of some errant breeze, and it was difficult to move because in his lightened state, every twitch caused a seemingly disproportionate reaction.

He'd come prepared for a lot of things, and though blasting through an outer wall wasn't something he'd anticipated, he didn't hesitate. He had several smaller pouches tucked deep in his pockets, and after only a few moments searching he pulled out a small, blue leather bag. It was filled with a white paste. He took this, being very careful not to touch the paste itself with his fingers, and spread it in a large, two foot circle by squeezing it out the top of the bag. He would have made it larger, but there wasn't much paste in the bag, and his reach was severely limited by the need to clutch a jutting brick ridge with his other hand. When he had completed the circle, he pulled back and gripped the wall with both hands. There wasn't much time left.

He glanced into the interior of the elevator. Just at that

instant one of the vampires rushed the glass and crashed into it with all the force he could muster. Startled, Donovan drew back. He lost hold with one hand and cried out. If his full body weight had come down unexpectedly like that on the one hand still gripping the wall, he'd have plummeted to the ground below. Cursing, he swung out from the building, wishing he'd been able to check the violence with which he'd kicked off. He needed to get back to that glass, to touch the circle he'd created and to finish what he'd started, but it was all he could do to hold on.

Inside the elevator, Bruno, who had panicked, was dragged from the glass by Vein and Kali, and held, kicking and screaming for release, as they all watched Donovan's fight for purchase. He didn't think he could drag himself back to the wall. His fingers were slipping. He felt his nails crumbling and his fingertips scraping painfully. His knuckles and wrist throbbed with the effort of maintaining his grip.

Everything slowed in that moment. He saw the faces of those trapped in the elevator clearly, the terror-stricken rage of the one, and the anxious attention of the others. He saw the circle he'd created on the glass, and knew he had to reach it.

A cry rose from above and behind him, and he cursed. He thought, just for a second, that it was another dragon, and his effort to whip about and verify this fear nearly dragged him from the wall. Then something heavy hit him in the back, and he spun toward the wall, gripping, clinging, finding purchase and hugging the brick. The second time the cry rose, he knew it for what it was.

"Three times, Asmodeus," he breathed. "I owe you."

He couldn't see the bird, but he knew it had risen to circle far above. Donovan didn't hesitate. It was now, or never. He reached out, pressed the tip of his nail to the outer edge of the circle of paste, turned his head from the elevator and pressed his cheek to the brick. He willed the heat down the length of his arm, commanding it to pick up speed at his elbow and flash through his fingers, where it erupted in a spark.

The paste didn't light. Instead, a reddish glow circled the ring slowly, starting at the point he'd touched the paste and working around until the entire ring turned rosy red, blue, and then white. The brilliance of it was unbearable; Donovan averted his eyes, and the vampires shrank back in fear. The sun might have dropped from the sky to pay a close, personal visit it was so hot. Donovan was bathed in sweat, and he felt the skin on the back of his neck searing. Then, with an odd, wet sound, the center dropped out of the circle and fell away. It tumbled through the air, its edges molten and dripping, and crashed into the alley below with a tinkle of shattered glass and a hiss of steam.

The vampires didn't hesitate. Though it was small, barely large enough to accommodate their shoulders, they were out that hole in seconds, ignoring the heat, paying no attention when their clothing, hair, and skin touched the molten glass and burned. They hit the wall like scurrying insects and crawled downward with incredible speed, hurrying toward the shadows, sewers, or whatever protection they could find from the rising sun. All but Vein.

The young vampire stood inside, stared out at Donovan, then reached through the hole and held out his hand. Donovan hesitated only a second then took the offered grip. He released his hold on the wall and swung out, and the moment he was directly in front of the molten hole in the elevator wall, Vein drew him through.

"You don't eat much, do you?" Vein asked.

"It will wear off. Get out. I can handle this from here. You only have a few minutes."

Vein hesitated, staring at the hole in the outer wall longingly.

"Go," Donovan said, pushing lightly on Vein's shoulder. "There's nothing more you can do here. Either I can stop this, or I can't, but you need to get out. The sun is rising."

It was true. Vein nodded, dove through the hole, and was gone. Wisps of smoke marked his passage, and Donovan wondered briefly if it was already too late. He hoped the vampire would reach the ground and safety, but there was no more time to waste on it. He stepped to the inner door, pressed his amulet to it and spoke the command sharply. He felt resistance; there were charms and wards on that door, but they weren't strong enough. There was a mechanical whir, the sound of heavy locks disengaging, and the glass slid aside. Beyond it the sliding metal doors opened onto an empty passageway, and Donovan dove through.

He sensed Amethyst's presence, though he didn't know where. He should have been able to locate her, but all he felt was the circle. It was huge, powerful, and no matter what the cost, he knew he had to stop it. He found the elevator shaft. The door was open, as Amethyst had left it. He glanced over the rim and saw that the car rested a ways below him. He reached out, gripped the ladder inside, and then dropped. He didn't bother to climb down because he was still light. He floated the two floors to the elevator's roof, scanned it, and found the maintenance hatch. He opened it and dropped through. Moments later he was in the passage, facing the large, ornate doors of Ezzel's inner sanctum.

He started forward, and then froze. A blood-curdling scream rose, and he recognized it. Amethyst!

Donovan dove through the door, rolled to the side, and stared at the huge, smoke-curtained circle across the room. A cry erupted behind him, but this time he knew it instantly, and he called the bird, Asmodeus, to his shoulder. It landed heavily, nearly knocking him sprawling. The Thunderbird bag was wearing off, but he was still only about half his full weight.

Amethyst lay limp squeezed in a long, dark tentacle of shadow. She struggled feebly, but there wasn't much fight left in her. Donovan turned away with an effort and concentrated on the circle. He knew he had to stop what was happening. He pulled a flat, clear crystal from his pocket and concentrated on it. He couldn't break the protections, even for a quick glimpse of what was happening on the far side. He could drag bits and pieces of images from the recent past of the surrounding room, however, and piece some of it together.

The crystal fogged; stayed that way for what seemed forever, and was likely about two seconds, and then an image shimmered to life. It was a vial, the vial that held Vanessa's blood. It rested on a long table, but that was all he could make out. He dropped the crystal back into his pocket and quickly walked the perimeter of the circle, as Amethyst had done. He found the crystals, felt their near resonance, and cursed sharply. His time was nearly gone.

Drawing a long, thin wand from a leather case on his hip, he held it before him with both hands. He dropped his head between his arms and concentrated, willing his essence up through his slender frame and into his arms. He sent it in waves down toward the thin strip of yarrow wood and the even thinner crystal tip. The stone was bound to the wand with a detailed weave of copper, bronze, gold and silver wire. As he drove his will down the length of the instrument, the crystal glittered, and then glowed brightly. The light was white and very bright, like that of the heat he'd used to melt the elevator wall, but somehow different. There was no heat, and though an aura of energy stretched up and out from that center, encasing him in a sheath of energy, there was no sound.

The old crow, Asmodeus, clutched his shoulder tightly, and Donovan reached out to it. He pictured what he wanted in his mind and pressed that image into the bird's thoughts, forcing aside the few barriers remaining between them. Their bond, which had strengthened slowly since their first encounter in the old church, solidified in that moment. The bird knew his thoughts and acted.

Donovan pressed his mind to the outer circle, wove through tendrils of smoke and the whispered voices of demons to the crystals, and the portal. It was nearly complete, and instead of trying to disrupt that harmony, Donovan hastened it. In the same second that the timeline stones resonated as one, Asmodeus launched off of Donovan's shoulder. The bird shot through that portal like an arrow, bursting through outer and inner circles without leaving a ripple, and disappeared from sight.

A heavy thump to his left told Donovan that the guardians of the protective ring had ceased their attack on Amethyst. Either she was dead, or they were coming after him. He couldn't afford to think about it. If he allowed the fear to seep in and taint his thoughts, the portal would fail, and they would all die. He stood very still, concentrated, and waited, keeping that slim hole in the fabric of smoke and dreams open.

The portal hummed to life with sudden intensity, and Ezzel very nearly lost control. He sensed it before he heard the sound, and that moment's warning saved him from total disaster. Something burst through into the circle, screeched like a banshee, and dove for the table. It was too late.

He had one final step to complete, and immortality would be his. None of the rest of it would matter. He didn't even believe that he would be destroyed if the circle's protections crumbled if the ritual was completed first. The building might cease to exist, but he would go on.

He heard his raven launch from its perch, and he braced himself against the pull of its mind on his own. The bird had been with him for nearly a decade, and their minds were linked very closely. He wanted badly to glance through the bird's eyes and see what had entered the circle, but he didn't' dare turn from the ritual. He poured the ashes of the priest's bone marrow carefully into a bowl in the center of the altar. He'd already added the other ingredients, one by one, stirring, mulching, pummeling some of it to paste and straining out imperfections. When the ashes were beaten in, only blood remained. The vial that held all that remained of Vanessa rested on a silver stand beside the bowl.

Something dark shot across in front of him, but he didn't feel the familiar lurch – it was not the raven. He continued to mix the ingredients, fighting the urge to watch, to look and see what it was. There was so little left to do. Then the shadow returned, closer, and with lightning precision, Asmodeus plucked the vial from its stand.

Ezzel cried out. As he did so, he reached for the speeding bird, missed it, and his hand collided with the raven, diving in pursuit. The bird's beak slashed Ezzel's wrist, and he drew back. Blood poured from the wound in his wrist, and he held it up instinctively. The blood splashed down into the bowl, and the mixture sizzled. Ezzel clutched his wounded wrist and stared at the bubbling formula in horror. He backed away from the table, but it was too late.

His bird, stunned, wobbled to its feet. It recovered fast and made a lunge for the portal, where Asmodeus had disappeared from the ring. Ezzel turned, watching in disbelief. He was afraid the bird would break the ring – then as he realized what had just happened, he hoped it would break – mercifully – and blast them all to oblivion.

The raven shot into the opening, and it seemed it would burst through to the other side, but something stopped it. Ezzel stumbled toward the circle, watching the rear end of his familiar twitch in the grip of something and feeling the dark tendrils of that something reaching into his mind through the bird's thoughts. It felt like ice.

On the altar, the bowl cracked, and he whirled, crying out a charm to prevent the mixture from spilling. It was only partially effective, and he saw the thick, viscous fluid leaking into jelly-like puddles on the altar. He started toward it, stopped, and dropped to his knees as pain shot through his limbs and stopped his heart.

Asmodeus shot back through the portal, past Donovan, and out of sight, clutching the vial of blood tightly. Donovan maintained the portal, shaking with the effort. If he released it suddenly, it would snap. The crystals would shatter, and all of them would cease to exist. He fought the hammering of his heart, watched the portal, and allowed it to close of its own accord. The crystals remained in resonance, but without the catalyst of his will, the portal was unfinished and incomplete.

As it closed, a dark head snapped through and Donovan gasped. He dropped his hold on the crystals too suddenly, but something prevented the portal from collapsing. Something dark and sleek. Its head protruded from the mist and it glared at him in wild-eyed anger and hatred, unable to move. Donovan watched in dark fascination as the portal, unable to remain open, slowly forced its way through the creature's flesh. The raven let out a pained squawk, but the sound died almost the second it was born. The bird hung loosely from the smoke, as Amethyst had dangled from the shadow tentacle moments before, and then it let go.

The bird's body, severed cleanly, slid down to the floor against a surface that Donovan could not see, but only sense. There was no blood. It appeared that whatever force had dropped half the animal on the outside of the circle had separated it completely – turned the one animal into two separate, lifeless lumps of flesh, bone, and feathers.

Donovan spared it no more attention. The portal was closed. He whirled and saw that Amethyst had managed to roll over and push herself groggily up on her knees. He ran to her side and lifted her carefully.

"Nothing broken," she said. Her breathing was pained, and she clutched her ribs tightly. "Might have cracked some ribs, but I'll live."

"We have to get out of here," Donovan said. He glanced toward the door. Asmodeus had landed on a small table just inside the door and stood beside a large, clear crystal globe, watching them intently.

"Ezzel?" Amethyst asked, glancing back at the circle.

"He's in there," Donovan replied, "But the ritual will never be complete. He's going to have to offer something to whatever he summoned, and I'm guess that nothing short of everything is going to do the trick. He won't break the circle unless he's certain there's no other way out. I'm guessing that buys us time to get the hell out of the way."

She nodded, shuddered, and he led her toward the door. When they reached Asmodeus, Donovan reached out and took the vial carefully from the old bird's claw.

"Good work," he said solemnly.

The bird ruffled its feathers, preened one wing, and stared back at him. There was no emotion to read in those dark, predatory eyes, but Donovan had no need to see. He felt the bond, and he smiled.

"Looks like your new friend is here to stay," Amethyst said.

Donovan shrugged. Asmodeus hopped to his shoulder, and the three of them hobbled out of the room. The elevator still stood where Donovan had left it, and they stepped inside. It operated with a set of only four buttons, and he punched the lowest of these. The doors closed silently, and they began to descend.

Amethyst leaned heavily against him, and he knew that she was hurt more badly than she was letting on.

"Just a little more," he said. "We'll get out of here and to my place. I can help you with those ribs once we're safe."

She glanced up at the roof of the elevator, as if looking through the walls and floors to the room far above, and the circle. She knew as well as he did that if Ezzel chose to try and break the circle and escape, they were not far enough away to escape the damage. If he did that, the building would collapse around them and bury them in a mountain of steel and dust, and there was no spell, charm, or wards that either could call on to prevent such a thing.

The elevator reached the ground floor, and they stepped into a dark room. Donovan whispered a word, and the buttons on his jacket illuminated. They saw the outline of a door directly ahead, and made for it as quickly as they could.

"Neat trick" Amethyst whispered hoarsely. "You'll have to show me how you made that work one day."

"It's a promise," he answered. When they slipped out the door and closed it behind them, it disappeared into a perfectly white stone wall. They stood in the outer lobby of the Tefft complex. The five regular elevator doors were lined up down that wall. They walked to the front of the building, exited quickly, and with Asmodeus flying high over head, started down the street as quickly as Amethyst's injured ribs would allow.

A few blocks away, Donovan led her into an alley, and after seven quick turns, they descended a short, dingy stair that opened onto the street across from Donovan's home.

In the circle, Ezzel worked frantically at the altar. He tried charm after charm, but he was frightened, and the fear caused him to slip words in where they didn't belong. He didn't have much with him, because he hadn't expected to need it. The bowl threatened to explode and plaster him with the imperfect formula, but he held it in check, barely, with a continually more complex web of containment spells.

At some point, his wrist began to throb where the raven had

cut it. He ignored the pain and concentrated. He wished that Le Duc had been a better magician. There might have been more in the journal on controlling this ritual, or an escape if things went badly. There was nothing.

The throbbing grew more intense, and he glanced down impatiently. When he saw his wrist, he screamed. He clamped his other hand over the wound, but it was too late. The cut had opened wider, and blood seeped down his arm to soak his robes. He turned and lurched toward the portal, determined to try and break through at that one weak spot. He took a step, then another, and then was lifted from his feet violently. The wound in his wrist erupted in a geyser of blood. The blood gathered in the air, whirled, and drained down to the bowl through an invisible tube of energy. He struggled. He tried to speak, but something gripped his throat and prevented it, and eventually the struggles weakened.

When the last of his blood drained away, he dropped headlong, breaking the bowl and shattering the stands and vials. The wand he'd stolen from Alistair Cornwell cracked as it struck the stone floor, and the murky, sticky fluid in the bowl dripped slowly to the floor, forming a puddle that clotted, and then grew still.

The mist snapped from the circle as though inhaled by a god. It was there, and then it was not. There was no breeze, and no flame burned in candle or brazier. Cold and dead as its owner, the room stilled. Broken on the altar, the desiccated carcass that had been Lance Ezzel crumbled to dust.

TWENTY

It took several days before Donovan was satisfied that the hidden rooms in the gut of the Tefft Complex were cleansed. When he'd entered the central chamber with Amethyst, Johndrow, and a select group of others, they'd found very little evidence of what had taken place within those walls so recently. Most of the Council was there, or had sent representatives. Vein was there escorting Johndrow, and Kali had come as well. The rest of their group had bowed out, having seen more than enough of the Tefft Complex to last them several long afterlifetimes.

Joel arranged for the contents of all the rooms they found to be inventoried. It had not taken long for the old banker to pull the proper strings and assume ownership. It was agreed up front that the money earned would be split between Joel, Donovan and Amethyst. Johndrow wanted only one thing from the place. Vanessa's remains were carried out carefully, wrapped in silk. The vial containing her blood was locked away in a safe.

Donovan did not recover the journal. Everything that had been within the interior magic circle was gone. The room was as colorful and filled with paraphernalia as ever, but that one bare patch, with its scorched braziers and inner and outer carved rings stood barren. Even the altar was gone.

There was no question of escape. Some part of what had been Lance Ezzel might not be dead, but he wouldn't be bothering anyone in San Valencez again, and though he might now survive the eternities he'd sought, they would not be pleasant.

The remains of the raven were a different matter. Half of

the familiar had been trapped within the circle when the portal snapped closed, and that half was gone. The other half of the bird, sliced cleanly and sealed as if it had been born that way, lay dead and cold on the stone floor. There was something eerie in that bisected corpse that sent a shiver down Donovan's spine. He needed no reminders of the power of the forces he worked with.

Amethyst still walked with a slight limp, but her eyes flashed bright with anger as she took in that space and her mind drifted back to the man who'd created it.

"It might happen to any of us," Donovan said, laying a hand gently on her shoulder. "I met him, remember? I didn't suspect a thing."

"I should have, though," Amethyst insisted. "I should have been able to detect something in his aura. He handled my crystals, pawed through my secrets, and I stood back and smiled and patted him on the back telling him what a good job he was doing."

"We all make mistakes," Donovan replied, turning away and leaving the room behind. "It's what we do with the lessons learned that defines us."

They departed the room together and rode the elevator to the ground floor. They stepped into the late night emptiness of the lobby and stood for a moment.

"I have one thing left to finish," he said. "I've promised it. When I'm done?"

"I'll be waiting," she said. "I think Cleo will let me in, and you still have to show me that trick with your buttons. Besides, you have a much better bar than I do."

Donovan chuckled. "It's true. I can show you a few more tricks with the buttons, if you like."

Amethyst grinned, leaned in, and kissed him deeply. "I can't wait," she said.

Donovan grinned in return, then added, "And don't forget to feed that damned bird."

Amethyst stepped out into the night. Donovan stood in the lobby, alone, and a few moments later he was joined by Johndrow and Vein.

"It's time," Johndrow said softly.

Donovan nodded. The three stepped out of the building and climbed into a long, sleek limousine waiting at the curb. When they were seated, Donovan noted that Kali was driving, and that Vein sat beside her in front. He smiled. He'd known Johndrow and Vanessa for a very long time, and the old banker, Joel, had been with his Ligaya for centuries. It was almost as if Vein had heard his words to Amethyst and determined to make use of his own recent lessons. Somehow, Donovan thought he was witnessing the beginning of a very long union.

They drove in silence, winding through sparse traffic and taking back roads whenever possible. It wasn't really necessary to maintain a low profile, but this night, of all nights, none of them wanted to be detained for any reason. Kali drove slowly and carefully, and before long they pulled into the private garage far below Johndrow's penthouse suite. There were few other vehicles present, and only a single guard watched from the shack near the elevator entrance.

You couldn't see it with the naked eye, but Donovan sensed the level of security that cloaked the building. Stine might not be around to supervise it, but his people had been working overtime. Every possible contingency was blanketed in wards and charms. The air crackled with the energy of it, and Donovan carefully avoided touching anything, lest he inadvertently set off some safeguard.

It was a somber group that piled into the private elevator. Though Ezzel was destroyed, or banished, there were still clouds hanging over the city that would be hard to erase. Johndrow and Vein had been through more in the past week than they'd seen in the past hundred years. Kali bounced her mood off of Vein's, and held her peace. She glanced at Donovan once or twice, her gaze calculating, but she said nothing. All of the younger vampires realized what he'd done for them. He could have fulfilled his obligation by entering the building and trying to save Vanessa, but instead he'd chosen to help them first. They hadn't said anything to him – not even an apology for their earlier attacks and accusations, but they owed him, and all of them were aware of it.

The elevator stopped and they stepped into Johndrow's hall, where it had all begun. There was no trace of Stine's death remaining. The penthouse was as opulent and decadent in both décor and ambiance as ever. Donovan had never been inside the home, and he stared about appreciatively. It had taken a lot of years, and a lot of money to make a haven so comfortable, and so secure. He hoped that the invasion and kidnapping would drive home the value of it all and keep Johndrow and his people attentive. It was never wise to accumulate wealth you weren't willing and able to spend the time to protect.

It wasn't his concern. Donovan had his own security considerations to look into once he'd completed the service asked of him. He followed Johndrow down a long hall, through the main room, where he knew the party had taken place.

They stepped through another doorway and filed down a long, narrow hall. There were doors to either side, but none was open. There was no sign that light had ever penetrated here, and Donovan suspected that few who still breathed and still possessed their own blood had ever been admitted there. The air was chilly, and he shivered.

At the far end they paused as Johndrow produced a key ring and opened a set of double doors. He entered; Donovan and the others followed. The doors were closed behind them. The room was absolutely dark. Donovan heard a rustle. It might have been the material of a jacket, or pants legs rubbing together. It might have been shuffling footsteps. He waited, and though he did not believe he was in any danger, his heart pounded. That pounding reminded him of whom he stood among, which increased his nervousness until it seemed like the blood was crashing through his veins, too hot and too loud to be ignored by those with the hunger.

When a match was struck, and a candle lit, the light was bright enough in that absolute darkness that he had to blink his eyes to clear his sight of the strobing video echo of the flash. The room took on boundaries and the interior assumed shapes and shadows. He saw the others standing nearby, and in the center of the room a long, ornate bench. It was draped with cloth that he could not make out the colors or designs of, and piled with pillows.

The air was scented. There were no braziers; it wasn't incense. Bowls of herbs and spices lined shelves on the walls. Fresh flowers were strewn about – lilies, Donovan thought, though he only felt them as his feet broke the stems and trampled the blossoms. The scent was of lilies and roses – and something else.

There was a stench underlying it all, a rotten, sickening tang of decay that even the multitude of flowers couldn't overpower. Somehow the sweetness of the blossoms mixed with that horrible stench was worse than it would have been on its own. Donovan tried not to breathe too heavily. He stepped forward to stand beside the table. Vein stepped up opposite him.

Kali stood at the foot of the table, furthest from the others. Johndrow assumed a position of authority at the head. Someone further back in the shadows lit a second candle, and Donovan was able to make out more details. Vanessa's remains had been laid out carefully on the pillows. With great caution she'd been positioned with her hands across her breasts in a death pose. The skin, scarecrow sticks that had been her legs lay limp and misshapen. The silence held for what seemed an eternity, and then Johndrow spoke.

"I have no words sufficient to thank you for what you have done," he said at last. "What was taken from me – from us," he gestured briefly at Vein, and the others who stood further from the table, "was irreplaceable. A life as long as mine is subject to many horrors, as well as joys. The horrors can last an eternity, and the joys can be extremely far between."

Donovan listened politely. He didn't require a speech; the two of them knew what had been accomplished, and somehow, with the rotting bones and flesh of the one he'd been sent to save lying in front of him it all rang hollow and empty.

"It is time," he said softly.

Johndrow nodded. Someone stepped up behind him and placed two objects in his hand, then withdrew. Johndrow held them, glancing first at one, and then at the other. Donovan thought the vampire smiled, but in the dim light it was very difficult to tell. There was a white flash of fangs.

He held out his hand, and Johndrow held out the first object that he'd been given. It was the vial Asmodeus had snatched from the circle; the vial that contained the essence of what had once been Vanessa. Donovan took it gently from the old vampire's hand, glanced at the second object Johndrow held, and frowned. He needed nothing more than the blood for the ritual.

"I'll explain this in a few moments," Johndrow said. "Please, continue."

Donovan put his questions aside and cleared his mind. His presence wasn't strictly necessary for this ceremony. Any of Stine's people, or possibly even Johndrow himself could have met the tenets of the simple ritual. It was an honor, he knew, something that most mortals would never experience. He did not fool himself into believing this made him anything special in the eyes of the undead. They had their own ways, and their own society, and he was not a part of it – could not be a part of it without experiencing death and dark rebirth, but he was respected. It was a memory to add to his long string of adventures, a moment to share over firelight in years to come. It was also a sign of trust.

He raised the vial before him and lowered his head. He turned to where Kali stood at the foot of the table, the South, and spoke the proper invocation, calling on elemental spirits and archangels alike to guard the proceedings. He turned to Vein, repeated this action, and did so again by turning fully away from the table. At the end, he turned to the North, and to Johndrow. He spoke clearly and closed the protective circle about them. The room rippled with – something. It was a sensation slightly different from any in his experience, but he didn't dwell on it. In this place, other powers were not far removed. The circle was complete, and if such a thing was possible, they were safe within that ethereal boundary.

"I must ask you all," he said softly, "not to move. Some of you are standing within, and some of you without, the circle I have drawn. Do not move, or that circle might be broken."

There was no sound. No one spoke in assent, but neither did they move. Donovan hesitated only for a moment, and then turned back to Vanessa's remains. He slid his hand down under the pillow directly beneath her head and lifted gently. He moved very slowly and deliberately. If he jerked, or stumbled, it could be disastrous.

When he held her head at an angle above the table, he turned to Johndrow and held out the vial. Without a word, the old vampire unscrewed the top. Donovan brought the open vial to the cracked, dried remnant of Vanessa's lips. He whispered softly. What he recited was a very ancient version of the last rites, but the words were spoken in reverse. He'd memorized the incantation long years in the past, and reciting them brought a stream of images and memories to haunt his thoughts as his voice, soft yet firm, carried through the small chamber.

At first, nothing happened. The blood ran down the parched, ruined throat and they heard it trickling and dripping as it wound it's way in and through, escaping through torn skin and staining yellowed, ancient bone a dark, shadowy hue in the dim light. Donovan paid no attention to the affect of the liquid, but concentrated on the words. There were not many, and he spoke them clearly. When the last syllable fell away to silence, he closed his eyes and waited.

Something moved in his hands. It writhed and slid but he ignored the sensation. A series of wet popping sounds echoed through the room, and a sound very like the tearing of rotten fabric followed. The weight he held shifted and grew, but still he did not open his eyes. The motion in and around his fingers stopped, and he felt something warm and silky. The weight lessened, and then lifted away from him completely. Still he held his silence, and did not open his eyes.

When soft fingers stroked his chin, he smiled, and when they slid down and he felt sharp nails tracing the pulsing vein in his throat, he finally opened his eyes.

She sat upright on the table, cradled in the pillows. The stench had left the air, as if drawn from the room by a giant vacuum. Her lips parted, as if she was going to speak, and Donovan reached out to place a finger across them, silencing her.

Pulling back very slightly, he turned, this time facing first to the North. He caught Johndrow's fierce, triumphant smile, but did not hesitate to enjoy it. He turned away from the table, and then across to Vein, whose expression was unreadable. He turned to the foot of the table last, released the ward, and returned his gaze to Vanessa's.

"It is safe now," he said softly. "You are safe. Welcome back."

She stared at him for a moment, holding her silence, and then glanced around the room at the others. Obviously the shadows that hampered Donovan's sight held no such power over hers. She stretched then, like a beautiful, silky cat. Her clothing had fallen away when she was removed from Ezzel's chains, and she luxuriated, pale, naked, and very much alive.

"Donovan DeChance," she said. "It has been a long time since I last saw you. My memory is hazy, but since you are here, I assume it was you who freed me?"

Donovan nodded slowly. He was on new ground here. She was very old, very powerful, and after her ordeal, no doubt ravenously hungry for fresh blood. The others would do what they could, he thought, none of them wanted the type of battle that might ensue if she attacked him, but his fears were unwarranted.

A small dark woman appeared from the shadows. She stepped timidly to the table, and with delicate grace she pulled back her long, dark hair from her shoulder and offered her throat. Vanessa watched her carefully. Her eyes glinted, and her limbs tensed, but she managed to control herself. She glanced at Donovan, almost an apology, then slid closer to the woman and leaned in. There was a gasp – pain? Surprise? The woman's eyes rolled slightly and her mouth worked. Vanessa held her gently, but firmly. In a moment, with a shudder of effort, she pulled back. The woman stumbled slightly, but Donovan caught her arm. Kali stepped to her side and applied a soft cloth to the punctures in the woman's neck and led her away.

Donovan stood, riveted. The site of Vanessa feeding jolted him. There was passion in the act, a sensual quality he'd never expected. The woman had groaned in – what? Desire?

Pleasure? She had offered herself freely, and been spared.

"Don't look so shocked," Vanessa said, laughing softly. "A girl's got to keep up her strength."

Everyone but Donovan laughed at this. Johndrow, unable to control himself, stepped forward and swept Vanessa into his arms. He lifted her naked body unceremoniously from the table and held her easily, gazing at her face as if he could drink her in and hold her there. He laughed, kissed her, and lowered her to her feet. She slid down his body, pressed close, and laughed gaily. Vein stepped around the table and slipped a robe over Vanessa's shoulders. She thanked him with a nod.

Johndrow turned to Donovan and held out his hand. Donovan shook it and met the vampire's gaze.

"Thank you," Johndrow said. "You brought her back to me. I believed that she was lost forever. We could not have done this without your help."

Donovan smiled.

"It was my pleasure." He turned to Vanessa, and bowed slightly. "I had almost forgotten how lovely you are," he said. "It would have been a shame, had the world lost you a second time."

She laughed and hugged him impulsively. As she pulled back, she stumbled a little, and Johndrow caught her.

"You aren't up to your full strength, yet," he said. "We should get you some rest, and you must feed again."

She shook off the momentary weakness, but nodded. "You are right, of course. But I want to know what happened. I remember, up to a point, and then there is nothing but a great darkness."

"There will be time for stories soon enough," Johndrow replied. "For now, Mr. DeChance needs his rest, as well."

"I'll be sleeping for a week," Donovan said. "I'll be happy to tell the entire story that I know soon."

He started to turn away, but Johndrow stopped him with a hand on the shoulder.

"Wait," he said. "I will arrange the payment for your services through more usual channels," he said, "But there is one thing more that I'd like to offer."

He turned to Vanessa. "I wish you could have been consulted on this, but of course it was not possible. I hope you'll agree that it's appropriate…"

He brought forth the second object he'd held while Vanessa was being revived. It was a small, dark gold flask. There were no labels or marks on the glass, and it was sealed with a cork, which was in turn held in place by wax dripped over hand-wrapped gold wire.

"I want you to have this," Johndrow said. He turned to Vanessa, who watched him carefully, as if seeking a sign, or a clue. "We want you to have this," he corrected himself. "It is a far cry from what that man – Ezzel – would have created. Still…"

"What is it," Donovan asked. He took the small flask and turned it over a couple of times, watching the dark brown liquid swirl around the inside of the glass.

Johndrow smiled. "You are probably aware of my collection," he said.

Donovan nodded.

"Even in my collection, this would be rare beyond price," Johndrow continued. "The cognac in that flask is nearly two hundred years old, and was sealed tightly all that time. Hermetically, I believe is the term. There isn't much – probably four small snifters."

Donovan stared at the flask and held it more gently.

"That isn't all," Johndrow said. "May I?"

He held out a hand, and Donovan returned the flask. Johndrow handed it to Vanessa, who grew very still at the touch. She glanced sharply at Johndrow and her fingers tightened momentarily on the neck of the flask. She looked at it again, and then she met Donovan's gaze."

"You will have a part of me," she said, handing it back and letting her fingers linger over his as he took it. "My blood. There is a very small amount, a few drops, I believe, mixed with the liquor."

"It is very old," Johndrow said softly. "Very powerful. Very … subtle. I don't believe that it will bring you immortality, but…if I am correct, it will lengthen your stay on this plane considerably. A century? Perhaps more?"

He slipped around behind Vanessa and drew her close against him. He rested his chin on her shoulder and added. "I think you will find the taste...intoxicating."

Donovan shivered and tucked the flask very carefully into one of the many deep pockets of his jacket. As he did so, he whispered a small charm of protection to prevent breakage. It was a treasure beyond anything he'd expected.

"There are those," Vanessa said, peeling free of Johndrow as those to either side snuffed the candles, and plunged them into shadow, "who say that a vampire has no soul. They say it is forfeited at the time of our transformation, and that we walk this world as hollow shells without spirit."

Donovan didn't answer. He felt her take his arm and turn him gently toward the door, leading him from the room. As they stepped into the hallway, she leaned very close and ran her tongue up the side of his throat to the lobe of his ear. She whispered then, words meant for him alone.

"I do not believe this. Our souls are liquefied and run through our veins. They become very thin, and each time we refresh the blood a part of something new joins itself with what remains of the soul and refreshes it. You have a part of me now, a part of my soul. It is a very fine vintage...drink it in good health, and think of me."

Then they were stepping into Johndrow's outer room, and one of Stine's security gnomes stepped forward to greet them.

"See Mr. DeChance to the garage," Johndrow said. "Have the driver take him wherever he'd like to go."

"Just outside will be fine," Donovan said, suddenly very weary, and ready to be home. "I can get where I am going more quickly on my own."

They watched as he turned away and followed the short, gnarled woman into the hall. When they were out of site, his guide turned.

"I thought you might like the last piece of the puzzle," she said softly.

Donovan frowned, wondering what she meant. She took three steps down the hall and stopped, and then turned seven times. A shimmering pattern emerged on the wall and Donovan gasped in surprise.

"We didn't know it was there," she explained. It was apparently built in without Mr. Johndrow's knowledge -- and whoever did it sold that information to Ezzel. He was out of here and gone before Johndrow even reached the hall. It leads to the garage below, among other places. We've sealed it properly, and now we control access."

Donovan shook his head in disbelief. He'd thought Ezzel must have used some amazingly powerful enchantment to invade this place, and the answer was now as obvious as it was simple. Someone had been planning to rob Johndrow all along. The penthouse had never been fully secure.

The small woman stepped aside, and Donovan entered the opening, which shimmered closed behind him. He stepped out of the familiar alley across from his brownstone, and smiled wearily. The portal closed silently behind him and he crossed to his door, the flask rolling gently over his hip, the promise of it burning like fire.

EPILOGUE

When Donovan entered his apartment, he noticed several things. There was a fire burning. Cleo was curled up on his desk, eying the old crow, Asmodeus, who was perched on one of the upper bookshelves and glaring back down at the cat, and Amethyst sat in his armchair waiting for him. She was reading a book, which she put aside with a smile.

He stepped closer to her, and she stood. As she did so, she let her arms drop, and the silk robe she wore slid over her shoulders and dropped to the chair. She approached him, long red hair tumbling free over her soft skin and her eyes sparkling. There were crystals glittering in her hair and as he stared at them he somehow lost track of seconds, and she was in his arms, pressing her warm lips to his. He blinked and drew her close.

"Wait…" he said softly.

She pulled back, pouting, and he turned to the bar along the wall. He drew out the small flask and placed it reverently on the bar, and then he chose two clear crystal snifters from the rack. He unwound the gold wire carefully and pulled it free of the wax seal, which he sliced evenly with the tip of one fingernail. Then, very slowly and carefully, he slid the cork from the top of the flask.

Amethyst watched him in silence. He poured the liquid equally into the two large snifters. He laid the empty flask aside, turned, and offered her one glass. She smiled at him almost quizzically, then accepted it and sniffed.

"My god," she whispered. "What is this?"

"Cognac," he replied, taking a sip and wrapping his arm around her shoulder. He turned her slowly until she was pointed at the door to his bedroom. "Cognac and vintage soul."

About the Author

David Niall Wilson has been writing and publishing horror, dark fantasy, and science fiction since the mid-eighties. An ordained minister, once President of the Horror Writers Association and multiple recipient of the Bram Stoker Award, his novels include Maelstrom, *The Mote in Andrea's Eye, Deep Blue, the Grails Covenant Trilogy, Star Trek Voyager: Chrysalis, Except You Go Through Shadow, This is My Blood, Ancient Eyes, On the Third Day, The Orffyreus Wheel,* The DeChance Chronicles, including *Heart of a Dragon, Vintage Soul, My Soul to Keep, Kali's Tale* and the stand-alone spinoff *Nevermore – A Novel of Love, Loss & Edgar Allan Poe.* His novels in the O.C.L.T. series include *The Parting, Crockatiel,* and the novella *The Temple of Camazotz* .He is also the author of the memoir / cookbook *American Pies: Baking with Dave the Pie Guy.* David can be found at: www.davidniallwilson.com and can be reached by e-mail at david@davidniallwilson.com .

Curious about other Crossroad Press books?
Stop by our site:
http://store.crossroadpress.com
We offer quality writing
in digital, audio, and print formats.

Enter the code FIRSTBOOK
to get 20% off your first order from our store!
Stop by today!

www.ingramcontent.com/pod-product-compliance
Lightning Source LLC
Chambersburg PA
CBHW061134200626
46817CB00016B/1396